# PLACE OF A SKULL

Keith Jacobsen

THAMES RIVER PRESS

# PLACE OF A SKULL

Place of a Skull

THAMES RIVER PRESS
An imprint of Wimbledon Publishing Company Limited (WPC)
Another imprint of WPC is Anthem Press (www.anthempress.com)
First published in the United Kingdom in 2013 by
THAMES RIVER PRESS
75–76 Blackfriars Road
London SE1 8HA

www.thamesriverpress.com

All the characters described in this novel are imaginary
and any similarity with real people is purely coincidental.

A CIP record for this book is available from the British Library.

ISBN 978-0-85728-006-0

Cover design by Svilen Radev

This title is also available as an eBook

# AUTHOR'S NOTE AND ACKNOWLEDGMENTS

For background information on the history of the conflict in Northern Ireland I am indebted in particular to Richard English's thorough, probing and well-balanced study, *Armed Struggle: The History of the IRA* (Macmillan, 2003). I am also grateful to those former members of the IRA whom I met in June 2011 for giving me such open and honest accounts of their own motives and experiences, and for showing me around locations which feature prominently both in the conflict and in this story, including the Falls Road area of Belfast, the Milltown cemetery, and the site of the Bloody Sunday shootings in Derry.

Though I place them in the midst of the all-too-real events of Bloody Sunday, Father Gerald and Father Burns are of course fictional characters. That day changes them forever, as it changed so many lives in reality. My story ends in 2005. But I like to think that they both lived long enough to see the publication in June 2010 of the report of the Saville Inquiry into the shootings and to hear David Cameron's apology on behalf of the British Government.

Keith Jacobsen
August 2012

# PROLOGUE

———

Two a.m. Silence, apart from the intermittent *rark* of an urban vixen and the distant growl of lorries heading for the Embankment. And behind him the steps he had at first mistaken for echoes of his own.

Patrick peered ahead, his eyes narrowing. His shoulders hunched under the weight of the massive black cloud bank as it sank slowly, filling the sky, masking moonlight, shrouding lamplight, finally squeezing out a few heavy drops onto the pavement and his bare head. He turned off the main road into the street where he lived, his pace slowing. The sound of the other steps had ceased at last. Whoever it was had turned down another street or into one of the houses on the main road. Something odd about those steps. They always seemed to be the same distance from him. He had varied his own pace to test that. When he slowed, the steps did not come closer. But when he speeded up he could not outdistance them. Ten feet? Twenty? Something else about them, something familiar. But what? It didn't matter. He was nearly home now. Only a hundred yards to go.

His destination was the corner house of an Edwardian terrace. Opposite the side wall of the house, on the other side of an intersecting street, was a patch of waste ground overlooked by a row of brutalist 1960s tower blocks. The waste ground was still covered in rubble from houses demolished after the war, their walls and foundations weakened by bomb damage. The Second World War, that is. Not Brendan's and Seamus's war. For those two there could only ever be one war. That was the one which had started in 1969 on the other side of the Irish Sea, which they had helped to bring to London's streets and to the house where now only Patrick lived. For Brendan and Seamus the house had been perfect. A small metal door in the side wall at pavement level, once used for coal

1

deliveries, barely distinguishable from the grime of the surrounding brickwork, gave direct access to the cellar. The back door led to a narrow passageway, useful for retreat when the front door was too risky. Everywhere near the house there were shadowy corners, ideal for hiding, watching and waiting.

Ten more steps. Just a few yards to the corner house and his own front door.

The corner! The man behind him could have turned down the street before his and then left along the pavement by the side wall of the house. If he had quickened his pace he would turn the corner before Patrick could get to the door. Of course it would have to be someone who knew where Patrick was heading and the other way to the house. Someone with a slight limp. He had remembered now.

Fumbling in his pocket for the key, he turned through the open iron gate and stumbled up the stone steps. He sighed with relief. Nobody had turned the corner to confront him. Nobody had been following him. The footsteps had been real enough, but they were only those of another lone denizen of the night streets, returning to the too long neglected warmth and safety of home and bed. He stabbed the key towards the lock, missing the entry point. He tried again, his hand shaking.

Another hand, this one firm and steady, heavy on his shoulder.

'Hello, Patrick. It's all right. Only me. Don't look round. Put the key down on the step. We're going to take a little walk over to the waste ground. You know why I'm here, don't you? You have been expecting me, haven't you?'

Patrick nodded. 'Hello, Seamus. Yes, I've been expecting you. I've been expecting you for twenty years.'

# PART I

---

# THE TROUBLES

# ONE

---

Seamus stood clutching a bunch of spring flowers at the place where the winds met and wheeled round him, from Belfast Lough before him and the Irish Sea beyond, from Black Hill behind him, from the Lagan Valley to his right. He turned down the grassy path to the part of Milltown Cemetery sacred to Republicans, where their heroes were buried beneath florid Gaelic inscriptions. He came to the most hallowed plot of all, reserved for those killed in action. It was where he had once dreamed that he and Brendan would be laid to rest side by side. Several yards of empty ground lay unmarked, waiting for the heroes who were now no longer needed. The space, as carefully tended as any of the graves, would remain empty as a symbol of peace. Brendan had not been killed in action. He had died of natural causes after serving his time, so his modest grave was a few yards further away. Seamus walked over to it and stooped to place the flowers. He looked around. Some family groups in the distance. A procession of large black cars. Nobody close enough to hear him.

'I did it for you, Da', as you made me promise. I did it for you.' He was almost shouting. 'So you would find peace. So why can't I find peace? Why is he still haunting me? What else do I have to do?'

He sobbed and walked slowly away. He no longer dared to hope they would find room for him near his father. He did not deserve it. He could not claim to be a hero. He had carried out his duties efficiently. He had killed traitors. But he had never been in real danger of being killed. He had never served time in a British prison. He had not been shot at by British soldiers or loyalist paramilitaries nor had he been beaten senseless by the RUC. The mainland police had detained him for a few hours, interviewed him politely and shaken his hand. Over time he had disengaged, ceased to be an active soldier, become part of the enemy nation. When he had at last picked up his gun again it was after the final cease-fire, after the Agreement had been signed. He had had no authority other than private revenge. He had killed someone who had never fought for or against the cause, who had offered no resistance. It was a cowardly killing. And, which was far worse, an unnatural one. None of the heroes buried there would applaud him for it or welcome him among their ranks. No, in his heart of hearts he knew this was a Valhalla where he did not belong.

He walked along the row of terraced houses where he had spent four years of his youth. No need to run this time. No need to keep looking behind him to see if eyes or steps were following. The street had been swept clean. All the houses were neat and tidy with freshly painted doors and windows, many of the doors open, inviting anybody, friend, neighbour or stranger, to drop in. The burned houses had been rebuilt. Children played outside, the older ones with bicycles, toddlers pushing miniature buggies or pulling bright toy cars or fire engines. They and their watchful parents called out to each other. Watchful, but no more so than in any other street in any other city. Was it his imagination or was the accent less sharp, less fearful? It was an accent he had fallen in love with the moment he had first heard it. Heard it for real, that is, in the cross-cut of conversation on the streets which had bred it, not in the softened, melodised form his father had had to use over on Merseyside to make himself understood. Within hours of his arrival in Belfast Seamus was using it like a native. He knew what he loved about it. It was that sense of stoic hurt which ran through every word, of not expecting to be believed even when stating the simplest and most obvious things, of suffering and grievance turned by time and imagination into something epic.

He crossed the road to the grey spike-topped fence which now separated the row of houses from the estate. A peace wall they called it. The new youth club on the site of the old one marked one end of the wall. It was a bright, modern building with large panes of glass, its vulnerability a break with the past and a sign of faith in the future. He heard sounds of laughter and chatter from within. He paused to read the plaque by the main entrance. The words were a tribute to John O'Hara, the man who had set up the original club in a disused school building during the early days of the Troubles in an effort to bring the local communities together. But the effort had been in vain. The club had been trashed and left derelict and John O'Hara had been shot. A paramilitary execution, it was thought, though neither side had claimed responsibility.

You'd be so proud, Uncle John, if you could see all this now. We still had some fun in those days, didn't we, despite everything? Remember those fireworks in the back yard? The ones that jumped along the ground and always seemed to be trying to get up your trouser leg? You pretended to be trying to escape them but I always suspected you were deliberately following them, just to make us laugh. You were always laughing. Your laughter was a beacon in the dark. But beacons fade quickly when they burn brightly.

He walked on through the streets of terraces off the Falls Road, overhearing snatches of pavement conversations, some of them in the Gaelic which despite his efforts he had never really mastered. Brendan had mastered it even though he was supposed to be slow with language, starting while still a boy and perfecting it in prison. The gable end murals, recently retouched to keep their colours vivid and their details alive, commemorated the armed struggle and celebrated its heroes. He thought he recognised some of the men who shuffled along the pavements. They had been prematurely aged by the times on those streets when snipers lurked behind corners and bullets raked the walls, when running feet, harsh shouts and the sounds of crunching wood from the back alleyways told of smashed doors and of men and women, old and young, pressed against the walls, searched and frogmarched away. He wondered if as a boy he had fought alongside those men in street fights. Although they greeted him in a friendly enough fashion none showed any sign of recognition. They were welcoming to him as they were to all strangers.

He came at last to the low, white-brick church crouching back from the pavement. Like a nun at prayer, he thought, so unlike the loyalists' churches, with their proud granite spires and towers rearing up to the sky as if with clenched fists. He entered quietly and reverently, dipping his fingers in the bowl of holy water near the door and making the Sign of the Cross. They were instinctive actions, ingrained from the times when he had regularly attended Mass and the sacraments. But that had been many years ago, when he was still a child, before he had learned to think for himself. Before he had found something more real than prayer and ceremony in which to believe. Before he had found the cause.

The priest who stumbled out of the confessional genuflected awkwardly before the high altar and shuffled slowly towards the sacristy. He was white-haired now, with a stoop. Not at all as Seamus remembered him.

'Father Gerald?'

The priest turned towards the voice, peering through the semi-darkness.

'I'm sorry, my son. You're too late for Confession this evening. Can you come back? Unless it's very urgent. I can see you in the sacristy. It's private there. Good Lord! Seamus? Is it really you?'

'Yes, Father. Really me.'

They moved towards each other and embraced. Then Father Gerald straightened out his arms, let his hands rest on Seamus's shoulders and gazed into his eyes, smiling broadly.

'God, you've changed, Seamus. So have I, I'm sure. We're all older now. And not much wiser, I suspect. But you look as if you've been in Purgatory.'

'I have, Father. And I'm still there.'

'Christ, man, what's been happening to you? How have you been since the funeral? How many years is it? Five or six? Funny, isn't it? We go for decades without changing much if at all. Then one day time taps us on the shoulder and says, hey, you owe me. Next time you look in the mirror it's a stranger staring back at you. Come on through to the presbytery and have a glass of something. Unless you wanted to make a confession first.'

'A glass of something would be fine.'

'Do you remember the meetings we had here in this very room?' said Father Gerald when they were seated in the presbytery lounge, each with a glass of whiskey in hand. 'It was a long time ago. You were only fourteen when you first came.'

Fourteen, beautiful with youth and hope.

'Of course I remember. Those were the days, Father. You and your friends made me feel I was a part of history in the making.'

'And you were, Seamus. You were.' And you aroused feelings in me which I thought had long passed me by.

'How did you do it, Father? Get those people there from all over the world?'

Father Gerald smiled and nodded, not wanting to reply right away for fear his voice would crack. They had dreamed and hoped so much, all those years ago. How could they possibly have known then that decades of blood and tears would flow before their dreams were even half-realised?

'Sure,' he said at last, 'they had a tale to tell, didn't they? And you listened, wide-eyed, drinking in every word. I'll never forget it. Those speakers brought their experiences. But you brought something else. You brought the wonder of a fourteen-year-old boy. And that energised us all. Because we knew that when we were gone or too old to be any use there would be a generation to follow us. So what brings you here today, Seamus? Are you missing the bad company of the old days?'

'Bad company? Not you, Father.'

'Especially me. I led a double life. I was a priest and a Volunteer.'

'You never killed anyone, Father.'

Only one, Seamus, one who intended great evil towards you. And I never meant him to die. You never knew it was all because of you.

'I gave shelter to those who had killed. I gave them Communion, knowing they were not in a State of Grace. I encouraged them to believe they were acting in a just cause.'

'It was a just cause.'

'But were we right to kill like that? The innocents, I mean. The ones who got caught up in it when they were only trying to get on with their lives. I've been thinking about it so much. That's the trouble when peace comes. You start thinking, and your thoughts grow inside you until they possess you like devils.'

'There are always innocent deaths in any war, Father. The ones responsible are the ones who provoked us to retaliate, who oppressed us all those years.'

'I know the arguments, for God's sake. Remember who you're talking to. I've spoken them often enough. But I'm a priest, Seamus. Did I forget that? I should have tried to get the sides together to talk peace right at the start, before it got out of hand. I should have said the cause was good but not worth a single innocent life. I only wanted civil rights, Seamus, for everybody. That was my dream. I didn't want to drive the loyalists into the Irish Sea and plant a flag at the spot where the last one left. My dream turned into a nightmare that day in Derry. Bloody Sunday. A local priest invited me to join a peaceful march for civil rights and the end of internment. The portals of Hell opened that day. I knew it would take years before they closed again but I never thought it would take decades.'

'We had to fight the war, Father. Nobody was going to give us civil rights simply because we asked politely for them. You realised that on Bloody Sunday. Brendan and I knew it long before. There had to be martyrs. You saw them gunned down in front of you. Innocent people. Yes, I lived by the gun as well. But the lives I took weren't innocent. They had betrayed us. It was us or them.'

'I know what you're saying, Seamus. I was the one who passed the messages onto you. But I sometimes wondered. Were we sure they were guilty? We never put them on trial. We never gave them a chance to defend themselves.'

'That wasn't our job. We weren't the interrogators. I never doubted the intelligence. Only…'

'Only what?'

'There was one, Father. More recent. Not like the others.'

'One you're not sure about?'

'I am sure. Or I was. It was five years ago. After Brendan had died.'

'Jesus Christ, Seamus! We had peace by then. We had peace before he died.'

'We had an Agreement. But there were still scores to settle.'

'Who are you talking about? Did you get orders to execute someone? You could have refused. You weren't under obligation anymore.'

'Yes I was. There are other obligations.'

'You mean…family obligations?'

'Brendan told me who shopped him. He made me swear.'

Father Gerald frowned and leaned forward.

'He knew? I always wondered who it might have been. It happened so suddenly. It was obvious someone gave the police a tip-off. Go on, Seamus. Tell me about it. That is why you came, isn't it?'

# TWO

---

Seamus had seen his father only a month before but now he hardly recognised him. Under the Good Friday Agreement there would be early releases from prison. But they had come too late for him. He had served nearly all his sentence. Now he was an old man with advanced lung cancer. Six months ago they had discharged him from the prison infirmary to a hospice in Belfast.

So Seamus knew what to expect on that last day. A hollowed-out face, wheezing lungs, shaking bony fingers, husky voice barely above a whisper. He had been like that throughout the months since his discharge. What was different about him now was that the shadow of death was on him.

'How are you feeling, Da'?' asked Seamus, offering him a strictly forbidden cigarette. Now his father was dying he no longer called him by his Christian name. It seemed sacrilegious.

This was usually the moment when Brendan would try a smile, tell him he would soon be back on active service or would be if it wasn't for that fucking Agreement and how the hell did he think he was feeling, the stupid git. But there was no time for that now. Not with death pointing a bony finger at him. Brendan struggled to push himself into a sitting position, refusing Seamus's offer of help. Then he raised his hand, calling Seamus's ear closer to his cracked lips.

'I'm on the way out, son, and don't you go saying anything stupid about me having years left and I'll be home soon. I know I won't be here tomorrow. So, will you promise me something? Will you shut the fuck up and listen to me for once in your life?'

'Sure, Da'.'

Seamus was fighting back tears and could not at that moment have said anything further to save his life. He gritted his teeth.

Whatever he did he must not let his father see him cry. He was a man, not like Patrick, and it was Brendan who had taught him to be one. He would always be grateful to him for that.

'That bloody Agreement. Good Friday they call it. Good Friday was the day Christ died for our sins. Not the day we betrayed Him and our cause and all the people who died for it. Black Friday they should call it.'

'Da', all that's in the past now. The fighting's over. We'll get what we want in the end. We'll get a united Ireland. Freedom and equality for all of us. Only the way we'll get it will be peaceful. You won't see it. I probably won't. But it wasn't wasted. They had to take notice in the end. And they did.'

There was a rattling sound at the back of Brendan's throat. A nurse entered the room. Seamus pulled the cigarette out of Brendan's mouth just in time but could do nothing about the smell. She frowned, shook her head and left the room.

'I thought you were going to shut up and listen.'

'Sorry, Da'. I'm listening.'

'That peace thing is a fraud. The men we entrusted to lead us to our destiny gave up the armed struggle before we got there. I don't agree with it, but I always followed orders. But peace? You can't call it that. There's no peace until the scores are settled.'

'You settled all yours, remember? And I helped you.'

'Yes. Except the last one. And now you'll have to settle that.'

'What are you talking about?'

'You know.'

'You said you didn't know who grassed you up.'

'No, Seamus. I told you never to mention it. I told you it was nothing to do with you. Only now it is. I never said I didn't know.'

'But who?'

'Don't be so bloody dim, son. I was always the dim one. You were the bright one. I thought you were a teacher now. How can you teach if you can't think or remember? Who knew where we were?'

'Your contact with the ASU. I never knew who he was. Only you did. That was the way things were done. Nobody knew the whole picture. Are you saying it was him?'

'No, you idiot. Why would he do that?'

'To get something off his sentence.'

'He never served a sentence, Seamus. He was never brought to trial. He was shot by the police in a bank raid. Who else?'

'Quite a few. We were a safe house for Volunteers waiting to go into action, or needing somewhere to hide afterwards. They all came through the ASU contact. Six altogether. Including the two we got rid of. It certainly wasn't one of those two. And then there were the ones who just delivered and picked up.'

'That's right. Six in total, apart from the contact and the ones we took out. Two of those six were also killed in raids. The others were picked up off the street after planting bombs. They were with me the whole time inside. They offered me use of their contacts to take out whoever had shopped me. All I had to do was name him. I refused. No reprisals on my behalf, I told them. It wasn't any of them, Seamus.'

'There was nobody else who knew. Except…oh, for fuck's sake! What did they know about it?'

Brendan seized his hand. Seamus winced, surprised at the sick old man's strength.

'Know? They knew what we were up to. They knew what we had in the cellar. They knew what came and went via the cellar door to the street. How could they not know, living in the same house? Why do you think they upped and left that day without a word of goodbye?'

'Da', you're talking about our family, for God's sake! They would never betray us, either of them. They could have done that any time, all those years here in Belfast. I'm sure they knew what we were up to here as well. And they knew we weren't moving to London for the sake of our health. They left because they had had enough. They wanted no more to do with us and what we were doing. So why do that if they were going to shop us? And why wait all that time?

We could easily have closed down by then or moved the operation elsewhere. If you had had the least suspicion you would have done just that.'

Brendan shook his head. 'Of course I didn't suspect. Not for a second. And it's not her I'm talking about. Your mother would never have betrayed me. If I know any truth on earth I know that.'

'You think...Patrick?'

'I don't think, son. I know.'

'Did the police tell you? Or the screws?'

'No. I wouldn't have trusted them. But somebody told me. Somebody very well placed to know. I can't say anymore. The intelligence was good, son. As good as it gets. You'll just have to trust me on that. We always did trust each other, didn't we? That's why we were such a good team. We were the best they had for the job we did. Anyway, he only confirmed what I already knew. It had to be that creep. That fucking weirdo. Your brother.'

'But why did he wait?'

'Maybe he needed that time to break away from her. And the first thing he did to prove he was a man at last was to betray his own father.'

'But not me. They never arrested me.'

'Maybe that was the deal. He told them he would never testify against you. It was me he hated. I don't know any more than I was told, which was that Patrick grassed on me.'

'But nobody needed to testify, not with everything they found in the cellar. And you confessed.'

'Only to possession of bomb-making equipment and firearms. And membership. Not to what we did to those two. They never found the bodies, did they?'

'No. Listen, are you sure about this intelligence? I know we were always careful, but couldn't someone have spotted the comings and goings and the deliveries and got suspicious?'

'Seamus, I've told you often enough what happened. They came and knocked on the door. They asked for me by name. Are you Brendan O'Hara, they asked. Polite as anything. They had a warrant in my name to arrest me and search the house. They had grounds for suspecting me of terrorist activities in connection with the Provisional IRA, they said. So how did they get hold of all that before they set foot in the place? I asked them, who grassed? Someone who knows all about you. That was all they said. It wasn't a fucking neighbour, or a passing tramp. After I had been arrested, before they let you come to see me, I had a visitor. Someone very senior. That's all I can tell you.'

Seamus's head was reeling. He had always assumed it was someone in the organisation who had turned traitor, one of those contacts of Brendan's whose identity had to be kept secret even from Seamus. Or maybe an agent planted by the Brits. But Patrick? Illiterate, backward, irrelevant Patrick? Impossible, surely. Yet Brendan's ruthless logic made sense. He had eliminated all other possibilities. And he had reliable intelligence from a senior source. Brendan would never lie to him about anything to do with intelligence. Their lives had depended on it on far too many occasions for that.

'But if you've known all these years, Da', why didn't you say anything?'

'Because it was between him and me. You weren't involved. I hoped I'd get out before it was too late and find him myself. I never wanted to drag you into it. Only it's too late for me now. That's why I've got to ask you to settle this for me.'

'But I haven't seen Patrick since the day he and Ma walked out. That was nearly twenty years ago. He might be dead. Or gone mad and in an asylum somewhere. You can't settle a score with a ghost or a lunatic.'

'But if you could, Seamus? If you could...? If chance were to put the two of you in each other's way...?'

# THREE

When Seamus had finished speaking a silence started to grow as if the ground between them was shifting and cracks were forming and widening. Father Gerald knew he had to say something before the cracks became a chasm that neither of them could cross.

'So you agreed, Seamus,' he said, in the near-whisper he always used in the confessional. 'To please a dying soldier who had forgotten the war was over.'

'He hadn't forgotten. This was nothing to do with the war. Patrick was never part of it.'

'So why would he betray his father?'

'It was personal. He knew Brendan was a wanted man. He was taking revenge for the way he had treated him in the past.'

'But Brendan had no idea where he was. Neither did you. So if this is just about an oath…'

For God's sake, Seamus, tell me this is just about an oath, a misconceived oath, an oath which it would be no sin to break, which it would be a mortal sin to carry out…

'I did find him. He had gone back to live at the house.' Seamus's voice was flat. 'I found him. I killed him.'

Father Gerald made the Sign of the Cross. He rose and paced up and down the room. When he spoke at last his voice shook with anger. At times he punched the palm of his right hand with his other fist.

'Christ, man, is it really all the same to you? Can't you see the difference? As a soldier, a Volunteer, working for a cause we all believed in, you were ordered to execute traitors. It wasn't what I would call due process but there was a kind of rough justice. I don't condone it but I can see it. But this? Cold-blooded revenge on a family member, your own brother? Did you hear his side of the story?'

'I would have heard it. But he was silent.'

'You weren't in your right mind when you swore, Seamus. Neither was he when he asked you to swear. He was dying after all those years in prison, burning up with anger and resentment. You were burning too, with grief. Neither of you were bound by what you said then. In the name of God, why didn't you come and ask for my advice?'

'I was afraid you would say what you just said. You might have talked me out of it. And I could never have lived with myself if you had.'

'And you can live with yourself now? Of course you can't. I can see that. Seamus, we both know that when the State fails to provide justice other forms take its place. I taught you that. Remember? When we first met. When you were only fourteen. The loyalists had their justice, only it was a byword for institutional injustice. We had the right to set up our own laws in response. But there are more fundamental laws. Places where we have to draw the line. All right, maybe Patrick overstepped your line, if he did. He betrayed his own father. That's what you say. I still don't know if I can believe it. But if it's true, do you think he didn't know that? Do you think he didn't have to struggle with his conscience every day of his life? And what danger was he? You said it yourself. He was never part of the cause. The Troubles were hard times and we had to be hard. But to execute a family member after peace had come, with no operational need, no order, just because of something a dying man not in his right mind made you say when you were off your guard? It's not right, Seamus. There's no way it can be justified. I said there are different forms of justice. And there are different forms of retribution. The Church offers Absolution through the Sacrament of Confession. I'll hear yours if you want. But I can only confer Absolution if I am convinced you are truly sorry in the sight of God. If you reject that way forward, other, more ancient, more primitive agents of justice will come for you. The ancient Greeks had a name for them.'

'I've heard of them. The Furies.'

'That's right. Your conscience will unleash them. They will torment you for killing your own brother. They won't care if you did it because of an oath. The line Patrick crossed, if he did, was something of the times, a line drawn in the sand. And by the time you picked up your gun to kill him those times had gone. And the wind had blown the sand, so it's hard to remember where the line was. But you crossed a line fashioned in granite, a line which will never be worn away by time and wind as long as the human race exists.'

Seamus rubbed his hands, looking down at them as if unsure they really belonged to him, rocking backwards and forwards in his chair.

'Did you use the same gun,' Father Gerald continued, 'the one I kept here for you?'

'Yes.'

'I wish to God I had never given it back to you, that time you came here and told me there was a man after you. Did you kill him as well?'

'No. I lost him. I never saw him again.'

'What did you do with the body?'

'It's in the same place as two other traitors we dealt with over there. Hidden cellar on a piece of waste ground.'

Father Gerald shuddered. 'You carried it there?'

'He went there with me. He just knelt there and let me kill him. He was silent. If he was innocent he would have said something. He knew I was there to kill him. I pushed the body in.'

'Did you come here to confess? To take the Sacrament, I mean.'

'Father, I don't want Latin mumbo-jumbo and blessings and exhortations to sin no more. I could go to any priest for that. I came to you because we're old friends. I need to talk to someone.'

'Then talk. I'm listening. You said you were sure he was guilty. That suggests you now think he might have been innocent.'

'No. Not when I'm rational. But I see him in my dreams. Nightmares, rather. I've been having them for years. They started after Brendan made me swear. My life was a wreck. My wife left me.'

Father Gerald shook his head.

'What, Carlotta? That lovely Italian girl? I'm so sorry.'

19

'I lost my job. I took to drink and drugs, anything I could lay my hands on. I decided I couldn't go on like that. I thought that once he was dead I'd be free. But the nightmares are worse than before.' He spoke in hurried gasps. 'I'm down there in the cellar with him. He's lying there where I left him. Then he gets up and walks towards me, pointing a finger at me. Each time I see him he's rotted away a bit more, but he still gets up and walks towards me, pointing. Now it's just a skeleton I see and it still happens. He's dead and he'll never just lie down and die. He'll always rise up and accuse me. I'll never be free of him.'

His voice tailed off into a sound somewhere between a choke and a sob. Father Gerald knelt by his chair and put his arm around his shoulder.

'It was so different with the others,' Seamus continued. 'I just went back with Brendan and we had a drink and I went to bed and slept like a baby. I never thought of them again, certainly never dreamed of them. But now…I started to wonder if he was still alive. But how could he be? I mean, I'm a trained professional. One shot in the back of the head, no chance of missing. I expected them to find the body. I thought they would come for me. I wasn't going to deny it. What would be the point? But nobody came. I waited. I had managed to kick the drink and drugs when I was searching for him. Now I was back on them again. In the end I decided I couldn't go on like that. I went back to see why they hadn't found the body.'

Seamus put his head in his hand and cried. Father Gerald rose, took the empty glass out of Seamus's hand, refilled it and brought it back to him. Seamus looked up at him, blinking away the tears. His hand shook as he took the glass.

'I'm sorry, Father. As you see, I'm not what I used to be.'

'Tell me what happened when you went back.'

'The land is still derelict. Corrugated fence all the way around. The developers must have gone bankrupt. I was going to go in and open the cellar and look at the body, reassure myself he was still there, but I lost my nerve. I lost my nerve for the first time in my life. I went back to the house a few times. Somebody must have seen me. He put these notes through the door.'

He passed them over. Father Gerald read them slowly, frowning, as if they contained numerous words in a foreign language rather than less than a dozen words in the plainest English.

'But if it wasn't Patrick, who could possibly know that?' Father Gerald asked at last. 'What about your mother? She and Patrick were always so close. Maybe she can vouch for his innocence. Though why she should do so by leaving anonymous notes I can't imagine.'

'She's dead, Father.'

Father Gerald's hand flew to his mouth, as if he was the one who had spoken the words and now wanted to call them back.

'Your mother, too? Oh, that's terrible, Seamus. What happened?'

'She left with Patrick, a few years after we moved to London. I traced her to Liverpool. She had killed herself there. There was no sign of Patrick.'

Father Gerald made the Sign of the Cross again. 'Poor woman. How dreadful, dying alone like that and in despair. Did she get a Catholic funeral?'

'Yes. Thanks to a good neighbour. I've been going to her grave to keep it tidy and put fresh flowers down. They couldn't trace any family or friends. I wish I'd known where she was, and how she was feeling. I could have tried to make it up to her. We were so caught up in other things we never noticed how it was for her.'

'She was lonely and depressed here. She never had a chance to belong. And she was so frightened by all the violence and the unrest. You're right. You should have helped her more, you and Brendan. I'll go and visit. Where is she buried?'

'St Anselm's. By Sefton Park. The headstone gives the name as Ruth Gibson. Her maiden name. The priest there can show you where she is. Father, do you believe in ghosts?'

Father Gerald smiled. For a few moments the warmth of his memories relaxed his features and dissolved the anger and sorrow which had taken them over.

'Of course. I'm an Irishman, remember? Dublin born and raised. When I went to seminary I was taught what all priests are taught, that the souls of men and women do not return to earth and that angels and devils are in Heaven and Hell respectively. I knew better. There are spirits here from our ancient past when the bards sang of times ancient even to them. They're in the mountains and the woods and the streams, in the towns and cities too. They come along the streets and down the chimneys and hide in the nooks and crannies of the houses. People here have told me about them so often that I started to see and hear them for myself. And during the Troubles we kept adding to the pile. Turbulent, howling spirits of men, women and children brought to an untimely end, who cannot bear to depart and cannot bear to stay.'

'I think Patrick's ghost has returned. He's coming after me and not just in my dreams.'

'Seamus, there's one thing I have never heard about ghosts, even Irish ones, and that's their writing notes and pushing them through the door. Try to think about this rationally. These notes can only mean one thing. There is someone else who knows. Someone who thinks you and Brendan made a mistake. And that person knows what you did. He knows where the body is.'

'If you're right he can do what he likes. He can kill me or try to blackmail me or report me to the police. I don't care.'

'There must have been somebody else. Try to think.'

'I have thought, Father. There isn't anybody. The more I think about it, the more I'm sure it was Patrick. If it was a real person who left these notes he's crazy.'

'Crazy or not, he's found out something, however impossible that seems. What are you going to do?'

'Give myself up. But not yet. I'm going back to the house to wait for him. I have to know who it is and find out how he knew. Then I have to kill him, if I get the chance. I owe that to Brendan.'

'Seamus, listen to me. You don't owe Brendan anything. Call a halt now, for God's sake. You asked for my advice. Well here it is. Give yourself up now. Maybe then the Furies will release you. Forget about the rest. Forget about finding and killing this mystery person. Haven't there been enough deaths? It's all over now.'

'I wish to God it were, Father. I wish it were.'

# FOUR

---

Seamus was desperate to leave right away. In vain Father Gerald tried to persuade him to stay for just one night. In the end he gave up and agreed to drive him to the terminal to catch the night ferry to Liverpool. They drove in silence through the deserted streets, Father Gerald's hands tense at the wheel, his palms wet. Even now, after all these years, he could not get used to the idea that they were in no danger of being stopped and the car searched by a patrol of the British Army.

He had hoped he could convince Seamus of the futility of his plan for yet another killing. Not just the futility but the danger. He had no illusions about Seamus or himself. Seamus had been a ruthless killer, and Father Gerald was as much a part of his violent past as anybody. But he had at last allowed himself the relief of believing that those days were over. Seamus had settled down in London. He had married, to Father Gerald's great surprise, and, he suspected, to that of Seamus himself. The Good Friday Agreement had been signed. Brendan had passed away. Paramilitary groups were disbanding. Weapons were finally being put beyond use.

So this visit from a ghost of the old Seamus had filled him with horror, all the more so since the visitor was not the cold, controlled executioner of the early days of the Troubles. By killing his own brother he had torn the heart and soul out of himself. He would barely be able to hold a gun. And he was going back to face someone who appeared to know what he had done, who was taunting him, who might not hesitate to exact revenge for a terrible crime. He was walking into a trap, and nothing Father Gerald could say could persuade him to change his mind. There had been a time when he had the eloquence and the authority to influence Seamus, but no more.

They were just in time, the few other passengers already on board. They embraced at the barrier, saying nothing, unable to meet each other's eyes. The boat creaked and groaned impatiently at its moorings, the ropes thick as a man's thigh straining and fraying against the oily stone of the quayside, the huge engines whirring and coughing, eager to embrace the dark waters of the Lough and the Irish Sea. Father Gerald watched Seamus's parting back until he saw the gate shut behind him. Then he made the Sign of the Cross and pronounced a blessing, the words carried away on the wind and the choking fumes.

Back at the presbytery, he went upstairs to his study, poured himself another glass of whiskey and settled down in the armchair which over the years had adjusted its springs and cushioning to his shape and posture. He wanted to sleep and at the same time he was resisting. He knew what images would come to him when he finally slipped into unconsciousness. Like Seamus he suffered from nightmares. Only those of Seamus were phantasmas bred by fear and guilt. His had happened before his own eyes, that January Sunday in 1972.

He had met Father Burns a year before, at a diocese meeting in Dublin. Afterwards they met whenever they could find the time, to discuss, even argue, often late into the night. To his parishioners and others of his acquaintance Father Burns was a mild-mannered, consoling figure who heard confessions and took tea on pastoral visits, nodded sympathetically and conferred all the appropriate blessings with a gracious smile. Only those who knew him better, like Father Gerald, were aware that his small frame and quiet manner hid a rare strength and energy of mind and spirit. In their discussions Father Burns argued that the expression of nationalist aspirations through armed conflict could only damage the burgeoning civil rights movement. The loyalists' reaction was one of fear, not only of the loss of their privileged position but of becoming in their turn a persecuted minority in a united Catholic Ireland. This fear had driven them into a position of fierce entrenchment, with no possibility of concessions on even the most reasonable demands for civil rights. Nationalist aims were legitimate but needed to wait until broader political developments could accommodate them. If the loyalists could be reassured, they would see the need to concede civil rights, for the benefit of all. Father Gerald had disagreed. He argued that the political and social structures in place were designed to perpetuate injustice. There were no mechanisms to deliver civil rights. The system was beyond reform and had to be replaced.

As they talked, they soon came to realise that they had created between them a zone of personal warmth and mutual understanding in which each could put forward any idea without fear of giving offence or risking ridicule.

When Father Gerald received the phone call from Father Burns inviting him to join him in Derry for a march for civil rights and the end of internment, he hesitated at first. He would be delighted to see his friend again. Father Burns had assured him that the occasion would be peaceful. The local MP would be sharing a platform with Catholic leaders. But Derry was a notorious trouble spot. How sure could the organisers be that it would not end in a way that would set back rather than advance their cause?

In the end, Father Gerald agreed to come. If peaceful methods could work in Derry, they could surely work anywhere. Perhaps the worst was over. It had been going on for nearly three years. Both sides had looked into the abyss. It was time to retreat, to get things into perspective again.

Some unease still lingered in his mind. It was the Civil Rights Association's march. But what if others in his own organisation wanted to turn it into something different? He rang the secret number for use only in emergencies and spoke to his local commander. He was reassured by what he heard. The IRA would be watching but would not interfere.

His dream of what happened that day always started in the same way. He would see in quick succession the huge banner of the Derry Civil Rights Association, dazzling white in the afternoon sun, the coal lorry on which the march leaders stood, the British Army barricade blocking their intended route to the Guildhall, the halting of the lorry by the mural announcing the entrance to Free Derry. Then he would hear the speeches calling for peaceful progress towards justice for all, those words he had longed in his heart to hear.

Then the shots, dismissed at first by the speakers as an attempt by the British Army to break up the meeting with rubber bullets. After that, events would cram and collide in confusion. Sometimes he saw and heard from within his own senses, sometimes as if he were a spirit hovering overhead. He linked arms with his neighbours. They sang that they would not be moved, until the screams drowned out the song. He turned to see armoured vehicles disgorging men with blackened faces, carrying metal tubes that spat fire and death. The crowds surged, carrying him up towards the Creggan Estate, where the marchers had first gathered. As soon as he could break free he sheltered behind a wall. They streamed past, men, women, boys and girls. All were crying. He fought his way back against the weeping, screaming torrent until he could see the place where he had stood.

The shooting had stopped. Sobbing groups huddled around bodies which had been carried into the shelter of the block of flats opposite him. He saw Father Burns at last. Still alive and unhurt, thank God. He was administering the last rites to someone lying on the ground in a pool of blood. He stumbled down towards them. Father Burns looked up at him, shaking his head, seeming not to recognise him. He moved on through the groups around the bodies. Eyes empty with shock and disbelief stared up at him. He helped to lift the dead and wounded onto stretchers and into cars and ambulances.

The army vehicles had gone. Finally, so had the bodies and the wounded. He led groups of shaking bystanders in prayers whose words he could barely recall. And all the time the shouting and the crying continued. Slowly, as evening became night, a silence began to fall. Unable to bear it, he knelt in the middle of the street and howled.

That was when he would awake from his dream, clinging for a desperate moment to the hope that it had all been wrought by his overheated imagination, remembering almost immediately that it had been only too real.

When finally they met again, it was at Father Gerald's presbytery a week later. They had stayed for three days, days which in their shock and fatigue had seemed to merge into an endless season of night. They had gone round houses on the Creggan Estate, knocking on doors, following the sounds of crying and shouting, desperately trying to offer prayer and consolation. Neither man had slept, until each had at last collapsed with exhaustion on a sofa in a front room, only to stagger out again into the street, not knowing where they were, nor the time nor even if it was day or night. On the following Wednesday, at St Mary's Church, they had joined thousands of mourners filing past the row of coffins. As the mourners dispersed to their homes, they knew there was no more they could do. Their own parishes would be missing them.

It had all happened in broad daylight, they reminded each other. There were witnesses, photographers. The dead and wounded, local people, all unarmed, were known. All they had done was to march peacefully. There would be an inquiry. Action would be taken to prevent further bloodshed. Maybe those who had died had not lost their lives in vain.

So they dared to believe for a while, until the official account, saying that it was the soldiers who had come under fire and who were only responding. How many now will decide that no peaceful means can ever serve, said Father Gerald to himself, as he watched his copy of the report burn in the grate.

A year later, Father Burns, convalescing from a nervous breakdown, retired to a parish in the far South-West of Ireland. The two men never met again, though they exchanged letters once or twice a year, always taking care never to mention the events of that day.

Night after night, for nearly thirty years, Father Gerald prayed alone before the high altar. His prayer was always the same. *Oh, Lord, Father in Heaven, why have You forsaken us?*

He shook himself just in time before sleep could claim him, went over to his desk and took out a folder of papers and old newspaper cuttings. He soon found what he was looking for, a report in a West London paper. September 1978. Police in London had arrested a man named as Brendan O'Hara, suspected member of the Provisional IRA. They had found firearms and bomb-making equipment in the cellar. He made a note of the paper's telephone number.

Twenty-five years ago. Twenty years in prison had not changed Brendan, not in his heart and soul. Seamus had tried desperately to change himself but now his past was reaching out to pull him back. And Patrick? Father Gerald had not seen Seamus's younger brother since he had left Belfast with Seamus and his parents, a shy, nervous fifteen year old who always gave the impression of being in a world of his own. Were Brendan and Seamus right to believe he had betrayed his father? If so, Patrick had changed more than any of them. Father Gerald had always believed and hoped the Troubles had passed Patrick by. But who could know what poisonous seeds they had planted within him that might have flowered into hatred and revenge?

He sat down again. He was feeling old and tired, far too weary for the task which he knew lay ahead of him. He dozed, fitfully. In the early hours of the morning he rose and made himself a strong cup of coffee. He had made up his mind. He picked up the telephone.

# FIVE

---

The smell of damp and decay caught Seamus's throat as he pushed open the front door. No sounds apart from those of mice scuttling away. Instinctively, he checked the floor space in the hall just in front of the door. No more notes, thank God.

The house had stayed empty since he and Patrick had walked away from it that night towards the waste ground. Nobody wanted to live there now, apart from the mice. Normally the boys from the estate would have smashed in the windows for fun. But even they avoided it. He had never known who owned the house. Whoever it was, they would have had a lot of explaining to do to the police. Once they had convinced them they knew nothing of what had gone on there they would have wanted nothing more to do with it. Nobody would want to buy or rent it so there would be no point in doing it up. Better just to leave it to rot.

He sat down in the front room on the same hard and lumpy sofa which had been there when he and Brendan had lived in the house. He took out of his pocket the notes he had shown to Father Gerald. He had found them only three nights before, though it seemed much longer. Five years by then since he had disposed of Patrick. Returning to the house for the first time since that night, he had spotted a plain sheet of paper which had been pushed through the letter box. The ink was faded and the paper thick with a layer of dust. How long had it lain there? All of those intervening five years, to judge from its appearance. The message was scrawled in a childish print in blue biro. He did not recognise the hand. The words screamed at him. *You got the wrong man.*

So, unbeknown to him, someone was watching the house the night he had killed Patrick. That same person had seen the killing and knew enough, or thought he did, to claim that Seamus had killed an innocent man. Now, five years on, was the house still being watched? He needed to know. He was staying in a nearby pub. He went back to his room there, returning to the house the same time the following day. He saw the second note, waiting for him on the floor in the hall. He picked it up. His blood froze. The message was as short and stark as the first. *It wasn't your brother.*

He rushed out of the house, ran up and down the nearby streets, pushing aside passers-by, swearing, sweat pouring from his face and through his shirt, searching frantically for he knew not what or whom, collapsing at last into a bar and downing three brandies in quick succession.

'Nobody knew…' he muttered to himself, so that nearby drinkers stared at him and moved away. 'Nobody knew I was going after him. Nobody knew who's still alive. And nobody saw me do it.'

Well, someone knew. And that someone had seen him. Unless… There was another possibility, though he could barely bring himself to admit it. His gun had failed and he had not even noticed. Patrick had slumped into the hole, pretending to be dead. Later he had simply got up and walked away. Or, more likely, the gun hadn't failed. He had lost his touch after so many years. His hand had shaken and he hadn't realised. He had cut out drinking and drugs so his hand would be steady, but it hadn't worked. He had missed the fatal entry point and Patrick had survived. It was possible to survive even a point blank shot to the head. Patrick had lain unconscious for hours, maybe days. Then he had woken up. Finding himself alive in the tomb Seamus had intended for him, he had climbed out. Now he was tormenting Seamus by pretending to be a witness to the shooting. Or maybe he really had risen from the dead, a spirit of vengeance who would not rest until he had dragged Seamus back down with him.

Seamus had always prided himself on being practical and down-to-earth. His understanding of matters of conscience and the spirit had never been strong. He was out of his depth. He would go over to Belfast to talk to Father Gerald. And while he was there he would visit Brendan's grave.

He had done both those things. Now he was back in the house, exhausted and dispirited. And yes, he was afraid. He had never felt so afraid, or so alone. His father had been as silent as the grave in which he lay. And his old friend Father Gerald had had no words of comfort for him. He had told him what he already knew, that the Furies were pursuing him for his crime of fratricide. So, in defiance of all Father Gerald's urgings, he had come back once again to face his unseen tormentor.

He saw it as he walked back into the hall. Another piece of paper, in the same place. Another note. Three in all. He knew it hadn't been there when he entered the house. So this time whoever it was knew Seamus was inside. So why hadn't he come in to confront him?

Picking up the note and cramming it into his pocket, he rushed to the front door, wrenched it open and ran down the front steps. He looked up and down the deserted street. Dusk was gathering. No retreating shadows, no sound of running.

He shouted. 'Come and face me, you bastard! I'm not afraid of you. I know you're afraid of me or you would have the guts to show yourself.'

He had killed, always knowing and seeing his enemy. But now there was an enemy he could not see. He could kill flesh and blood but not shadows. He was helpless, impotent. He clenched his fists and cried out. He took the note out of his pocket, straining to read the faintly scribbled words.

*Tomorrow morning. Ten o'clock.*

He walked the streets all night. Occasionally he was aware of the familiar flutter in his heart which warned him he was being followed. But each time he turned round he found only silent and deserted pavement.

At seven he took up a position across the street from where he could see anyone approaching the front of the house. He put his hand in his pocket and fingered the cold metal of the gun. He had checked it several times during the night and early morning. This time there must be no mistake.

At ten he crossed the street to the house. He had seen nobody go near it. He walked round slowly, looking for signs of movement inside. He pushed open the front door quietly and crept in. He knew how to move silently, but something must have given him away. A slight creak of the hinge perhaps. The voice, distant and muffled, came from the back room.

'In here, Seamus.'

He drew the gun from his pocket. The stranger, if stranger it was, might have one trained on the door. But Seamus would have the advantage if he stayed where he was. He would call the other man out into the hall. He would have to come out eventually. All Seamus had to do was stand his ground and wait. He opened his mouth, then hesitated. There was something about that voice. Whoever it was did not mean to kill him. He could have done that already from the depths of the hall when Seamus had stepped over the threshold. And whoever it was did not seem to care about being killed.

'I know you've got a gun, Seamus. You won't need it. Put it away. Come in. I just want to talk to you.'

Very slowly, one step every few seconds, listening to the rasp of his breath, he stepped into the room. The gun dropped out of his hand and clattered to the floor.

'For fuck's sake,' he whispered. 'You're dead.'

# SIX

Brendan and his older brother John were born in Belfast. From the start John was the livelier and noisier of the two. He was popular and made friends easily. Although Brendan was quiet and shy John never excluded him from the dangerous games which he and his friends played, such as stealing from sweetshops underneath the owners' noses, or dragging ramshackle homemade wooden carts around the streets until the planks fell off and the wheels went their separate ways.

With the arrival of their teenage years, differences in the personalities of the two boys became more pronounced. John remained cheerful and outgoing. Brendan, deemed by their parents the more thoughtful of the pair, did not ignore the political history which seemed to wash over his brother, despite their parents' efforts to instil its secrets into both of them. On the contrary, he relished it. The more he listened to his parents and tried with painful slowness to read the books they pressed into his hands, the more he relished Belfast, not as a place in itself but for the way it gave access to a hinterland of the mind and heart.

His parents had settled in Belfast soon after their marriage. But they came from 'the South,' words which readily caused a mist to form in their eyes. They had never called it 'the Republic.' For them it was still 'the Free State.' They told Brendan they would only talk of the Republic of Ireland when it was united, when the British had given up the six counties of the North. Brendan took the words into his heart. While John was out playing football in the street with his friends, they taught Brendan about the history of the island of Ireland and its legends and its songs. From the mists of pre-history they created a myth for him and his boyish, impressionable soul drew nourishment from it.

Neither boy had done well at school except in practical subjects such as woodwork and metalwork. When they left they both took up apprenticeships to become welders. They sought work locally, expecting to spend their entire lives close to their place of birth. But only John found the sort of work for which they had trained, at a factory that made metal components for Harland and Wolff. They take some Catholics, John had told Brendan, but never two from the same family. Two Catholic brothers are only going to cause trouble, they had said. So Brendan moved to Merseyside, soon finding work at the Cammell Laird shipyard in Birkenhead. He met and married Ruth, a Liverpool girl, and settled down there to bring up their two boys, Seamus and Patrick. He pined for his home town but never expected to move back. Catholics don't go back to Northern Ireland in pursuit of a better life, it's the other way round, he would say to himself during occasional moods of fatalistic homesickness.

Brendan was valued by his bosses and fellow workers as a skilled and reliable workman. At home he spent much of his spare time maintaining the car or doing jobs around the house, showing the same skill and concentration as he did at work. He did not join his fellow workers for drinks after work or at the weekend, gaining a reputation as a loner. Even while he was engaged in jobs requiring a high degree of focus he gave the impression of being elsewhere in his thoughts. A good workmate but not easy to know, that was the general opinion in the yard after he had been there for a few months.

He had only one hobby. He joined a pistol club, quickly earning admiration for his coolness and accuracy. After a session there he would sometimes join fellow members for a drink at the bar, and would begin to relax and even smile a little. It was as if the controlled violence of the act of shooting had released something inside him, something which could erupt dangerously if it remained suppressed.

After he had spent fifteen years at Cammell Laird orders began to dry up. He was made redundant. He searched for work fruitlessly. Nobody seemed to want his particular combination of skills and experience. Although he was barely into middle age prospective employers seemed to regard him as already too old. In desperation he contacted John. Things are beginning to open up here a bit more, John told him over the phone. I'll see what I can do. A week later Brendan took the ferry for Belfast for an interview at the factory where John worked. They agreed to take him on, so long as he and John worked in different units. After another week he rang Ruth to tell her to sell the house and bring the children with her to Belfast.

Work was one thing. Housing was something else altogether. He knew it was difficult enough for a Catholic family who had lived all their lives in Belfast, never mind one moving in from outside. So as a temporary measure they moved in with John and his wife, Linda. They had a comfortable enough terrace house and having no children of their own could just about fit them in.

It was very obviously a Catholic house. There were pictures of the Sacred Heart of Jesus in each room. John's and Linda's First Holy Communion certificates hung opposite each other in the hall. In their bedroom a crucifix hung over the bed. On their bedside table was a plastic statue of Our Lady of Lourdes, a memento of a pilgrimage there. John and Linda went to Confession every Saturday evening, and to Mass at least once during the week as well as on Sunday. Of the new arrivals only Patrick was anything like as rigorous in following the prescribed rituals.

John was a laughing, larger than life presence, constantly on the move. He never sat down except to eat and not always then. He would circle the room, telling jokes and stories, slapping the backs of anybody within reach, serving drinks, rushing out to the kitchen to make tea or a meal, whatever time it was. After dinner he would dash out to spend time with friends who never came to the house. There was a reason for that, John explained. While the row of houses was mostly Catholic, it was what he called an enclave. Seamus, who hung on his every word, asked what it meant. Words, especially unfamiliar ones, were becoming of increasing interest to him. It means we're surrounded by the proddies, John laughed, slapping him on the back. His friends were scared to come through the Protestant areas to visit though he was never afraid to go to see them.

Seamus could not imagine John ever being scared. He was huge and muscular with massive hands. As if he had been built at Harland and Wolff, said Brendan. That's right, said John, except for my shoes. You built those at Cammell Laird, along with your own. Only fucking thing you ever did build there. Linda told him off about his language. He slapped her on the back as well, winding her.

John lived for the big occasions, birthdays, Christmas, bonfires and barbecues. If no big occasion was due he would invent one. He loved firework parties in the back yard, especially when the July marching season was approaching. Although the Orange Parade marches did not come along their street the sounds of the pipes and drums could always be heard, as could shouts from the crowds around the bonfires on the nearby Protestant estate. I can't see why we can't have a bonfire if they do, he would say. If those bastards can burn the Tricolour we can burn sausages, can't we? Brendan once suggested that they burn the Union Jack in response but John refused. They can have a political bonfire if they want, he said. Ours is just for fun.

For Seamus they were fun beyond anything he had experienced, although there was barely enough room in the yard for them all to stand. John laid everything out like a military operation, rockets in bottles, Catherine wheels pinned to the fence, sparklers in everybody's hands, sausages on the grill in the kitchen. The boys were assigned the task of setting off the rockets at pre-arranged intervals, while the women would hold the sparklers, waving them around to create circles of fire in the darkness. Patrick left his duties to Seamus to carry out for both of them, being nervous of the explosions, preferring to stay close to his mother, though she was sometimes able to persuade him to hold a sparkler. Once, as John moved around directing operations, Brendan placed a cracker near his feet. It was a mischievous little firework designed to go off in a series of explosions while jumping around at random. At the first explosion John jumped sideways but the cracker followed him. He jumped again. This time the cracker found the inside of his trouser leg. Seamus laughed until he cried. Patrick ran indoors.

Linda always watched John's behaviour with bemused tolerance, hand on hip, shaking her head. She was a plump, nervous woman with a habit of crossing her arm over her face as if to ward off blows from an invisible attacker. Her husband was something of a puzzle to her. He had none of the intense seriousness of most of the men she had known, a seriousness which in times of company and relaxation was more likely to turn to sentimentality than to light-heartedness. He did not seem to realise that life in Belfast for a Catholic was not a laughing matter. Perhaps it was this difference in him that continued to bind her to him. She found relief in his ability to rise above circumstances which bore so heavily on others, including her. Unlike him she was naturally serious. There was a permanent frown on her face and a watchful darkness in her eyes. John seemed to appreciate these qualities in her, though he teased her relentlessly for them. He understood that they were needed to get by, even though he could never aspire to them himself. It was sufficient that she had them, giving him freedom to enjoy himself.

The move back to Belfast soon began to bring about a profound change in Brendan and in his relationship with his elder son.

During his early years in Merseyside Brendan took care to suppress the nostalgic side of his personality. He did not expect Merseysiders to understand it or sympathise with it any more than he could share their sharp, ironic humour. He did not seek out the company of fellow Irishmen who might have tapped into his nostalgia, for fear of falling into moods of painful homesickness. He only allowed it to emerge again when he met Ruth. She seemed to sense its presence from the start and encouraged him to talk about it. In her company there was no danger of it turning into morbid loneliness, so he let her tease it out into the open. He was not sure she really understood where it came from or how deep its roots were. There was nothing in her background with which she could compare it. But he soon realised that it was that part of himself to which she was most attracted, however little of its real nature she grasped. Maybe the power of the attraction lay in the fact that it was beyond her understanding. He did not question what was happening between them. He was too full of gratitude and delight that this girl who had first appeared to him across the dance-club floor as a vision of dancing, mini-skirted joy on the edge of womanhood, still too young to realise how she could take a man's breath away with a shake of her hair, was ready to open herself to him in every way.

With the arrival of the responsibilities of a husband and expectant father he packed away his dreams once more and concentrated on the practicalities of life. To his surprise and joy the arrival of Seamus released and at the same time absorbed a new tide of emotional energy. He was aware that Ruth was becoming less and less important to him. He assumed that her failure truly to understand his inner nature, a failure which had once drawn them so powerfully together, was now creating distance between them. The birth of his weak and sickly second son seemed only to accelerate the process. He had once thought that he had found his destiny when Ruth became his wife. Now he realised that it was Seamus for whom he had been waiting. He dared to dream once again, this time not of his own destiny but of a joint one for him and Seamus, whatever form it might take.

His return to Belfast had seemed at first a backward step in his life. Now he saw it as his and Seamus's first steps towards a new future. Nostalgia would play a part, but not as self-indulgence in a bittersweet mood. It would be a source of energy and inspiration for what was to come, not just for him and for Seamus but for all who drew strength from their awakening awareness of themselves as members of a lost people who would once again find themselves.

He knew he was right almost as soon as they arrived in their new home. From his earliest years Seamus had modelled his speech patterns on those of his father, ignoring both the Merseyside accents which surrounded him at school and his mother's speech. It had been a natural choice. He would never have dreamed of trying to imitate his mother, whose speech reflected the efforts of well-intentioned elocution teachers to eliminate all traces of the Liverpool accent from their pupils. But Brendan had had to modify the way he spoke to fit in with his work colleagues. Now, back in the town of his birth, he was delighted when almost overnight Seamus picked up the authentic accent of one born and bred in those streets. When he first called him 'Da" Brendan's heart surged and tears came into his eyes.

As a young man Brendan had a tenor voice which, while unschooled, had an expressive quality which compelled anyone who heard it to stop and listen. But he had not sung since before his marriage. He had inherited from his father an old gramophone and a collection of John McCormack 78s, all of which had lain unused in an attic room. He had brought them back to Belfast, where with their help he rediscovered his ear and his voice. He would sing along to the 78s, teaching Seamus the words so he could join in with him. There were other records in the collection, Celtic bands, folk groups, often singing in a language of which Seamus could not recognise a single word. It was Gaelic, Brendan told him. The real language of his forefathers.

But the words of his favourite song were in English. He and Seamus would sing it together every evening after they had finished the other songs and it was Seamus's bedtime. When the words of the refrain came, they doubled the volume and broke into harmony. *A Nation Once Again.*

# SEVEN

While Brendan and Seamus felt increasingly at home in their new surroundings, Ruth remained uncomfortable. She was impervious to John's warmth and openness. She cringed when he walked into the room, and retreated to a chair in the corner. She rarely spoke in his company. With Seamus and Brendan absorbed in their explorations of the music and history of the past she kept to a tight circle of her own, confined to Linda and Patrick. She did not make friends with her new neighbours, aware that her speech would mark her out as a foreigner, and only ventured to the shops in Linda's company.

Sometimes she would confide to Linda her worries that they were an imposition on their hosts. Linda always hastened to reassure her. John was delighted to have acquired a new family at a stroke, Linda told her, while she found it a relief to have female company in the house to offset John's raucous presence. When the two women talked, more often than not in the intimacy of the kitchen, the frown would ease on Linda's face and traces of a smile could sometimes be seen around the edges of her mouth.

But Ruth remained ill at ease. She was morbidly sensitive to the tensions in their neighbourhood. John's cheerful talk of the hostile 'proddies' who surrounded them made her acutely nervous. She also suffered bouts of intense homesickness.

She could not talk to Brendan or to Seamus about her feelings. Neither of them seemed even remotely aware of her discomfort. Seamus might have noticed when he was younger. He might even have asked her what was troubling her. But now he said nothing. That was because Brendan didn't, and by then Seamus always took his cue from his father. For the comfort of physical closeness she still had Patrick, but he was too young to understand her troubles.

But at least there was someone to whom she could talk, one woman to another. There was always Linda.

Did ever a mother have two more different sons, she sometimes asked herself. She had once hoped Seamus would bring her and Brendan even more closely together. Instead Brendan had simply taken Seamus and ignored her. He had the son he wanted, one he could make in his image. He did not even say thank you. Perhaps they had never been close. Perhaps she had only imagined it.

So she had taken Patrick. And Brendan could not have cared less. Take him, you can have him, he might have said, if he had been bothered to say anything. He's no son of mine, he might have said. He was of course. She had always been faithful to Brendan.

They had met in a dance-club in Bootle. She was seventeen, apprenticed to a hairdresser. He was twenty-five, strong and well-built. She knew at first glance that she had fallen in love. It was not just his physique. There was something in his eyes. They seemed to look both at her and through her. They saw the present and a distant dream at the same time. She loved to dream. She wanted someone she could dream with. She wanted Brendan.

As the youngest of six she had been left alone, her mother far too busy with five older boys to bother with her. She read, went to the cinema and dreamed. She listened to music, mostly from the musicals. Her music teacher at school told her she was gifted with the violin, though her brothers complained about her 'screeching' when she played at home. Perhaps she did screech. But in her mind's ear her sounds were those of angels.

Brendan took her out every week. At first he was reluctant to talk about himself. Gently but persistently she pressed him. When he began to speak she put her head to one side and opened her eyes wide, gestures which he seemed to find encouraging. The more he spoke the more attentively she listened. He told her about his family and their life of poverty in the countryside near Dublin. How they had moved to Belfast in search of a better life but found only prejudice and hatred. How he dreamed of a better world where there was love and friendship. Her heart ached as she listened. She longed to tell him she too dreamed of such a world. But she was afraid he would laugh at her. So she let him take her to bed instead. The following week he asked her to marry him. There was only one problem. He did not believe in mixed marriages. She would have to convert.

She agreed and went to see the priest. She liked him very much. He spoke with such a soft musical voice about such wonderful things. He spoke about everything she believed in. In kindness and love, especially love. She knew all about love now. Brendan loved her. And now she knew that God loved her too.

After a few weeks the priest heard her first Confession. She was visibly pregnant by then and he had already noticed. He asked her why she had not confessed to that. But surely it's not a sin to be pregnant, Father, she had asked. Not when you love the father and you're going to marry him. But sex outside marriage was always a sin, he told her. God would forgive her because she had not known at the time. She accepted Absolution. But in her heart she knew it could not be a sin, not when she had given herself out of love. Love was never a sin.

When Seamus arrived she was doubly sure that nothing that could produce anything so beautiful could be a sin. He had his father's eyes. He too would dream. They would all dream together. She was pleased when Brendan took Seamus out on his own, in the pram, then the pushchair, then in toddlers' reins. She was pregnant again and often sick in the mornings. She tired easily. She liked the way Brendan showed him off to his friends. She liked the way he bathed him. She liked the sound of laughter from upstairs when he was bathing him. She liked the way he told him bedtime stories.

But why did Brendan not love her all the more for having given him Seamus? She loved Brendan more than ever since Seamus had arrived. Her love for one fed her love for the other. But now Brendan hardly spoke to her. When he was not at the yard or at the pistol club he devoted all his attention to Seamus. She felt lonely and excluded. He no longer touched her, even though her pregnancy was still in the early stages. She wondered if the time he claimed to spend at the pistol club was really a cover for an affair. She did not dare to confront him directly for fear of what his answer might be. She thought of hiring someone to find out, but knew she could never find the money without arousing his suspicions.

So Patrick was a joy and consolation to her when he arrived, late and tiny and running a whole gamut of infant illnesses from the start. Brendan took one look and snorted. 'A runt in every litter,' he said. She held Patrick protectively, trying not to show how the remark hurt. It's all right, she whispered to the pink scrap in her arms. People will be cruel to you. They will say hurtful things. But I will always be here for you. I will always love you.

Seamus followed his father's example in showing little interest in Patrick at first. Later he realised that there was fun to be had in teasing him and ordering him to do things on Seamus's behalf for which Patrick would take the blame. When the misdeeds were committed in or near the house, Brendan was always happy to take Seamus at his word and punish Patrick with well-aimed slaps across his cheek and the side of his head, though only when Ruth was out of the house. Patrick never cried or protested or told his mother what had happened, nor did he ever blame Seamus for instigating his wrongdoing. Brendan did of course suspect the truth. He continued to administer the punishments in the hope that Patrick would at last learn to stand up for himself. When he never did, Brendan began to conclude that he must be simple, so much so that he was unaware of the injustices being heaped upon him. When Patrick started school and received poor reports from the start, Brendan's suspicions were confirmed. The boy's backward, he would say, eleven pence halfpenny short of a shilling. Ruth ignored him and refused to be concerned about Patrick's school reports. She knew Patrick was not like other boys. He had special qualities which would emerge in their own good time.

By the first anniversary of their move to Belfast Seamus had ceased to have any interest in teasing Patrick. Brendan had had no interest in him at all for a much longer period of time. They ignored him. The household split into two. Brendan and Seamus would spend the evenings in the front room listening to their Irish songs, John joining in on the rare occasions he was at home. In a small parlour at the back Ruth sang romantic songs from the American musicals to Patrick. Linda would join them when she was not busy in the kitchen, sitting quietly in a corner and knitting. Ruth had brought her violin with her, a battered old school instrument which they had let her have for nothing when she left. Sometimes she took it out of its case and played it to them. She warned Linda that she wasn't very good and her brothers had always told her to stop screeching. But according to Linda she did not screech at all. Patrick also seemed to love the sound, though when she invited him to try he produced results which nobody could deny to be screeches.

One day while out shopping with Linda she saw a six-stringed Spanish guitar for sale in a second-hand store. Considering that the instrument was in good condition it was surprisingly cheap, though much more than she could afford. She wondered aloud to Linda if she might get it for Patrick. She could just imagine him playing it. It would surely suit him better than the violin. It was so beautiful, she thought, varnished and shaped in voluptuous curves, suggestive of passion and freedom in a distant, sun-baked land she had only ever seen in films and photographs. Go on, said Linda. Get it for him. I'll help you out. I've got some savings. It can be a present from the two of us for him.

When Patrick first brushed his fingers against the strings they trembled, then released a shimmer of sound, like the pang of a long repressed heartache. His eyes shone though he said nothing.

A music teacher at school agreed to give him lessons on the guitar during school time and at no extra charge. He stayed behind at school to practise. That was when he was not sick, which he frequently was, with vague symptoms such as sweating and headaches. Then he would be put to bed instantly and Ruth and Linda would nurse him devotedly.

# EIGHT

Seamus's one clearly understood responsibility towards Patrick, which he accepted though with great reluctance, was to take him with him to school.

In England their school had been run by the Irish Christian Brothers and John had found a similar one for them in Belfast. It was a short bus-ride away. To get to the bus-stop they had to walk through the nearby Protestant estate. The first time they did this John went with them, having taken a day off work for the purpose. Young men in worn denim jackets and jeans stood about in small groups on the corners of the pavements and walkways, looking them up and down, puffing at cigarettes already reduced to their tips, scuffing their tattered pumps against paving stone edges or pieces of rubble. One of the groups moved towards them, blocking the way. Then their leader noticed John, smiled at him and signalled for the group to let them pass. He called out to John in a friendly way as they did so. John waved and smiled.

'You'll be all right now, coming this way on your own,' he said. 'They know you're with me. I run a youth club round here. That's how they know me. No religious divide there. We all muck in, organise football matches and stuff like that.'

Seamus was always relieved when the time came to drop Patrick off at the separate school entrance for first year boys. His own classmates teased him about bringing his kid sister to school. Patrick's black hair had grown long by then. Ruth would not cut it or let Linda do it. So beautiful, she would often say to herself. Such lovely hair, such large, sad eyes. But after a few weeks at the school Patrick was ordered to have his hair cut, something which he seemed to accept with equanimity though Ruth broke down in tears when she heard.

Although Seamus had picked up the local accent very quickly he was still treated as an outsider. There were gangs in school and on nearby Catholic estates but he was never invited to join. In the evenings and at weekends Protestant gangs from another part of the city would visit their neighbourhood. They fought with each other and with any visiting Catholic gangs, though they kept their distance from the row of houses where John and Linda lived. The fights were not that serious at first. Stones and bottles were thrown, injuries were mostly slight. Seamus was desperate to go out and join in, but did not know how to attract the attention of the leaders on the Catholic side.

Brother Carey changed all that. It was impossible to tell his age. A particularly cruel combination of natural inheritance and life experiences his pupils could barely imagine had scarred and reddened the skin of his face and rearranged its features. One of Seamus's classmates suggested that whoever had brought him up had disciplined him by the use of a threshing-machine and a tub of boiling water. He taught Latin, or he tried to. When normal methods failed he liked to use his strap. Not like the others. Most of the strap length was flexible leather, designed for use on the palm of the hand. The handle was much harder. There was a narrow neck, to be gripped between thumb and forefinger. The head was fan-shaped, to fit comfortably in the user's palm. The usual ritual followed by most of the teachers at the school was to call the miscreant out to the front of the class where he would be told to hold out his hand. The maximum was six per hand, the usual four. During the punishment the other boys would watch out for any signs of weakness or flinching. This would be dealt with later in the playground by relentless teasing. Afterwards the boy would thank the teacher and return to his desk with a studied air of insouciance.

Brother Carey had a different approach. He attacked without warning while his victim was still seated. The reason could be a mispronunciation or mistranslation or a word whispered to a neighbour or simply a look he did not like. He would hold the strap by the soft end and use the hard handle to lash out around the face and temples. One day it was Seamus's turn to translate a passage out loud. It was part of the homework set for the previous evening but he had neglected it. As soon as he made his first mistake Brother Carey pounced. To his own horror Seamus seized the strap handle as soon as he felt it on his cheek. It was an instinctive reaction. Brother Carey stumbled towards him, the end of the strap which he was holding slipping out of his hand. The whole of the strap was now in Seamus's hand. The class let out a collective gasp, wondering what terrible fate awaited him. Sheepishly, Seamus handed back the strap and apologised. Brother Carey said nothing. The class continued as before. For the rest of that day the class treated him with awe. He was given sweets and lemonade in the break. He felt like a prisoner condemned to die.

The next day a Physical Training lesson was scheduled. Seamus loved it. Their teacher, Mr Clayton, was popular. He treated the boys as mates and cracked jokes with them. One of the weekly outside routines was four laps of the school perimeter. The school estate was not large. Four laps should have been easy. But it had a reputation for being something of an ordeal because nearly everybody went off too fast for the first two laps and staggered to the end with wheezing lungs and aching sides. Seamus soon learned to pace himself and usually came in near the front.

On this occasion he noticed that Brother Carey was standing next to Mr Clayton at the start, whispering something to him and pointing at him. When he had finished he was still there.

'O'Hara! Four more laps!' Mr Clayton called out.

His legs were still fresh and he continued. He lapped several of his slower classmates. He was enjoying it. The torture began with two laps to go. His legs seized up and he could hardly breathe. He crawled over the finishing line when the rest of the class had already changed for the next lesson. Brother Carey had stayed throughout at the finishing line. He shook his head and walked away.

The next week the same thing happened and again the following week, with Brother Carey there to watch. But after a few weeks it was no longer an ordeal. He would finish the first four laps well ahead of the field, and continue, still fresh, lapping about half the class. Some would still be on the last lap of four when he finished his eight.

He became a hero. Classmates and younger boys sought his company. At last he was invited to join a prestigious gang, one that didn't wait for the Protestant gangs to come but went in search of them. At home Brendan beamed with pride when he heard that at last his son had been accepted.

Eamonn was one of his classmates, a leading member of the gang he had joined. He was tall and gangly, with a premature and cruelly simultaneous attack of acne and an obsession with girls. Because of the number of boys in the class with the surname Murphy, each was known as Muff, preceded by the initial of his first name. Thus Eamonn was E-Muff. John Murphy, who sat next to him and was no relation, was J-Muff.

One evening after school E-Muff invited Seamus to his house. Seamus went round, after dropping Patrick off at home. E-Muff was alone in the house. He told Seamus his father had gone round to a nearby club for a drink with his mates from work. His mother had left home the year before and he had not seen her since.

'Where does he work?' asked Seamus.

'Warehouse down by the shipyard.'

'Do they take Catholics on there?'

'Not usually. Listen, I want to show you something.'

He took Seamus out to the garage and showed him a small black box with a dial and a metal rod. He plugged it into the wall.

'It gives you electric shocks. Not serious. You hold the rod and press this button here. You have to wait while it warms up. Do you want to try it?'

'Have you tried it?'

'No. You first.'

'After you. It's yours.'

E-Muff hesitated. 'It's not really mine. I saw Da' bring it home the other night. I asked him what it was. He told me. Said he and a mate had been talking to a snitch at work.'

'A snitch?'

'Someone told the boss my da' was a Catholic. The boss is keeping him on anyway because they're short. But Da' hadn't told him. He could have lost his job. So he got together with his mate that night, took this snitch down to this empty house and gave him a bit of a talking-to. With this machine to help the conversation along. He said it was only mild. The guy's all right.'

'Where did your da' get it from?'

'The mate who was with him. He told my da' to keep it. Said he always knew where to get things like that. Said he had contacts.'

'What sort of contacts?'

'He never said. I've got an idea, but I can't say.'

'So try it then.'

'I thought you were going to go first.'

'Look, I've got an idea. You've seen my little brother.'

'Yes. The weird one. Used to have his hair long like a girl.'

'That's right. He'll do anything I say. We'll get him to try it out first.'

It was E-Muff who introduced him to the back of the bicycle shed as a suitable place for furtive smoking during break. At least it was suitable until a prefect caught them and marched them off to the headmaster's study. Their hands were still smarting hours later. Another classmate and part-time member of the gang told them they had been snitched on by a boy in the year below, wanting to get into the prefect's good books.

They took the boy to the garage the following evening, after E-Muff's father had gone out, picking him up on the way home, each holding one arm and pretending to chat to him in a friendly way.

'Keep moving and don't make a fuss,' said E-Muff, 'or we'll break your arms.'

49

In the garage they made him sit in a chair while they charged up the machine. The setting was the same as the time they had tried it out on Patrick. The boy started to cry.

'It's all right,' said E-Muff. 'It won't hurt much. We know. We've tried it ourselves. This is just a warning.'

Patrick had dropped the rod the instant he felt the charge, shaking his head when they asked him if he had felt anything. Seamus had tried it, then E-Muff, each managing to hold onto the rod for a few seconds. But what if their victim let go right away, as they had done? What kind of a lesson would that be? So they tied his hand to the rod. A few minutes later, the boy staggered outside, sank to his knees and retched.

'What if he tells his da'? Or the teachers?' asked Seamus.

'He won't. He knows now what happens to snitches. Anyway, it wasn't that bad. He's just a cry-baby.'

Seamus was still frustrated. He knew important things were going on around him, but he did not know how to get involved. He was tired and bored of the petty activities of his gang and of his father's songs and dreams and stories from history. He wanted real action. He wanted to know about the contacts E-Muff's father had, the sort of people who could get their hands on machines like the black box with the rod. He knew a little about the history of the organisation his father had told him about. He knew they were active in the nearby Catholic neighbourhoods. E-Muff had referred, in a tone filled with awe, to his father's 'contacts' but would not say anything more about them. Were they members of the organisation? If so, how could he get to meet them? And, more to the point, how could he get to join?

# NINE

Brother Downie could not have been more different from Brother Carey. His skin was smooth, his features regular. Still some years short of middle age, he had tousled brown hair which bore only traces of grey. Tall and athletic, he taught chemistry and coached cricket and rugby.

The chemistry laboratory was his domain. During lunch breaks, when all the pupils were supposed to be in the dining-hall or the playground, he would lock himself inside to conduct secret experiments, so the rumour went. Every day there was an expectation in the air that this would be the day he would blow himself up and take half the school buildings with him. There were other rumours. That he did not spend those lunch-time sessions in the chemistry lab on his own. But nobody thought to have been in there with him would ever speak of it.

One day he was taking Seamus's class in the lab, just before the lunch break. At the beginning of the class he handed back their homework but kept Seamus's back, telling him he wanted to discuss it with him later. As the class filed out into the corridor for the break, he told Seamus to remain behind. Telling Seamus to sit down at a bench in the middle of the room, he walked slowly towards the door. Seamus could see he had a key in his hand.

He had never really been afraid of Brother Carey. Though Brother Carey's reactions were unpredictable it was always obvious when he was angry, and, much more rarely, when he was pleased. But he was afraid of Brother Downie precisely because he never knew what he was thinking. Brother Downie did not lose his temper. His only reaction to substandard work was to ask the culprit, in even, measured tones, to do it again and better this time. If someone misbehaved in his class, which was a very rare event, he would do no more than fix them with a stare. It always worked. He never used the strap. Now Seamus would be locked in the laboratory with him. He was shaking. He knew it had nothing to do with his chemistry homework. He knew that what was about to happen to him had happened to others, but nobody had talked. What would he have to do? Would it hurt? Would he be able to speak of it afterwards, or would he be silent like the others? What was it that had forced them into silence?

Just as Brother Downie reached the door and began to close it it was pushed open from the other side. Brother Carey stepped in. He looked across at Seamus and into Brother Downie's eyes. He shook his head.

'Sorry, Brother.' Brother Carey spoke so quietly Seamus could hardly hear him. 'Not this one. This one's mine.'

Brother Downie put the key in his pocket and walked out without a word and without turning round. Brother Carey walked over to Seamus, took him by the arm and eased him up from the bench to which he had become frozen.

'Come on, Seamus. Time for break.'

It was as if nothing had happened, as if Seamus had simply become so absorbed in his work that he had not noticed the class had ended and the other boys and Brother Downie had left.

When they reached the corridor, Brother Carey turned to him.

'Are you free on Sunday, Seamus? After Mass, I mean.'

'Yes, Brother.'

'Do you know Father Gerald?'

'Yes. I mean, I know who he is. He's our parish priest. I haven't met him.'

'He is a close friend of mine. He's a remarkable person, in many ways. Would you like to meet him on Sunday? He's asked me round to lunch and I can bring a guest.'

'Yes. I'd like that very much.'

'Good. I'll meet you outside the church at one o' clock.'

# TEN

'You mustn't mind John,' said Linda, as if reading her thoughts. 'He's a bit of an intimidating way with him at times, that's all. I don't claim to understand him. The worse things get the more cheerful he seems to be and to want others to be. Perhaps it's just his way of coping. But he's a good man and his heart's in the right place. He's pleased to have you all with him. And so am I.'

Ruth and Linda were out shopping and, weary of walking and carrying, had stopped for a cup of tea in a café. It was a week after Patrick's thirteenth birthday.

'I know he's a good man. And a brave one. The work he does at that youth club. There must be many who oppose what he's doing there.'

'There are. But that doesn't bother him.'

'I'm sorry Seamus was so rude to him when he invited him to come along to the club.'

Linda waved her hand as if to dispel the thought from the air into which Ruth had released it.

'Sure, he wasn't rude. Not at all. And John would never have taken it that way. He accepts that Seamus has his own friends to be with now. And he knows Patrick wouldn't be interested.'

'We're all grateful, really, for everything. I had hoped we would have a place of our own by now but you know how difficult it is.'

'Ah, get away with you. Don't you be talking about gratitude now. It's me that's grateful now there's a woman in the house I can talk to. The neighbours keep their distance, as you'll have noticed.'

'Why is that? I mean, I can understand their keeping their distance from me. I'm an outsider. But you're a native here.'

'Not really. My family came from a suburb a few miles away, further up the coast. My father had a grocery business. We had a nice house with a garden and a car. John and I were about to get married when the business collapsed so we had nothing to contribute. We lost everything. They know where I come from and I suppose they think I've got airs and graces. I don't think I do but that's what they think. And then there are John's friends and the work he does at the youth club. It's no secret that he tries to build bridges. Some people resent that on principle. But I don't mind, not now you're here. There's Patrick to keep me company too. I don't mind him being quiet. He's such a sweet boy.'

'As opposed to Seamus, you mean. It's all right, Linda. I know what you're saying. Truth is, I'm worried sick about both of them. I'm worried Seamus is falling in with the wrong sort of people. Rough types. And his father only seems to be encouraging him. And I'm worried about Patrick because I think the other boys are picking on him at school. He comes home with cuts and bruises and won't say where he got them. I know he'd never pick a fight himself. And his schoolwork's not at all as good as it should be. Brother Francis told me he might have to repeat his first year. Again, he won't talk about it. He just goes into his corner and plays his guitar. When he's upstairs he writes sometimes. In a notebook. I caught him once and asked him if it was his homework but he said it wasn't, it was private. He wouldn't let me see it. He takes it to school with him.'

'Oh, don't be worrying about him now. He'll come out of his shell soon enough. When the girls notice how good-looking he is and he notices them back. What's the matter, Ruth? You've gone pale like you've seen a ghost.'

'Linda, for God's sake! The boy's only twelve.'

Linda stared at her.

'Ruth, are you going and forgetting already? His birthday was only last week. He's thirteen now. A teenager already. You sound as if you don't want him to grow up. He's not a baby anymore. Look how tall he's grown since you both came here. Tall and good-looking already. Maybe he's met someone and he's writing love-poems in that secret book of his. Ruth... Wait a second!'

Ruth had slammed down her cup and rushed towards the door. Pushing her way through the shoppers on the pavement she took the first left turning and ran on, stopping only when she was out of breath. She looked around. The street was deserted. No shoppers, no cars, no buses, only two rows of tightly packed terraced houses.

She turned and began to walk back towards the reassuringly crowded and busy street where she had left Linda. It should have been directly ahead. If she could not yet see it she should at least hear the sounds of traffic, of conversation and the laughter of children. But there was nothing, only more terraces. And an eerie silence. She must have taken another turning, possibly more than one, without realising. She was lost. Every step could be taking her away from the shoppers, the buses, the cars, the children, Linda and home. She slowed and finally came to a stop. She had wanted to slap Linda's face in the café, but if she had appeared then she would have hugged her. Should she knock on one of the doors?

Footsteps behind her. She turned round slowly. Three men stood looking at her, one of them in his forties, the others teenagers, wearing loose denim jackets, their hands in their pockets. A father and his sons, perhaps.

'What's the matter, darling? Are you lost?' the older man said. An accent so blade-sharp she could barely understand him. She nodded. They came nearer, each in step with the others.

'I thought so,' continued the older man. 'People don't come down this street unless they belong here. Unless we know them. We don't know you. Where are you from?'

She tried to speak. Not from here, she wanted to say. Not from Belfast at all. I don't know my way around. I didn't want to intrude. I was out shopping with my friend. Not a word came out.

'Where do you live?' he asked. She saw that all three of them were fingering objects inside their pockets. 'Come on, say something. In this town we can tell where people come from to the street, just from the way they speak.'

She opened her mouth again. If she had had a strong Liverpool accent it would have saved her right away, but her parents had always tried to discourage her from 'talking common' as they called it. What traces she once had she had almost certainly lost. What she had acquired of the local speech might place her in the Catholic row or in the surrounding Protestant estates. She had no way of knowing which it would be. And what would be the right way of speaking for them, the one which meant they would let her go? She was aware of gable ends decorated with murals, of flags flying from some of the houses. She tried to look out of the corner of her eye. There were no walls or gable ends visible from where she stood. She realised she was trying to recall fleeting impressions from minutes before, when she was hurrying on in a frantic attempt to find her way back, impressions of a different street from the one where she now stood. Those walls, those murals, those flags, held a vital clue to the sort of neighbourhood into which she had blundered. Nationalist flags or Union Jacks? She tried desperately to remember.

'We can take her in and search her, Da',' one of the teenagers said. 'See what she has on her.'

'All right, gentlemen.'

Linda's voice? It had come from behind her. It must have done, though she had not heard any approaching steps. Her senses were so blurred she could not be sure. She did not dare to turn round in case she was wrong.

'This lady's with me.' Linda. Thank God. 'She's visiting from Liverpool. We got separated. She came down here by mistake, looking for me. I know I don't belong here either, but I'm only here to get her out safely. Neither of us means any disrespect or any provocation. So do the decent thing and escort us to the main road. Or your leaders will get to hear that it takes three of you with whatever you've got in your pockets to bully two defenceless women.'

The older man glared, then smiled.

'All right, you heard the lady. She called us gentlemen and that's what we are. So do as she says. Escort her to the main road.'

Ruth turned and walked behind Linda, the two young men either side of the couple, like an armed guard. When they reached the main road the men disappeared. Linda turned to her.

'Christ, Ruth, what in God's name were you thinking of? You must never go out round here on your own. Promise me you'll never do anything like that again.'

Ruth nodded.

'Come on, let's go home now.'

They walked home in silence. Ruth realised she was shaking. She still did not dare to try to speak for fear of what strange sounds might emerge from her mouth. She glanced sideways at Linda and realised she was shaking as well.

'I'm sorry if I upset you,' said Linda, after a few minutes. 'I was only teasing. I thought you'd be glad that someone had noticed Patrick was…I'll never talk about him in that way again, I promise. All right?'

Ruth stopped and turned round, hoping now that her voice would be back under control.

'No, Linda, I'm the one who should be sorry. How could I have been so stupid? You should have just left me there to learn my lesson. It's just that…Brendan doesn't seem to notice or care about me anymore. Seamus is in his own world now. I know John is well-intentioned but I seem to go to pieces when he's there. Patrick is all I have and with you talking about him growing up and leaving…'

'I mentioned him growing up because that's what happens in the nature of things. But did I say anything about him leaving? Listen, Patrick isn't all you have. You have me. Come here.'

Linda hugged her. When she pulled back she was smiling.

'Ruth, when you were at school did you have special friends, ones you swore to be friends with forever?'

'Yes,' said Ruth, dabbing her eyes with a tissue. 'We drifted apart of course.'

'Well, it'll be different with us. Because we're not silly schoolgirls. We're grown-up women. We'll always be there for each other, won't we? And as soon as we get home I'll get you an appointment with the doctor. He'll prescribe you some sleeping pills and tranquillisers. He does it for me sometimes. A good night's sleep is all you need to get everything back into perspective. Let's go. Oh shit! We've gone and left the shopping in that café.'

# ELEVEN

'So, Seamus, how old are you?' asked Father Gerald.

'Fourteen, Father. Fifteen in a few weeks.'

'And are you a good Catholic?'

'Not really, Father. I don't always come to Mass. Or Confession.'

'You're from Liverpool, is that right?'

'Birkenhead. My da'... my father had a job there, until he lost it. Does it matter, Father, about me not always coming to Mass or Confession?'

Father Gerald was thirty-five, plump, with a shock of unruly, greying hair. Speaking or listening, he had a habit of raising his widespread arms in a gesture which seemed to embrace everybody and every sound and movement that surrounded him. When he smiled, which he did often and eagerly, a mischievous boy from many years ago reappeared in his face.

He had studied Politics and Irish History at Trinity College, Dublin. After graduating he enrolled at a seminary near Liverpool. Throughout his time there he had constant doubts about his vocation but he kept them to himself. He took the final step of becoming ordained because he could by then imagine no other role in life for himself, certainly not that of a husband or father. But the idea of the priesthood as an escape from the realities which would otherwise face him troubled him profoundly. If he was to spend his life detached from those realities it would only be because it would place him in a better position to help others cope with them.

As part of his duties as a parish priest in Liverpool he was appointed confessor to the Irish Christian Brothers, who ran several schools in the city and elsewhere in the North of England.

In this way he came to know Brother Carey. Brother Carey confessed freely and frequently to outbursts of uncontrolled temper. But in their conversations outside the confessional he convinced Father Gerald of the sincerity of his combined vocation as teacher and member of a religious order. Why didn't you become a priest, Father Gerald asked him once. Because education was the way out of poverty for him and his brothers, he had replied, and he wanted to pass on the gift. If only God had given him the gift of patience as well as learning. None of us is perfect, Father Gerald had said.

Another of his contacts was with a local branch of the Liverpool IRA, run by one of Brother Carey's elder brothers. Though they called themselves a branch they were little more than a social club with a dozen members who met occasionally in the backroom of a house in Bootle to drink whiskey or Guinness, listen to Irish music and talk about the old times. Some had taken part in the anti-Treaty Civil War in the early 1920s. They still felt a visceral sense of betrayal towards those of their former comrades who had decided to support Partition and the establishment of the Irish Free State. War would come again and afterwards would come justice, they prophesied, even though few if any of them would be around to see it.

Father Gerald made up his mind. Christ had said that His kingdom was not of this earth. But whatever parish he served in would always be of this earth. And the part of the earth where he wanted to serve his fellow-man was Northern Ireland. He applied for a transfer to Belfast. After a few years his request was finally granted. Soon after his move Brother Carey got in touch with him. He too was being transferred. Father Gerald was overjoyed at the prospect of once again being together with his old friend.

Their IRA friends in Liverpool had given them the names of contacts in Belfast. Father Gerald was welcomed among them as a spiritual adviser. But within a year he decided he wanted more. He wanted to be one of them. He became a Volunteer, offering the resources of the presbytery as a meeting-place and, if necessary, hiding-place.

During all this time he knew no other emotional life than that which flowed from being part of a movement which he sensed was gathering momentum with each passing day. There was no room for any of those special feelings for one individual which others described as love or attraction or infatuation and which seemed so central to their lives.

Not until the day when Brother Carey brought along a fourteen-year-old boy called Seamus to the presbytery.

'Well, I wouldn't be minding too much about that sort of thing now,' said Father Gerald in reply to Seamus's question. 'The rituals, I mean. I'm not saying they're not important. But being a Catholic over here is not the same as it is over there. Here it hurts. I mean, hurts where it matters, in your livelihood, your ability to provide for your family. But things may be changing, slowly.'

'Too slowly, Father. If it wasn't for Uncle John, my father wouldn't have a job and we wouldn't be able to live where we do.'

Brother Carey laughed. 'I told you he could speak up for himself, Father. He's a tough one and a bright one, just the sort we need.'

'And I'm thinking you were right about that, sure enough. I like that in a lad. There are some things you shouldn't just put with. Is that what you're saying, Seamus? You're saying we should help to move things along a bit?'

'Yes, Father. Why not?'

'Seamus, did they tell you at school what Jesus said when the people asked him if they should pay tribute to Caesar?'

'Yes. He asked them to show him a coin and he asked whose face was on it. They said, Caesar's. Then he said, give to Caesar what is Caesar's and to God what is God's.'

'Quite right. But what if Caesar took your home and your job and ordered his soldiers to attack you because you objected? Would it be right to pay tribute to him then?'

'No. Because Caesar has a duty to the people who pay him tribute.'

It was Father Gerald's turn to laugh.

'You've done really well with him, Brother. Seamus, are there any more like you at home? Have you got any brothers?'

'There's Patrick, my younger brother. But he's a bit weird. A dreamer. Lives in a world of his own. I don't think it's really his fault. He's educationally subnormal. That's what my father says.'

'A dreamer, eh? Dreams are good but not on their own. It's action we're needing now. What about your father?'

'I think you might like him. He's a dreamer as well. But about things that matter. About our past and our future. There's my Uncle John as well. Everybody likes him. But he doesn't take things seriously.'

Father Gerald leaned forward and lowered his voice. 'Listen carefully, Seamus. There's a Bible on the sideboard. Bring it over.'

Seamus obeyed.

'Put your hand on it. That's right. Swear not to tell anybody outside this room about the conversation we are having today. Not unless I say you can.'

Seamus swore, using Father Gerald's exact words.

'Dreams on their own aren't enough, Seamus, as I said. And actions without dreams are for mindless thugs. We need the two together. The right dreams and the right actions. I'd like to meet your father. You can tell him everything we have talked about here today and everything I am about to say to you. But strictly in private. Don't say a word to your uncle or your mother or anybody. Do you understand?'

'Yes. But don't tell them about what, Father?'

'Have you heard of that business at Burntollet?'

'No.'

'It was at the start of this year. Before you came over, I suppose. A march for civil rights. One-man-one-vote in local elections, fair electoral boundaries, houses allocated according to need, jobs on merit. All good stuff, eh? Nothing wrong with any of that. But the marchers were attacked near Derry, by Burntollet Bridge. By loyalists as they call themselves. Of course they're loyal, to a system which gives them unfair advantage. Some were off-duty policemen. So tell me, Seamus, when the police attack Catholics on a peaceful march for basic rights, and the police are an organ of the state, what duty do we owe to that state?'

'None, Father.'

'Listen very carefully, Seamus. I'm not just talking about outbreaks of trouble here and there. What's coming will be on a much bigger scale. It will be civil war. Everybody will need to decide whose side they're on. We, that is, Brother Carey and myself and others of a like mind, use this house for certain meetings. Very secret meetings. I want you to come to the next one. Next Sunday, at eight o'clock. Talk to your father and persuade him to come along. Tell only him, Seamus. Nobody else. Talk to him only when nobody can overhear you. Lives could be at risk if you talk carelessly.'

After Seamus had left, Father Gerald and Brother Carey sat together in the lounge, each with a glass of whiskey in his hand.

'So, what do you think, Father?'

'I like him. Very much. You've a good eye for talent, Brother. The father sounds promising as well. Fox can have a look at both of them next week. The boy's too young now, but he can serve his time as an apprentice until he's ready. We need him and ones like him. If the father joins, it will be because the boy inspires him.'

Brother Carey coughed. 'I'm not the only one who's spotted him, Father.'

'What do you mean?'

'You know that Brother I told you about? Downie?'

'The one with an unhealthy interest in the young ones?'

'More than an interest. He went for Seamus last week. If I hadn't intervened... It's all right, Father. He'll leave him alone now. I warned him off.'

'And Seamus will always be grateful to you for that, won't he?'

'He'll be loyal but not just because of that. It'll be because he's found something he can believe in. That's what young people need these days. We had the faith, but I'm afraid that's not enough for the youngsters in this day and age.'

And it was never enough for me, thought Father Gerald. I have a faith of sorts and now I have the cause, but they are still not enough. There's always been something missing. Someone special in my life, someone I can love and protect and look out for. But now maybe God has brought that someone into my life, and there is something I can do to help him.

'This Brother who approached Seamus. Downie. Are you sure it wasn't just a friendly interest?'

'I'm sure. He was about to lock the door of the lab. Just he and Seamus inside. I stopped him just in time. I know he's done it before. I reported my suspicions to Brother Francis, but none of the boys will talk. There's nothing we can do without proof.'

'Tell me everything you know about him.'

'Seamus? I've told you all I know.'

'No, not Seamus. Brother Downie.'

# TWELVE

The week following Linda's rescue of Ruth was Easter week. Both families attended the Good Friday service together. Ruth was appalled by the story of the Passion as enacted in the church step by awful step through each of the Stations of the Cross. How could they have done such dreadful things to such a beautiful, innocent man?

That night she had a dream. She was once again in the street with the three men. She was naked because they had told her they had to search her. One of the two younger men was beside her, touching her, exploring her body. She turned towards him. He too was naked. It was Patrick. The other men took hold of him and dragged him off.

'Where are you taking him?' she cried. 'You know,' they said. 'To Golgotha, of course. The Place of a Skull.'

She shuddered awake. She was alone. More often than not Brendan slept downstairs on the sofa, telling her he did not want to disturb her when he came in late. Even when he did come to bed he never touched her and it was touch she craved. The loving touch of another, not the furtive self-touch which she sometimes allowed herself and which since becoming a Catholic she knew to be a sin. Not that she ever confessed it. It only made her loneliness more intense and wasn't that punishment enough?

She had known a moment of closeness when she and Linda had embraced, after she had been threatened by the three men. But there had been no such moments since. Yes, she and Linda would now always be friends. But the warmth of that embrace would remain only a memory. Though they had lived their early lives on different sides of the Irish Sea, the upbringings of both women had been very similar. They had learned to treat physical contact with deep mistrust. For a moment their relief at Ruth's escape and Ruth's gratitude and admiration for Linda's courage had broken through lifelong habits of distance. But back in the house and on their normal shopping trips the barriers had gone up again.

She wondered what comfort Brendan found in the house he visited from time to time. She recalled her conversation with Linda about it, one afternoon in the front room over tea and knitting.

'Linda, I think Brendan might be having an affair.'

'What makes you think that?' Linda took the question so much in her stride that she did not pause in the middle of an intricate manoeuvre with the needles.

'He never touches me. He avoids me as much as possible. He often sleeps down here. And I have no idea where he goes when he comes in late at night.'

Gently, Linda put down her knitting and lifted her cup to her lips.

'Listen, my dear. Of course he's not having an affair. Men round here don't have affairs. Certainly not secret ones. They don't have the skill or the imagination or the nouse. When it comes to sex there's places they can go where it's cheap and easy. That's all he's doing. And it's absolutely no reflection on you. I'm sure he still loves you in his way. In the way of the men around here. He may not come near you anymore. But you can be sure if any man or woman bad-mouthed you he'd defend your reputation to the death. That would be a matter of honour, you see.'

'How do you know? About these places, I mean?'

'John told me.'

'What! He told you he went there?'

'That's right. Years ago. We tried for a couple of years to have children but it didn't work. He assumed it was my fault and he lost interest.'

'Was it your fault, as you put it?'

'I have no idea. We didn't have tests. There was no point by then. When he lost interest I had the same idea you had. I asked him outright if he was having an affair. I got a black eye for my question. Then he told me where he went.'

'Did he tell Brendan?'

'He probably took him there.'

'So John…'

'…is no different from the others. Not really.'

'That surprises me. I would have thought he was different. I mean, if anyone did have the nouse for secret affairs it would be him.'

'I know what you mean. Maybe I was generalising a bit before. Men round here can think and talk and plan as well as any in the world, probably better. It's just that none of that is focussed on women. They're brought up to regard women as weak inferior beings and at the same time to put them on a pedestal. Either way they don't have to talk to them or listen to them. That frees up their time and energy and intelligence for putting the world to rights. Which they haven't quite managed to do yet but it's not for want of trying.'

'How did you and John meet?'

Linda laughed. 'You mean, how did two such different people manage to get to know each other well enough to get hitched? We didn't. Get to know each other, I mean. I'm not sure we ever have. Our fathers were old friends. His father used to come round every Sunday for lunch. He started to bring John with him. John was eighteen or nineteen by then. Good-looking, with plenty to say for himself. But he hardly ever addressed a word to me. After about a year I discovered why he had been coming round. He had been courting me and I had no idea! Neither had my mother. That was his idea of courtship. Now, if you're thinking that's an odd way of going about things, then you'd be wrong. It's quite common round here. He asked my father for permission to marry me. At some point he casually mentioned it to me. Within a month we were married. I didn't mind. I knew I was doing well for myself. He was quite a catch. There were much prettier girls around than me but for some reason he had chosen me. I wasn't going to object. Just thought it would have been nice if he had asked me at some point. What about you and Brendan?'

'We met at a dance. It was love at first sight. On my part anyway. I would have done anything for him.'

'You did. You converted.'

'That didn't seem such a big deal. Until the priest told me I had sinned by becoming pregnant before we were married.'

Linda dropped her knitting and squealed.

'Ruth O'Hara, you wicked woman! If I had known… Jesus, Mary and Joseph, here's us sheltering a scarlet woman under our roof. You should be off and never darken our doors again. You of all people, I would never have thought it.'

Ruth smiled and clasped her hands in an attitude of feigned supplication.

'Oh, don't throw me out, please. I was only seventeen. He was twenty-five. A man of the world. What chance did I have to defend my virtue?'

'It doesn't sound as if you wanted to give your virtue much of a chance.'

'You could be right about that.'

'Well, I may give you Absolution,' said Linda, in a mock-serious tone. 'So long as you can assure me you have never strayed since from the path of righteousness.'

Ruth laughed. 'No, Father. I have never strayed since. There was only ever him.'

Linda shrugged her shoulders. 'Oh, very well. Say ten Hail Marys and tell Our Lord you're sorry.'

'I think that's exactly what the priest said. I said the Hail Marys but I couldn't say I was sorry because I wasn't.'

Linda sighed. 'It was a bit different with me. I never fell in love with John. I don't claim to understand him. I'm not sure I even like him. But I've always been faithful. Perhaps that's why he married me. Because he knew I would always stand by him.'

Ruth had meant it when she said she had never been unfaithful. However intense her physical loneliness she could not imagine herself going out on her own to a bar to meet someone, or going up to a stranger in the park to start a conversation which had only one purpose in mind. No, she could never seek out temptation.

But what if it came to her? What if the stranger of her occasional fantasies approached her in the street? What if all she had to do was to respond? How strong would she be then?

That would never happen, of course. She liked to think she was still attractive. But since she had come to live in Belfast the burden of worry had deepened the lines in her face and dulled the light in her eyes. There were no signals, not even accidental ones, for a passing stranger to pick up.

She still had Patrick, of course. But she could find no physical comfort there anymore. Until quite recently he had let her be in the bathroom with him when he took a bath, to scrub his back and wash the hair she was allowing to grow long again in defiance of the school rules. How she had looked forward to those times. Now he locked the bathroom door. Now whenever she tried to hold him he squirmed away.

But at least there were the pills Linda's doctor had given her. And there was the bottle of gin in the sideboard, which with a nod of mutual understanding they replaced each time they went shopping.

# THIRTEEN

Brother Downie's widowed mother lived alone in a cottage near Crossmaglen. He visited her every Sunday, often taking with him essays he needed to mark for the following day. She had little sight or hearing left, so he did not need to make conversation once the initial enquiries about her health and the state of the cottage were out of the way.

He usually enjoyed the drive, particularly through the remote border areas where traffic was light and he could slow down to let his eyes rest from time to time on the rolling green hills and copses he knew so well. However for the last two weeks the journey had not been as relaxing as he would have wished. He had been disturbed by a Land Rover which had come up close behind him on several occasions, horn sounding and headlights flashing. He only managed to lose the other vehicle when he made the final turn up the track to his mother's cottage. Not like the old days, he thought. Farmers got around on horses and carts. Not much else on the road apart from the odd brightly-painted travellers' caravan.

On the third Sunday he did not see the Land Rover on the way there. He was relieved he could put it out of his mind and enjoy the drive once more.

The Land Rover was waiting for him on his way back. He saw it as he turned left out of the track, blocking the narrow road. Definitely the same vehicle. What the hell was it doing there? He sounded his horn. He was about to sound it again when he realised that there was nobody in the front seats. Then steps running towards him from behind, the door of his car being pulled open, masked faces close to his as they dragged him out.

He was pushed into the back of the Land Rover. He stared at his captors. Two men in the back with him, each with an Armalite, one up front driving.

'You've made a mistake,' he stammered. 'Whoever you're after, you've got the wrong man. I'm a teacher. A member of a religious order.'

'That's right,' said one of the men. 'A fucking pervert. You're the one all right.'

The driver stopped after half an hour, pulled over to the side of the road and switched off the headlights. They pulled him out and dragged him into nearby woods.

The two men who had been in the back with him held his arms, forcing his back against a tree. As one of them pointed a torch in the direction of the third man there was a momentary flash as a long curved blade reflected the light.

Brother Downie screamed. 'For God's sake, why don't you just shoot me?'

To his amazement the man with the knife laughed.

'All right, boys, let him go. You don't really think we'd do that to a man of the cloth, do you? We were just having a little joke. We'll take you back to your mother's now. We'll leave you there so you can say your goodbyes. Just make sure you're over the border by tomorrow morning. We'll be back to check you're gone. And don't dream of coming back or next time we won't be so friendly. Don't you be worrying about your mother now. We'll make sure she's looked after.'

# FOURTEEN

Somewhat to Seamus's surprise, Brendan readily agreed to attend the Sunday evening meetings at Father Gerald's presbytery. Seamus had thought his father might take offence because it was Seamus who had been approached first. But Brendan had shown nothing but delight to learn of the new friends his son had made.

The meetings took place around a large, oblong dining table. Father Gerald sat at one end, with Brother Carey to his left along with a man in his thirties with close-cropped hair, dark suit and tie and briefcase. Seamus and Brendan sat to Father Gerald's right.

Brendan, who struggled much more than Seamus with the intellectual challenges which the meetings presented, did not share Seamus's excitement and was growing increasingly impatient. After one meeting he took Father Gerald to one side, asking him if they could have a private word together.

'Look, Father, don't get me wrong. We appreciate you inviting us along here. We've heard some really interesting things. I'm not into the political theory stuff. But Seamus has been taking it all in and he tries to explain it to me afterwards. But what I'm wondering is, where does all this lead? I mean, there are still all these things going on. The injustices and the killings and the beatings. How do charts on a blackboard going back to 1916 help us with all that? I want to help, Father. But I'm a man of action, not words. And Seamus wants action too. I can tell that. I have something to offer. I can handle a gun. I trained at a pistol club back in England. I have certificates of proficiency to prove it. Seamus could learn too. He takes after me.'

Father Gerald sat down with him in a corner.

'Listen, my son. If I've been testing your patience, I'm sorry. It's for a good reason. I'm a priest, not a man of action, but I do understand what you're saying. You want to get on with it. You have experience with firearms. Yes, that could be useful, though there's a difference between firing at cardboard targets and firing at real people. You understand that.'

'Of course I do. But I could do it for real. With the right training.'

'I believe you, Brendan. But anybody who knows how to use a gun can go out and target someone because they live in a different street and go to a different church. That's what our oppressors do already. But we're not like that. There is change coming. I can sense it. And there is trouble coming. And if people like you are going to be involved you need to understand why. You need to understand the history and geography of the revolution of which you will be a part. You need to understand in depth exactly why our cause is just. So, will you trust me? There is a place for you and Seamus in the fight ahead. We're sure of that now. And when the time comes you will be contacted.'

As Father Gerald was speaking Brendan realised that the man in the suit who always sat next to Brother Carey was standing close to them, looking down at them, listening.

'Yes, Father, I understand. I'm sorry if I spoke out of turn.'

'You didn't, Brendan. Not at all. God bless you now. Take heart and take courage. You will need them.'

The man in the suit nodded to Father Gerald and walked away.

# FIFTEEN

The following Saturday Father Gerald and Brother Carey met in the church. They needed total secrecy so they used the confessional box.

'I didn't know what had happened,' whispered Brother Carey, his face pressed close to the grille. 'When he went missing Brother Francis told us he had gone on extended study leave. He arranged for a replacement. I thought he'd just been told to stay away, maybe roughed up a bit to underline the warning. Then they found the body.'

'It's my fault,' said Father Gerald. 'I was hasty, thoughtless. I was so angry about what you had told me. I said too much. I asked Fox if he could arrange for him to receive a warning. Fox asked what he had done. I told him what you said. They warned him all right. Took him into the woods. He thought they were going to castrate him. Then they told him to get over the border and stay there. They took him back to his mother's to say goodbye. When they went back the next day to check he had left, they found his body. He had cut his throat in front of her. She never saw or heard it. She's in a nursing home now.'

'Maybe it's for the best, Father. Not the way it happened but the fact that it happened. He might have carried on doing those things somewhere else.'

'I'd be dishonest if I tried to console myself with that thought, Brother. It's happening as I always feared. We have let loose something terrible in the land. And soon it won't just be a few thugs and one terrified man in a lonely forest at night. The guns will roar and our cities will burn.'

# SIXTEEN

Father Gerald was right. Belfast streets burned that summer and British troops arrived.

Brendan, Ruth, Linda and the boys stayed indoors. Afraid of breaking glass from stones through the windows, they kept them open, letting in the distant sounds of the riots. They watched in horror the televised images of families being forced from their homes.

John was the only member of the household who was not afraid to come and go as he always had. One evening Linda confronted him in the hallway as he was on his way out.

'For God's sake, John. We have to do something. Those poor people are losing their homes. It's not just Catholics. It's both sides, just for living where they do. We're in the minority here. This is a Protestant area, for God's sake. We have to go. If we stay in, they'll burn us alive.'

John shook his head and patted her on the shoulder. He was gentler with her since the violence had started.

'Don't worry,' he said, in a soothing voice. 'Nothing like that will happen here. It'll be all right. Just stay indoors.'

Linda returned to the front room and crouched behind the sofa. Ruth was already there, grateful that Patrick now allowed her once again to hold him in her arms. Once John had left, Seamus and Brendan took up defensive positions in the hall for hour after hour, armed with kitchen knives.

This scene, including Linda's confrontation with John in the hall, was repeated night after night. But to their relief the violence always seemed to stop at the end of their row. There were no attacks on the houses. Nobody threatened the occupants or demanded that they leave the area. In time their enclave came to be seen as a place of safety. Friends and relatives of John and Linda came to stay, carrying what few belongings they could. At one time several people were sleeping in every room of the house, on cushions and mattresses, carpets or bare boards, wherever they could find space.

One evening Linda had a panic attack and could not get her breath. One of the refugees in the house, a nurse, urged her to take deep breaths while she took her pulse.

'Has she had anything like this before?' the nurse asked Ruth.

'No. She was very brave once and kept calm throughout. Only shook a bit afterwards, that was all.' She told the nurse about the episode when she had been lost and Linda had rescued her.

'Could be some delayed shock from that time,' said the nurse. 'The problem with courage is we only have a limited stock of it. This trouble on the streets has brought back memories of that time.'

When at last Linda could breathe more easily she struggled into an upright position and tried to speak.

'It's all right,' said Ruth. 'Just keep calm and rest. Angela here is a nurse and she's been helping you. I'll get a blanket to put round you.'

Linda caught her hand. 'No,' she gasped. 'Get John. You must get John. He's out there. They'll kill him. I dreamed about it last night. Men shooting him. He keeps the peace between the gangs here so they want to kill him. The ones who don't want peace. Get him now, please.'

Seamus was watching and listening. 'I'll go, Ma,' he said.

It was Ruth's turn to panic. 'For God's sake, no, son. You'll get yourself killed as well.'

'I'll be all right. I can look after myself. Where do you think he'll be, Linda?'

'He never tells me where he goes. Try the youth club. Even he wouldn't be so stupid as to go towards the streets where there's rioting. God bless you, Seamus.'

Ruth realised that Linda had already taken Seamus's offer as a promise and that it was too late to stop him.

'I'll come with you,' said Brendan, putting on his coat.

'No, Da'. Someone has to stay and look after these people. Look, if there's trouble I'll run. I promise. I'm the best runner in my year. Nobody can keep up with me. But if you were with me you'd slow me down, no disrespect.'

'All right, son. No offence taken. You're right. Just no further than the club, understand? If he's not there, leave a message with anyone that is, or pin it to the door and get straight back. And if there's trouble you come running back here, not into more trouble. Is that clear?'

The youth club was deserted. Windows had been broken. The front door was off its hinges. Seamus walked through the main hall, picking his way carefully through a carpet of glass pieces. Tables and chairs had been overturned, some thrown against the walls. He went out through a side door. Uncle John was sitting on a bench a few yards away, smoking a cigarette, looking out over a patch of waste ground towards the estate. With him on the bench was a powerful-looking bald man, about the same age. They were whispering together, stopping abruptly when they realised there was someone else there. The bald man stood up and whirled round in a single movement, reaching for something in his pocket. It was not fear, Seamus was sure of that. This man was like his uncle. He knew no fear. But in another sense he was not like him. He was trained. The movement was a well-rehearsed routine.

'Ah, it's you, Seamus. It's all right.' He nodded to the bald man. 'This is Seamus, my nephew. He's a fine brave lad, as you see. Only a little foolhardy at times. Seamus, you don't want to be coming creeping up on people like that at times like this. It could be dangerous. We could have been anybody.'

Seamus noticed that the bald man did not speak and John did not introduce him. The man stared at Seamus for a few moments, carefully, as if trying to memorise his features, then sat down again.

'John, it's Linda. She sent me out to get you. She's been having panic attacks. Says she's been having dreams of you getting yourself killed out here. She's a lot calmer now. There's a nurse there looking after her. But she wants you to come back now. Jesus, this place is a fucking mess.'

John nodded to the bald man, who rose and walked away briskly without a word.

'Sit down, Seamus. Join me for a cigarette.'

'I shouldn't. Linda will still be worrying about you. And Ma will be worrying about me. We should get back.'

'Sure, you said she was calmer now, didn't you? And your da' is there to look after them, isn't he? I hate being cooped up there with all those people, though I'm glad we can offer them shelter. I need to get out. I need some freedom. So do you, don't you, son? Come and have a cigarette.'

'All right. Just for a minute.'

'Good lad. No need to worry. It's safe here. Look at the estate over there. It's quiet. The gangs are busy elsewhere.'

Seamus took the offered cigarette and matches and lit up, trying to ease himself into the surreal mood of calm which emanated from his uncle. Sounds of shouting, crashing glass, whether of windows or bottles they could not tell, explosions, running feet, cheers, came to their ears from a distance.

'I know Linda's worried,' said John, puffing on a fresh cigarette. 'But will you be listening to them now? Sticks and stones. A few petrol bombs. Toys for amateurs. But wait until the real weapons come. They'll see the British troops on the streets with all their firepower and want the same. And there's plenty around the world ready to give it to them.'

'Quite right, too.'

'What? That innocent people will die?'

'No, I didn't mean that. Of course not. I mean, right that we should have real weapons. If nobody can protect us we have to protect ourselves. It's up to us to use them properly to make sure innocent people don't die.'

John put his hand on his shoulder.

'It's funny. I talk about "them" and you talk about "us." But we're both on the same side, aren't we? I'm a Catholic, but I don't want to be part of any violence, that's all. But you talk as if you do.'

'I don't want violence any more than you do. But sometimes you have to fight for a cause. You have to fight for justice if there's no other way.'

John laughed. 'Oh, what it is to be young and to see it all so clearly. You're right of course, in principle. Only if things are out of control the way they are now, do you think it will be possible to control it when the Armalites and the Semtex arrive? I hope you're right, Seamus. But I fear you may not be.'

Seamus turned his head towards the building behind them. 'What happened to this place?'

'Young kids. Too young to know about the divide or its causes. Kids I'd brought here from both sides to play together so they would learn we're all people first, people who in the end have to live together. So they would learn to shake hands rather than fists. So they would learn to ask first, what sort of man are you, not what side are you on. But the riots started and they didn't want to be left out. They thought it must be fun, smashing things up. So they smashed up the club. Father, forgive them for they know not what they do. That was what Christ said on the Cross, wasn't it? I say it to myself a hundred times a day. I hope He has forgiven them. Because I sure as hell know I haven't. Come on. Let's get back.'

# SEVENTEEN

---

Seamus told Linda she had no need to worry about John. He spent his evenings smoking on a bench outside his club. Seamus described the bald man to her.

'I don't know him,' she said. 'From the estate, I suppose. Comes over for company when he sees John there.'

As the summer wore on, Seamus and Brendan tired of remaining indoors. They persuaded John to stay in one evening to look after the occupants while they went out for a breath of fresh air. By then the house was less crowded. Some of the refugees had returned to homes which no longer seemed in danger, while others had dispersed to friends or relatives elsewhere. Some had gone over the border, while several had crossed to England, vowing never to return.

Ruth begged them not to go out, but John put his arm around her and assured her they would be safe in the house with him to look after them.

'It's not me I'm worried about,' said Ruth, 'or anybody left in the house. It's the two of you. Just don't go looking for trouble. Promise me you'll go no further than the end of the street, you hear?'

They promised. They did not tell her they had armed themselves with a kitchen knife each.

Once outside, they filled their pockets with stones from the waste ground near the former youth club and headed towards the sound of the riots.

They joined a street fight a mile away. Seamus recognised members of his own gang, despite the faces smeared with oil and charcoal.

---

Proudly he introduced his father to them. They sensed their opponents were in retreat and pursued.

As they followed, Seamus noticed that some had taken refuge in an alley, or so he thought. He followed them into the alley. It was a trap. Four of them surrounded him. In a few moments they had him on the ground and were beating him with sticks. They left him where he was, motionless, blood pouring from his arms and legs and the side of his head. It was Brendan who found him. He had noticed he was missing and gone back to look for him. Knowing that no ambulance would get through at that time he somehow found the strength to carry him back to the house.

Ruth screamed when she heard the frenzied knocking at the door. When she saw Brendan carrying Seamus over the doorstep she fainted.

Linda looked after her in the kitchen, mopping her brow and trying to get her to take some brandy, while Angela looked after Seamus in the front room. She did her best to dress his wounds with what was available. She made a bed for him on the sofa. Ruth had by then recovered enough to take over nursing him, with Linda's help.

It was several days before they could get him to hospital. He was there for a week, Brendan by his side day and night. Ruth was too frightened to leave the house. When he could talk, he told Brendan it had been the proudest moment of his life when he had gone into that alley on his own, and the happiest when he was dimly aware that Brendan was carrying him in his arms.

Brendan came home from the hospital the day before Seamus was due to be discharged to tell them how pleased they were with his progress. Ruth had not said a word to Brendan about that night, but now she turned to him.

'So what the hell were you up to, the two of you? I told you not to go seeking trouble. And what did you do? Go and walk right into the middle of it and nearly get yourself killed.'

'It wasn't like that, Ruth. We did what you said. We only went up to the top of the street. There was a gang there, waiting.

Someone must have seen us come out and tipped them off. They took us by surprise.'

She stared at him. She knew he was lying. Because if it had been like that he would have been ashamed. Instead she only saw pride in his eyes, for himself and above all for Seamus. It was a pride she would never understand. It was a stranger standing before her. And it was a stranger who came home from hospital the next day, applauded by everybody in the house, even by Patrick. Even by Linda. Everybody but her.

I'm the stranger here, Ruth said to herself, in this town, this street, this house. A stranger in my own family.

Seamus could walk without too much difficulty, though ever after he had a slight limp. His running days were over. He never tried to hide the limp. He displayed it like a badge of honour.

# EIGHTEEN

One Sunday evening after one of Father Gerald's meetings the man in the suit handed Brendan a piece of paper. On it were written an address and date and time. 'Both of you,' he whispered.

'At last,' said Brendan to Seamus.

The address was a farm some ten miles outside the city. Brendan did not have a car of his own and had to borrow John's. The man in the suit greeted them at the door of the farmhouse and took them through a yard into an empty barn. In the centre of the floor space was a table and three chairs. He signalled for them to sit down.

'You want to volunteer, right?' he asked. His manner was crisp and business-like, his speech precise with only a slight trace of a local accent. He did not wait for a reply.

'Seamus, you're still very young. We've decided to let you be a novitiate. Sorry, that's not an official term, it's one of mine. An aunt of mine went to be a nun. I should say apprentice. On your next birthday, if you're still with us, you can join. You'll be seventeen then. Understand?'

Seamus nodded.

'Now, listen to me very carefully, so you both know what you're letting yourselves in for. You've heard this before so I'll just state it again as simply as I can. We are in direct linear succession to the 1916 Provisional Government of Ireland and the Dáils of 1919 and 1921. The Treaty with Britain partitioned the nation and left it under imperial control. By accepting the Treaty in 1922 the Dáil made itself illegitimate, so the succession fell to the remaining faithful Republican Deputies. They delegated executive powers to the IRA Council. But the leaders in Dublin proved useless against loyalist aggression in the North. They wanted to go down the route of political change while our streets were burning. So a couple of years ago the IRA split and the Provisional IRA was born. That's me, and after today that's you. There was only one surviving faithful Republican Deputy from the Second Dáil by then. Tom Maguire. He declared that the powers that those Deputies had granted to the IRA Council had now passed on to the new Provisional Army Council. We inherit those powers. We are the provisional government of the future united Ireland, with the right and the duty to resist foreign aggression by force.'

'I understand all that, sir,' said Brendan.

'He does, sir,' said Seamus. 'Honestly. I've explained it to him many times.'

'Good. The important thing is to remember it when people call you criminals. Now, answer me this, both of you. Are you here to volunteer by your own choice, solely because of your convictions? And are your objectives political freedom and social and economic justice for your people?'

They answered yes in unison.

'Good. Now, the enemy. That's everybody who has a vested interest in maintaining the status quo. We're talking about politicians, the media, the judiciary, the British war machine, the UDR, the RUC. If you had friends in these establishments they are now your enemies. You are in a permanent state of war. You cannot be friends with such people at night and enemies during the day. You are a Volunteer first. After that you can be a husband, a son, a lover, a student, a worker, to the extent that it does not conflict with your duties as a Volunteer. These are your priorities from this day forward.

'Now, let's get something clear. As a Volunteer on active service there are two things which are very likely to happen to you. You might get killed. Or you might get a long prison sentence. Be prepared for those possibilities. You are soldiers and you may be captured. There is no shame in that. The Brits will try to break you and get information out of you. Expect the worst and prepare for it.'

Seamus felt himself grow dizzy. He wanted to yell with pride and delight.

'Remember that this is an army,' the man continued. 'You do not carry out unauthorised operations in any circumstances. You must obey all orders and regulations issued by the Army Authority and any superior officers. Brendan, I'm going to ask you now to make the Declaration exactly as it is written out here.' He handed Brendan a sheet of paper. 'Read it through, and if you agree, read it out loud. Seamus, for you this will need to wait for another day. But you must regard yourself as bound by an oath of secrecy concerning everything you have heard and seen today. You are old enough to understand the seriousness of an oath, in my judgement. Brendan?'

Brendan read out the Declaration, haltingly, stumbling over the words several times. He sighed with relief when he got to the end.

'Seamus, do you swear to secrecy, and to follow the principles of all you have heard, pending making the Declaration yourself on your seventeenth birthday?'

'I swear.'

Of course I do. Of course I fucking swear, he wanted to scream to the heavens.

'All right. Now to practicalities. I am your unit commander. My codename is Fox. On no account will you attempt to contact me directly. Your attendance at the meetings with Father Gerald, so long as I am present, will discharge your obligation to remain in contact with me. At those meetings you will give no indication that you know me or what I am. If in an emergency you need to contact me, do so through Father Gerald. Any questions?'

Seamus put up his hand.

'Sir, is Father Gerald...'

'A Volunteer? Of course he is. And the one thing you must never ask anybody or of anybody is if they are a Volunteer. Understood?'

Seamus grinned, glowing with inner satisfaction. So his instinct about Father Gerald had been right.

'Now you know he's a Volunteer you need to know his codename. It's Squirrel. I suppose you'd also like to know about Brother Carey. He's a civilian. He helps us out with things like talent-spotting. He does a good job. He spotted you, didn't he, Seamus? We've selected you two to train in the use of small arms for special operations. This is where the training takes place. Stay here when I leave. The staff captain in charge of training will come to take you to the range. Now, some personal issues. Brendan, your wife is English, I understand.'

'That's right, sir. Is that a problem?'

'But she is a Catholic?'

'Yes. She converted so we could marry.'

'You must keep your membership a secret from her. But if she did suspect anything, do you think she would cause difficulties?'

'You mean, shop me? Never. She's totally loyal.'

'That's what we think.'

Brendan stared at him. 'You've been investigating her?'

'We have Squirrel's opinion as to her personal loyalty. That's enough. But I wasn't actually thinking about her shopping you. I was thinking more on the lines of getting in your way or trying to stop you doing what you have to do. She won't understand the politics of the cause. She may have scruples.'

'She won't get in the way. I promise.'

'Good. Seamus, do you have a girl-friend?'

'No. Not yet.'

'But he's interested,' added Brendan quickly. 'And I know they like the look of him.'

Fox smiled at last.

'I'm sure they do. But it wasn't his love life I wanted to talk about, not as such. You're both fairly new here. It can be hard to know who to trust, even when you've been here all your life. There are spies and informers. The Brits set honey-traps. Send girls in to pretend to be on your side so they can get information to pass on. Think of the girls you know, Seamus. Have any of them approached you? Shown a special interest?'

Seamus nodded. 'One or two.'

'Avoid them like the plague. If you go out with someone be very careful what you say. If you can't help getting attached to someone, let us know and we'll check them out. Now, this is even more important. Young lads like you can get into trouble with the law.

You mustn't. Live cleanly. Dress respectably. No petty crime. No thieving. No more street fights. Be a model citizen. If the boys at school make fun of you, too bad. If you upset the gang members, too bad. You must not on any account get known to the authorities. That applies to both of you. Any more questions? Then goodbye for now and good luck.'

He shook hands with each of them and walked briskly away.

After several weeks' training they took a small supply of handguns and a stock of ammunition back to Father Gerald's and hid them in part of his huge garden shed. 'Last place the Brits will think of searching for guns is a priest's garden,' he said, with a wink.

On the way back, Seamus turned to his father.

'Da', I've done what Fox told me. I've kept out of trouble and I've steered clear of the girls. But it's very frustrating. I can tell they're interested. And so am I. I want to be a man, Da'.'

'You are, son. They like you and trust you. And I'm not talking about the girls. You'll soon be using that gun in earnest.'

Seamus turned away, feeling his cheeks burn.

'That's not what I meant. You know what I mean.'

Brendan nodded. The next day he took him to a house on Lisburn Road, paid the middle-aged woman who emerged from the back in answer to his knock and waited while she took Seamus upstairs. He was back in ten minutes.

Brendan smiled proudly. 'Don't call me Da' anymore,' he said, tears in his eyes. 'We're men together now. Call me Brendan.'

# NINETEEN

For over a year their involvement was limited to the provision of armed cover during a number of night-time raids on business premises. There were no shootings, only thefts of cash and valuables. During all this time they continued to train rigorously, each time at a different secret countryside location.

One evening, a few weeks after Seamus had made the Declaration, Father Gerald rang their doorbell and handed Brendan a note. On it were scribbled the name of a pub outside the city, a time and a date.

The main bar was deserted, apart from a burly man drinking in a corner. After they had bought their pints Brendan glanced at the man, who seemed to nod towards a side-door. They went through it to a tiny snug with one beer-stained table and a corner-seat. There was a single stool by the bar. The snug was empty.

After a few minutes the burly man came in, holding a freshly-drawn pint. He wore baggy trousers held up by braces and a large, badly worn brown pullover. He smelt of manure. Brendan wondered if he was a friendly local farmer rather than their intended contact. He swore under his breath. If their contact had come in and was watching from the main bar, would he suspect them of meeting an informer and abort the meeting? What would happen to them then? Brendan breathed a sigh of relief when the man extended a hand to each of them.

'Good evening to you's. I was wondering if you could give me a lift?'

They drove several miles deep into the countryside. The man signalled to Brendan to pull over by a field with a broken-down fence. He took out a packet of cigarettes, offered one to Brendan, who accepted, and to Seamus, who shook his head. He puffed slowly and thoughtfully for a minute. At last he spoke, very quietly so that they had to lean forward to catch his words.

'Now listen carefully, the both of you's. You need cover. Seamus, I can give you a Saturday job on my farm. It's near here. Only pocket money, I'm afraid. But the fresh air and exercise will be good for you. You can drive him there and back, Brendan, and also do some collections and deliveries on the way. I'm talking about genuine stuff for the farm. Your cover must be real. You'll need your own wheels. I'll give you the name of someone who'll get you something cheap and reliable, good for country roads. Drive around in the rain and get it nice and dirty. Get manure and farming tools on board so it won't look suspicious, you driving around the country lanes. We want you to do some clean-up jobs for us, as and when needed. You're just right for them, both of you's. Cool under pressure, no nerves. You don't have to go and find people. We'll find them for you. We'll tell you when to come out. If you're ill or you get raided, get a message to Fox via Squirrel as soon as you can. Otherwise, don't make any attempt to get in touch. This is where they'll be handed over to you. Hide the guns in among the farm stuff in case you're searched. Inside a bag of manure works well, in my experience. Always check your guns before you set out and bring a spare. Your targets won't give you any trouble. They'll have been worked over. You take them to this field. The trench will already have been dug. One shot in the back of the head and into the trench. Then get the hell out of there. Don't attempt to cover up the bodies. Somebody else will do that. It'll be one at a time. Take it in turns to do the actual shooting, so one of you's doesn't start to feel guilty or get nightmares. The two of you's will always work together, never separately. That's Fox's order. You have a joint codename. Mamba. I think that's a snake. Fox's idea, not mine. Like all the bloody silly animal codenames in his unit. His way of taking the mickey out of the Brits.'

'Who will they be?' asked Seamus. 'Brits? Protestants?'

'No soldiers and no police. They're out of your league for now. But still big stuff. The worst scum in the world, I'd say. Our own side.

Traitors. Informers. Don't talk to them. Don't listen if they try to talk to you, which they probably won't because they'll be in no state to. They're guilty. That's all you need to know. The first is timed for next week. Anything else? If not, I'll show you the field. I'm Badger, by the way. I know. Bloody silly codename.'

Ruth simply shrugged her shoulders when Brendan told her about Seamus's Saturday job. She did not even react when Brendan bought a second-hand Land Rover and loaded it with tools and bags of manure and fertiliser. She's no danger to us, thought Brendan. She couldn't care less what we get up to.

The following week Father Gerald delivered another message. They drove to the spot and waited. An hour later another car arrived. A man, bound and gagged, was pulled out and bundled into the back of their vehicle. It was too dark to see his face. The man did not move and made no sound. After the other car had left they drove to the trench, dragged the man out, shot him in the back of the head and pushed him in.

Five times in all, at intervals of a few weeks, sometimes months. Five bodies in the trench. Five fewer traitors to worry about.

# TWENTY

One day when Linda and Ruth were alone in the house, the boys at school, the men at work and all the refugees at last dispersed, Linda took a phone call from John. He told her the firm were sending him to Liverpool. They had a branch factory there. It was doing badly and needed someone with John's experience to join a team to help turn it round. He had to leave right away. He gave her an address where he would be staying and a phone number where he could be reached in an emergency. Linda recognised the address. A cousin of John's lived there. John had stayed with him when he had gone over to visit Brendan. She remembered having been there with him once.

'Who was that?' asked Ruth when Linda came into the front room. Ruth was knitting. Linda had taught her but she was still not very good at it. 'Why are you crying?'

'It's John,' said Linda. 'He's going to Liverpool. Something to do with the firm. He's going in such a hurry there's no time to say goodbye or even to come home and pack. I'm to send his things after him. He rang from the ferry terminal. I'm sure he's known about it for some time. He just couldn't face telling me, knowing how I would react. You know how he hates a scene.'

Ruth put down her knitting. 'Linda, I'm sorry. He should have told you before. But it won't be for long, will it?'

'He said two or three weeks at most.'

'Well, there you are then. Don't worry. He'll be fine. I wish to God I were going with him. I don't know if I can stand it here much longer. Did I ever show you my old photographs? Some of them are a real scream. Shall we have a look at them, cheer ourselves up? Then we can have a drink.'

Linda nodded, wiping away her tears, trying to smile. 'Let's have a drink at the same time, not afterwards,' she said.

'I'll just go upstairs to get them. You get the bottle out.'

Ruth kept her old albums on the top of the wardrobe. She had not looked at them since coming to Belfast. She did not know whether she was going to laugh or cry.

They pored over the fading images, each with a glass of gin in hand, giggling at Ruth's brown, shapeless bathing costume on the beach at New Brighton.

'God, look at me! I had a figure in those days, didn't I?'

'You certainly did. You still do. I envy you. The belle of the ball. I mean, the beach. Can you have a belle of the beach? Shit, I think I'm drunk.'

'Already? I'd be too fat these days. Did you see the pictures in that magazine of that model? What do they call her? Twiggy. You could get three of her into that costume. Look at these. Taken when I was about ten. Making a sandcastle in the freezing cold and pouring rain. There's British seaside holidays for you. I look happy enough, though.'

'Where was this?'

'Holiday camp near Ainsdale. Along the coast near Southport.'

'I know where that is. I went there once. Southport, I mean. John took me with him to visit his cousin. We took a train to Southport for a day out. Very elegant. Lots of old ladies dressed up in furs, walking their puddles along the promenade.'

'Puddles?'

'No. No puddles. It was a nice sunny day. I remember.'

'No, you said "puddles." You said the ladies were out walking their puddles.'

'I did not,' replied Linda, indignantly. 'I said, they were out walking their... poodles.'

She paused before pronouncing the word, drawing out the sound of the vowels so there could be no mistake. She rose and attempted to imitate the walk of the Southport ladies, before collapsing in a heap on the floor. Ruth flopped down beside her.

'I think they were the happiest days of my life, those holidays,' said Ruth. 'We went back every year. I suppose it's closed down now. But if I get the chance I'll go back there. Even if it's deserted. Just for old times' sake.'

She stood up and walked to the window.

'Linda, do you know that man?'

Linda rose unsteadily and stood beside her.

'What man? I can't see anybody.'

'He was there, on the opposite side of the road. He's gone now. All I could see about him was that he had shaved his head. He seemed to be watching the house. He went away when he saw that I'd noticed him. Didn't Seamus say there was a bald man with John when he went to fetch him from the youth club that time?'

'Yes, I remember. Maybe he's wondering where John is and why he hasn't seen him.'

'In that case, why doesn't he come and knock at the house?'

# TWENTY-ONE

When Linda had not heard from John for a week she rang the number he had given her. It was a pub opposite the flat where he was supposed to be staying. The landlord promised to get a message to him. When another week passed with no news, she rang again. The landlord told her John's cousin was away. Nobody staying in the house had seen John. She rang the factory.

When Brendan returned home that evening she confronted him, before he had even taken off his coat.

'Brendan, do you know where John is?'

'He's in Liverpool. You know that.'

'When did he tell you he was going?'

'He didn't. He never said a word to me about it. You told me yourself. He rang you from the factory to tell you about it.'

'No. He rang from the ferry terminal. So he said.'

'I swear the first I knew about it was when you told me. You know we work in different units. We very rarely see each other there. What is this?'

'I've heard nothing from him since he left. He's not where he said he would be staying. So I rang his foreman today. He asked me how John was enjoying his holiday in Dublin.'

'Dublin?'

'That's right. He told him he had the chance of a couple of weeks there, house-sitting for a friend, only he had to leave right away. The foreman was a bit taken aback, but as John's so reliable and was owed a lot of leave he gave him permission. So where the hell is he?'

There was a hard, nearly hysterical edge to her voice.

'Linda, I have no idea. It's obviously something he didn't feel he could tell you or the boss about. He told you one story and the boss another. So all we can do is wait until we hear from him. Now, I need a drink.'

The weeks passed, with no more news of John. Violence was increasing again on the streets and this time it was coming closer. Messages were pushed through the doors of all the houses in the row, warning the 'papist scum' to get out or they would be burned out. The family in the first house left almost immediately. The next night the abandoned house was set alight when a petrol bomb was pushed through the door. By the time the fire brigade had it under control it was little more than a shell.

More messages came, this time wrapped around stones thrown through the windows. The message was always the same. *YOUR NEXT.*

Brendan convened a family council in the front room with Seamus, Ruth and Linda. Brendan spoke first.

'First of all, Linda, has there been any news from John?'

She shook her head.

'I spoke to his foreman today,' continued Brendan. 'He hasn't heard anything, either. One thing seems clear. Whatever protection John was able to give us and our neighbours has gone.'

'We have to leave,' said Linda, in a quiet, flat voice, her eyes unfocussed.

'Ruth, what do you think?' asked Brendan.

Ruth shook her head. Her eyes were lowered. She was shaking, as she was nearly all the time now. For weeks she had barely spoken to any of them. Brendan could not be sure she had understood his question or even if she realised what was going on. The silence was broken by the strum of Patrick's guitar from the next room.

'Jesus Christ!' said Brendan, raising his eyes to the ceiling and pounding his right palm with his left fist. 'That fucking guitar! He's so fucking out of his head he thinks he's in the middle of some fucking hippy love-in with dope and incense instead of a bloody war zone. They could burn him out and he wouldn't even notice.

If I didn't have better things to do I'd go and break it over his fucking imbecilic head.'

Whimpering, Ruth stood up and left the room. Seamus rose to follow.

'It's all right, son,' said Brendan. 'Leave her be. Somebody needs to be with Patrick. Neither of them has a clue what's happening so neither of them has anything to contribute to the discussion.'

'Discussion!' shrieked Linda, jumping to her feet. 'Discussion! We're Catholics in a Protestant area. We're being burned out of my house and my husband's gone missing. And you say we're having a discussion! There's nothing to discuss. We've got to get out or we're all going to die. End of story.'

'Sit down!' shouted Brendan.

Linda glared at him. When she spoke at last she forced the words out through clenched teeth.

'What in the name of God gives you the right to order me about in my own home? John and I offered you a home when you needed one. You don't own this house. You're only a guest here. You certainly don't own me. John is the master of this house and in his absence I take his place. Do you understand?'

Brendan rose and glared at her. For a moment Seamus thought he was going to hit her. Then he sat down again, breathing hard.

'All right, Linda.' He was struggling to keep his voice under control. 'I know you're upset so I'll forgive you for speaking to me like that. These are difficult and dangerous times and there are decisions to make. In John's absence the task of taking these decisions falls to the man of the house and at the moment that is me. I am responsible for you, in John's absence and on his behalf, and for my wife and children who happen to be under this roof. We are having a discussion because I would prefer us to talk about these things calmly and agree on them. But if we can't discuss things calmly I will tell you what we are going to do. First of all, Linda, you will sit down.'

Linda opened her mouth to speak, then decided to say nothing. She sat down.

'Right,' continued Brendan. 'Now it's clear to me that we have to leave.'

Linda laughed harshly. 'I just said that, didn't I? Why does it take so long for a man to realise what's so fucking obvious?'

Seamus signalled to her to be quiet. Brendan ignored her and continued.

'For some time now Seamus and I have been planning to return to England. Seamus has done well at school, unlike his idiot brother who hasn't passed a single exam and has just been expelled. Seamus tells me he wants to go to an English university, preferably in London. I'll go with him to support him.'

'When were you planning to tell me?' They had not noticed Ruth, who was standing in the doorway, staring at them. Brendan turned to her.

'You and Patrick are of course welcome to join us. We can find a house together. I don't want to break up the family.'

It was Ruth's turn to let out a harsh laugh.

'You did that a long time ago, Brendan. Long before we came over here. And just for the record, Patrick hasn't been expelled. He's left school by mutual agreement.'

Brendan's face twisted into a sneer as he spoke.

'You've suddenly got a lot to say for yourself who's hardly said a word for weeks. What's given you the courage? Is it that bottle of gin you've got hidden away next door? I notice you've stopped shaking and there's a certain smell on your breath.'

Ruth rushed at him but he stepped aside and pushed her onto the sofa next to Linda.

'What about me?' whispered Linda.

'You come from round here. Have you anywhere you can go? Friends, relatives?'

She shook her head. 'They've all gone.'

'Then come with us. You can join us, or you can try to find John. It's up to you. What I'm going to do now is pin a notice to the front door, telling those bastards that we're going, so they don't burn the house until we've gone.'

Within two days they had packed and caught the ferry to Liverpool.

Linda parted from them at the bus-station near the pier head, giving Ruth a prolonged and tearful hug. She told her she was going to the address which John had given her. She had to see for herself that he was not there. If he wasn't, she would try to find out if anybody nearby knew where he might be. She was convinced by then that he had left her for another woman and had not had the courage to tell her.

Brendan, Seamus, Ruth and Patrick went on to Lime Street to take the train for Euston. As they walked up the platform they saw a train pull in and a unit of British soldiers get out, chatting nervously, hoisting their huge kitbags onto their backs.

'It's the enemy,' said Seamus to Brendan. Ruth and Patrick were walking on ahead, so there was no danger of their being overheard.

'Good job we've no orders to attack Brits on sight,' said Brendan, 'or we'd be gunned down in seconds.'

Seamus grinned. 'We could tell them they're going the wrong way. They're going over there and the war's coming over here.'

They found a cheap hotel where they stayed while Brendan looked for somewhere permanent. After a week he told them he had found a house to rent which would be perfect for them. He had also found a job. There was a garage nearby which had agreed to take him on as a panel beater and general repair man. They were ready to start their new life.

# TWENTY-TWO

It was all a lie, of course.

Ruth realised it soon enough. Yes, the house and the job were real, though she was not interested enough to ask where Brendan worked or what he did there. But the reason for the move was a lie. She knew about the IRA only from what she read in the papers and saw on television, but she had long suspected that Brendan and Seamus were involved. Stupefied as she was most of the time with pills and cheap gin, she found it hard to care. If it wasn't for Patrick she would have killed herself long ago, she told herself. She had protected Patrick all that time in Belfast. Now she had to do it again because she knew the war had crossed over with them.

It was true that Patrick had failed miserably at school in Belfast. But she was sure Brendan was wrong when he said he was stupid. How could he be when he played the guitar so beautifully? And he wrote. She knew that, although he never let her see anything. He could not be illiterate. For a time in Belfast, towards the end, the dangers of their situation had brought her and Patrick closer together again. Now the immediate danger of physical attack had gone she sensed him once again withdrawing from her. He spoke to her as rarely as he did to the others.

His beauty, increasing every day, made her heart ache. Of course she could no longer be with him as he took a bath. She had not been able to do that for years. But at least she had found another way to watch him, without his knowledge. The thought of other women seeing that beauty, with his connivance, at his invitation, drove her to a frenzy of jealousy. Not that there was any immediate danger. He never went out on his own and Brendan and Seamus were too busy with other things to bring girls to the house. But one day he might fulfil Linda's prophecy. He might come out of his shell. And he would only have to walk down the road with his eyes and ears open to realise that there was a different world out there. But he would not realise what dangers lay in that world. What would they do to him, those women, if he let them near him? They would tell him they loved him and offer to look after him. But they would never appreciate him. Not the way she could. They would never understand him. They would never be able to give him what he needed.

But neither were they safe in the house. The police could come at any time. They were likely to suspect that the whole family was involved in illegal activity. She would gladly accept a prison sentence for herself. Had it not been like that for her for years? But the thought of Patrick in prison made her sick with dread.

She was torn, agonisingly. To stay in the house was to leave Patrick exposed to the danger of arrest. To take him away would risk his leaving her and plunging into a world for which he was not prepared.

She stuck it for three bleak, anxious, silent years. Then one day she told Brendan that she and Patrick were leaving the next morning. Brendan did not even ask where they were going. She did not know herself. There were no goodbyes. Brendan and Seamus were out when Ruth and Patrick let themselves out of the front door and into a waiting taxi, taking with them a suitcase each and the housekeeping Brendan had given her for the next few weeks.

# TWENTY-THREE

Seamus had, to his own surprise though not to Brendan's, obtained good grades in his A-levels in Belfast and succeeded in getting a place at King's College to study history.

His was a strange life when he took time to think about it. On the one hand he was studying with supposed academic objectivity the history of the nation he considered to be occupying and oppressing his own, at a university established by and within the heart of that enemy nation. On the other hand he continued to support Brendan and their unnamed visitors in an armed struggle to defeat the enemy on its own ground. Surrounded every day by evidence of the sheer power and size of the British State and the apparent stoical indifference of the people he met, he began to believe they could not possibly succeed by force of arms alone. They could rob banks and blow up pubs and shopping centres. But their impact on the state and society as a whole could never be more than a pinprick.

He kept quiet about his misgivings, which it was clear Brendan did not share. Brendan remained convinced that the mainland campaign was the key to success. Mainlanders did not care about violence in Northern Ireland, he would say, but when it is on their own doorstep they will care all right. They will force the British Government to withdraw.

Their work was routine and low profile for the most part, stocking and supplying firearms and bomb-making equipment, providing a safe house when asked to do so. They carried out their duties efficiently, all the time missing the excitement of their night-time missions back in Belfast.

At last a chance came to bring those times back, to let them feel once again the pulsing of blood through their veins, the pounding of their heart-beats, the gathering of sweat on their brows and palms, the surge of power and relief as they extinguished the life of yet another traitor. Seamus shouted with delight when Brendan told him about their new mission.

Brendan had a single contact with the Active Service Unit to which he and Seamus were attached, knowing him only by a codename. Seamus knew nothing about him other than his existence. Brendan was under orders to keep it that way. If we get caught, the less we know about the ASU the better, he told Seamus. Brendan and the contact met only when there was urgent and serious business to discuss, as was the case that evening in the secluded corner of a Soho pub.

The contact was a dapper, neatly-dressed man in his thirties. He had the look and manner of a bank clerk or an accountant. Brendan found it hard to believe what he knew to be true, that the contact had masterminded and taken part in several bank raids, two of them on the same bank in the Falls Road, where he had been born and raised, two much more recently in London and Birmingham. The contact put his briefcase on the beer-stained table in front of them, refusing Brendan's offer of a drink. He handed Brendan a slip of paper.

'We need Mamba's services again,' he said, as if enquiring about the availability of a reliable plumber. 'Don't react, man, for God's sake,' he continued, noticing that Brendan had raised his hands as if to clap them together.

'Sorry.' Brendan forced a serious, frowning expression onto his face and leaned forward. 'So, who are they?'

'Natives, Volunteers, like us. Only they're working for the Brits. These are the codenames we know them by. Will you remember them? Give me back the paper.'

Brendan handed it to him. The contact took out a box of matches, placed the piece of paper in an ashtray, set fire to it and watched it burn.

'They're good, bloody good,' he continued. 'They got hold of intelligence about some of our arms-smuggling operations and tipped off the border patrols. But they underestimated our counter-espionage people. Their cover's been blown and they have no idea. Now they've volunteered for the mainland campaign, to try and disrupt our operations here. The orders are to get them when they arrive. Not over there. They have a network of escape routes. They could easily slip away if they caught even a whiff of danger. Over here, they're much more vulnerable. They'll be on their own. They'll arrive within a couple of weeks of each other. They'll need a safe house. Yours. I'll meet them, show them to your door and leave once I see they're safely inside.'

'Won't the second get suspicious when the first doesn't make contact?'

'They won't be in touch with each other, only with me. That's the rule and it suits everybody. We keep them apart. They build up a fuller intelligence picture by getting fed into different parts of the campaign. Each will arrive separately at your house. Within a few days I'll contact them to give them further orders. That's what they've been told. Instead, you will take each one out within twenty-four hours of arrival. The second won't know what's happened to the first. You'll be in sole charge of the operation. There's no back-up. If you're caught, you're on your own. That means getting rid of the bodies yourselves, without anybody seeing you or knowing what you are doing. You get a message to me when each job's done. You don't tell me where they are. I don't want to know. You don't tell anybody where they are. Think you can manage that?'

Brendan decided to permit himself a smile.

'No problem. I know just the place. Very secret. Execution and burial, all in one. Are you sure you won't have a drink?'

Only once did Brendan and Seamus disagree openly with each other about the campaign. A year had gone by since they had disposed of the two spies. Seamus had gone for a walk in a park in Central London. He sat on a bench by a lake, watching the ducks. He had bought a sandwich. As he unwrapped it he found it unappealing, so he tore the bread into pieces and fed it to the ducks. There was a bandstand nearby. He watched a little girl playing on it, jumping on and off it. He envied the innocent, carefree life she was leading and could expect to lead. The campaign would continue but she would be unaffected.

The following week the bandstand was blown up without warning, the IRA belatedly claiming responsibility. By chance nobody was hurt. Seamus and Brendan saw it on the news while having dinner.

'For fuck's sake,' said Seamus. 'I was just by that bandstand only last week. There was a little girl playing on it. If it had happened then she would have been blown to pieces. Why did they go for that target? It was a mistake, surely.'

Brendan glared at him. 'A mistake? What's the matter with you? Are you going soft or something? That bandstand was used by military bands.'

'So that makes it a legitimate target, does it? Are we at war with men playing cornets?'

Brendan thumped his fist on the table. 'We're at war with the British Army, in case you've forgotten. It doesn't matter whether they're playing their imperialist tunes in the park, drinking down the pub, marching up and down in front of Buckingham Palace dressed up like the prats they are, or murdering innocent civilians in Derry on Bloody Sunday. It's still the army and they're always a target. And that was a warning. The bomb didn't go off while the band was playing. But the next time it might.'

'Don't those idiots know that children play on those things when they're not in use?'

Brendan picked up a glass, made as if to throw it at him, then smashed it onto the floor.

'The guys who plant those bombs are heroes.' His voice was thick with anger. 'Don't you ever forget that. They take far more risks than we do. They're on the front line of the fight for freedom. Don't you ever dare call them idiots again or you leave this house and never come back. I'm beginning to think it was a mistake to bring you back over here. You've forgotten what we're fighting for, now we're no longer there.'

Seamus wanted to cry. 'I haven't, Brendan. I'm sorry. I'll never speak like that again. I promise.'

Brendan sat down. 'All right, Seamus. Let's forget it. Anyway, how do you know there wasn't a warning? The British establishment are in charge of the media here. It's in their interests to put out a false story, knowing people will react the way you did. Maybe they blew it up themselves and pretended we had claimed responsibility.'

'Yes. I'm sure you're right. I expect that's what they did.'

They were sure the arrangements at the house were foolproof. They conducted the middle of the night arrivals and departures and the deliveries of materials with great care, always on the watch for anybody who might be following them or observing them, or for chance passers-by whose suspicions might be aroused. They were satisfied nobody knew about their activities, other than Brendan's contact and those who came to the house. They could surely be trusted. There could not be informers among them, or they would already have made their move.

After graduating Seamus continued to study, obtaining a postgraduate diploma in Irish History at a college in West London, then a certificate qualifying him to teach in schools. Brendan asked him if he intended to go on studying and getting qualifications for ever. Seamus assured him he was looking for work. Shortly afterwards he got a job as an assistant lecturer in a college in Brighton. He lived there during the week, returning home every weekend.

Finally, five years after their move to London, Brendan told him the house would soon cease to be used as an operational base. The campaign was to be stepped up. The leaders wanted out-of-town premises with more storage capacity for larger stocks of weapons and better security. Soon the house would be cleaned out. 'Disinfected' was the word he used.

It did not happen in time.

# TWENTY-FOUR

Two uniformed policemen picked Seamus up from his digs and took him to Brighton Police Station. They searched him and took his fingerprints, behaving with impeccable courtesy but telling him nothing about the reason for his detention.

There were two plain-clothes officers in the interview room, one sitting opposite him asking questions and taking notes, the other pacing up and down behind him. Both were dressed in grey suits and ties. The one who asked the questions was softly-spoken, tall and slim, with a handlebar moustache and receding hairline. Quite young for his rank, early forties possibly. From his brief impressions of the other man Seamus would have said he was in his thirties, tough and not very bright. The muscle and rough to go with the other man's intellect and smooth. An effective team when they worked together.

The man with the moustache stared intently at Seamus, glancing down only occasionally to write something on his pad.

'Are you Seamus O'Hara, of 4 Bell Street, Brighton?'

'Yes.'

'How old are you?'

'Twenty-three. What is this about?'

The interviewer stared at him for nearly a minute.

'You don't know?'

'I've no idea.'

'What do you do for a living, Seamus?'

'I'm an assistant history lecturer at Hove College.'

'Is your father Brendan O'Hara?'

'Yes.'

'When did you last see him?'

'I visit him each weekend. What's this about?'

'We've arrested him.'

'Where is he?'

'Paddington Green.'

'On what charge?'

'Interesting that you didn't ask that first, Seamus.'

'What do you mean?'

'We told you we had arrested him. You asked where he was. Then you asked on what charge. I would have asked those questions in the reverse order. It's as if you weren't surprised we arrested him, as if you knew on what charge.'

'I am surprised. And I didn't know. Of course I didn't. So are you going to tell me? And are you going to tell me why I'm here? Am I under arrest as well?'

'We found bomb-making equipment in his cellar, along with a supply of small arms.'

Seamus sat back in his chair and laughed. He hoped it did not sound too forced.

'Bomb-making equipment! You've got it all wrong. He had a chemistry set down there. He liked to do experiments.'

'Did you see them?'

'No. He wouldn't let me down there. Said it might be dangerous.'

The interviewer leaned forward. 'You know, you two should have got your stories straight. He said he told you he made model aeroplanes down there. He didn't want you to go down unless you knocked them over. He said you were clumsy. So you never went down there? Never saw what he had down there?'

Seamus shook his head.

'Never saw the guns?'

'What guns?'

'The ones we found there. Don't tell us they were toys as well.'

'He could never have made bombs. He'd have blown up the house long ago. And why would he be so stupid?'

'Where did you live before?'

'Belfast.'

'Both of you?'

Seamus nodded.

'Address?'

Seamus gave it.

'Your father's house?'

'No, my Uncle John's. We lived there with him and his wife.'

The interviewer looked down at his notes. Then he nodded at the man standing behind Seamus.

'Where is your uncle now?'

'I don't know. He left just before we did. Said he was going to Liverpool. Only there was no trace of him at the address he gave his wife.'

'So he disappeared?'

'Yes.'

'Why did you leave?'

'We're Catholics. We were being burned out. They were going down the whole row. If we had stayed they would have killed us.'

'Who's "they"?'

'The loyalists. The Protestants.'

'Why did you come to London?'

'I wanted to study at university here. I graduated a couple of years ago.'

'So you and your father came over from Belfast to escape the Troubles.'

'Yes. And my mother and brother.'

'How long did you live together in London?'

'My mother and brother left after a few years. I have no idea where they are. I lived there until two years ago.'

'And all that time you lived there you never went into the cellar?'

'None of us did. Only my father. It was what you call his personal space. Every man needs his personal space, he used to say. We respected that.'

'Seamus, your father has confessed to possessing bomb-making equipment and illegal firearms. He told us he never made bombs himself. He passed the material over to specialists in the organisation.'

'What…organisation?'

'Oh, did I forget to mention it? He also confessed to being a member of a proscribed organisation. The Provisional Irish Republican Army, to be precise.'

'I've heard of them.'

'We all have, Seamus. Especially since they began their campaign here in England. Just at the time you and your father came over.'

'I told you why we came. We were getting away from all that stuff. He got a job, I went to college.'

'What stuff, Seamus?'

'The Troubles, I mean. I told you, they were burning us out.'

'Are you a member of the Provisional IRA, Seamus?'

'Of course not.'

'You were never a member in Belfast?'

'I was only a kid. I was fourteen when I went there.'

'And eighteen when you left. Lots of boys joined younger than that. Why did you come over to London?'

Seamus sighed. He told himself he must not lose his temper. That was what they were trying to make him do. He had to keep calm.

'I've already told you. I wanted to go to university.'

'Not to help your father in his activities in support of the PIRA mainland campaign?'

'I didn't know anything about that. If it's true. If you're not making all this up. If your London colleagues didn't plant that stuff.'

How did they know? The words whirled repeatedly round inside his head. How did they know the address? How did they know where to look? Was there an informer, after all? But why make his move now, after all these years?

The interviewer took out a packet of cigarettes and offered one to Seamus.

'No thanks. I don't smoke these days.'

'Do you mind if I do?'

'Not at all.'

It was not what he expected. The man's gentleness and courtesy. He had heard how they had treated those suspected of the Guildford bombings. Was he being softened up? Would the man behind him start to get rough as soon as they sensed he was weakening?

'You work at Hove College.'

'Yes. I told you.'

'Under the name of George Hughes. Why?'

'These aren't good times to have an Irish name. Lot of prejudice about.'

'But you sound Irish.'

'A few traces from my time in Belfast. Most people don't notice.'

'So, Seamus, what do you think about the PIRA's aims and activities?'

'I support the aims. I don't deny that. I don't support the methods.'

'Are you in favour of the mainland campaign?'

'No.'

'How do you feel about your father being part of it?'

'I'm shocked. Surprised. Are you sure he really confessed? You didn't beat it out of him? That sort of thing has happened, you know.'

The interviewer ignored the question. Seamus began grudgingly to admire him for his refusal to be provoked.

'How did your father get his job in London?'

'I don't know. We came down to London and stayed in a hotel. He went out looking. One day he came back to tell us he had a job and had found a house for us.'

'Very quick and convenient.'

'He gets things done when he has a mind.'

'Where did your father work?'

'In a garage. Didn't he tell you?'

'How much did he earn?'

'I've no idea. It was none of my business. Why don't you ask him?'

'When you arrived in England he was still the only breadwinner in the family.'

'That's right. He worked hard.'

'Yes. In a garage. Do you know how much the rent is on the house where you lived?'

'No idea. He looked after all that sort of stuff.'

'Nice big house. Cellar and attic. The rent must be quite a lot. How could he afford it, working in a garage?'

'I don't know. You'll have to talk to him about it.'

'We have, Seamus. Would it surprise you to learn his job was, shall we say, below the radar? No tax or national insurance, cash wages only?'

'I don't know anything about it.'

'Who was the landlord? How did he pay the rent?'

'I don't know. Why don't you ask him?'

'We have. He tells us he went to see the landlord each month and paid him in cash. It's a strange way to live, isn't it?'

'What do you mean?'

'Below the radar. Off the grid. No way of tracing him. No tax return, no insurance card, no rent-book, no bank account.'

'That was his business.'

Then how the fuck did you find him if he was off the grid?

'Do you know this man?'

He pushed a photograph across the table. Seamus stared at it for a moment, then gasped and nodded. He felt the colour drain from his face.

'It's my uncle. What happened?'

'We've been in touch with our colleagues in Belfast. He was killed there. The case is still unsolved. He was found a few hundred yards from where you lived. So, wherever he was planning to go, he never made it.'

'Where exactly?'

'In a bin at the back of a building once used as a youth club.'

'Shit! That was his place. He built it up. Then kids trashed it.'

'The body wasn't found for some weeks. Nobody emptied those bins any more. It was starting to smell. Some kids went to look.'

Seamus pushed his chair away from the edge of the table, leaned over and retched. The other men left the room. After a few minutes the interviewer returned with a glass of water for him. Seamus sipped it slowly.

'Are you all right, Seamus? Can we carry on? I'm sorry about that. Must have been a shock.'

'I'm all right.'

'Was your uncle, as far as you knew, involved in any paramilitary activities?'

'No. He couldn't have been. He was a man of peace. He tried to bring the communities together. How did he die?'

'A shot in the back of the head. Standard execution method, used by paramilitaries on both sides. Obviously someone didn't appreciate the work he was doing. Have you any idea who might have killed him?'

'No. Of course not. What about his wife?'

'They managed to contact her. She was in Liverpool. She went back to Belfast to arrange the funeral. Her current whereabouts are unknown. They couldn't find your father to give him the news. He had disappeared. As we all know.'

Then how did you find him?

'Only one more question. Do you know where your mother and brother are?'

'No. I haven't seen them since they left. They just walked out one day.'

'All right, Seamus. Thank you for your cooperation. That's all for now.'

Seamus stared back at him. 'I can go?'

'Yes. We can find you at the same address if we need you again?'

'Of course.'

'Let us know if you're planning to leave for any reason. I'm Inspector Rees. If I'm not here, just leave a message for me.'

'I want to see my father.'

'Of course. I'll ring them as soon as you've gone and ask them when you can go up to London to see him. I'll let you know.'

Inspector Rees put out his hand. Seamus took it, barely able to believe he was about to walk out of that police station a free man, that he had just shaken hands with a member of the British police force, that he had not been beaten by the other man to within an inch of his life.

# TWENTY-FIVE

There was a look of weary defeat in Brendan's eyes as he sat huddled in a chair in the interview room. He seemed much smaller and thinner than Seamus remembered him from only a few weeks before. His jacket was loose around his shoulders. There was the beginning of a sunken look to his cheeks. He was unshaven. His hands shook slightly as he spread them on the table in front of him as if searching for something to hold. Could he have changed so much in a few weeks? Or had Seamus with the blindness of his love failed to notice what their way of life had done to his father over the years? Brendan barely glanced at Seamus as he sat down in front of him.

'Hi, Da'. Are you all right? How are they treating you?' asked Seamus, trying desperately to sound cheerful. Brendan looked up slowly, screwing up his eyes.

'Oh, it's you, son. They told me you were coming.'

His voice was wavering, drained of all the passion and certainty which had animated it for as long as Seamus could remember. Seamus felt a tide of fear and anger welling up inside him. What had the bastards done to him?

'They didn't beat you up to make you confess, did they, Da'?'

'No, son. There was no need. Not with all that stuff down there. I decided to go quietly. They seemed to know everything. Who I was, what I had been doing. They got a bit angry when I couldn't tell them the names of my contacts. But they soon realised I couldn't tell them what I don't know.'

'Do you need anything from the house? Any of your books?'

Brendan shook his head. 'You bought them. You take them. I could never get the hang of them. I was never a reading man, as you know.'

'I don't want them. I don't want to go back there. Ever. I'll leave them there. The landlord can sell them. Or let the next tenant use them.'

'He'll have a job finding someone with tastes like yours. Are you all right yourself?'

'They had me in for questioning. They're suspicious but they can't prove anything. I don't think they're going to charge me. And they won't expect you to shop me. So it's up to me.'

Brendan leaned forward and grasped his hand. He whispered, although the only policeman in the empty, windowless room was well out of earshot, reading the *Daily Mirror*, his shoulders hunched in an attitude of boredom. He glanced only occasionally in their direction.

'Listen, son. I had to tell them where you were, or they would have got much more suspicious. And I wanted them to tell you what had happened. I wanted to see you.'

'That's all right, Da'. I understand.'

'I told them I was the only one involved. None of the rest of you knew anything about what was going on. That's the way I want it to stay. No point in both of us going down, is there? You've been going cold on us for the last few years, haven't you, son? Don't interrupt. It's true. I could tell. Some of those conversations we had. You didn't approve of our methods anymore.'

'I never opposed killing informers. I still don't. I'd do that again. But some of the other things...'

'I understand. You're not like me. I was born to be a soldier. A private who just obeys orders. You're clever. Thoughtful. Did well at school. Then university. I'm so proud of you. But I always knew you'd think for yourself and maybe come to a different perspective on things. I'm going to be inside for a very long time. I accept that. You won't. You can move on. I want you to. I want you to make a new life for yourself. Get a steady job. Get married and have kids. Have you got a girl-friend?'

Seamus shook his head.

'What do you do? I mean, for...company?'

'You mean sex? I do what you showed me. That place you took me to in Belfast when I was sixteen. They have them everywhere.'

Brendan sat back in his chair and grunted. 'Have you got a fag, for fuck's sake?'

Seamus pushed a packet and lighter towards him. 'Help yourself. I got these for you. I've given it up now.'

Brendan lit a cigarette, inhaled strongly and coughed violently for a few moments.

'Listen, son, I wanted you to be a man. Like any father who loves his son. Maybe I wanted you to grow up too quickly. I wanted us to be men together. I wanted you to be initiated early because I didn't want it to be with you the way it was with me. Waiting all those years. Your mother was the first, you know. The first and only one. When you wait so long, dreaming and thinking about it all the time so you think it will be like an ocean of joy and blessings when it finally comes, the reality can't help being a disappointment. I only felt those joys and blessings when you came along. You were my world. You still are. I know I wasn't the man your mother deserved. I let her down. But I was never unfaithful to her. It's not unfaithful to go with whores because it doesn't mean anything. I wanted to open the door for you, Seamus, when you were just old enough. But I meant you to understand it was only a door. I wanted you to go through it. I didn't want you to stand there by that door forever, thinking that was all there was. It was an initiation. You're good with words so you know what that means. A beginning. You're still stuck there. It's time to move on. You know what I'm saying, don't you? Find someone you can be with. Have a family with. Have a life with. Have the sort of life I never did. You can do that. The war will go on but we're both out of it now. I'll be serving my time and you will grow up and find yourself. Do you promise me, now?'

Seamus nodded. 'I'll try. I promise. Christ, why did you never talk to me like this before now?'

'I suppose it's because now I've got time to think. I'm not used to doing that. But I'll have to get used to it, won't I? Because I'll have twenty years ahead of me for thinking and not much else.'

'They won't give you as long as that. I'm sure they won't. Just a few years. You cooperated. You confessed. And you were never a big fish. A stage hand, not the leading man.'

'They know I was never high up. But they don't like the fact that I'm older than most of the ones they've caught. They think I'm some kind of father figure. A sort of spiritual leader, like that Dally Lama bloke who wears those funny robes. You know…bald, with rimless glasses. You've seen him on television. A bad influence on the young. No, I'll get twenty years all right.'

'Christ, Brendan. It was the other way round. I was the bad influence on you. No point telling them, though. They'd never believe us.'

There was a loud knocking on the door and a shout of 'two minutes' from outside.

Seamus leaned forward and lowered his voice.

'We haven't much time. Did they show you the picture of Uncle John?'

Brendan nodded. 'Yes. Poor bastard. Terrible, him being found like that. Not what he deserved at all. How could they do that to him? He was my brother, for God's sake, not a piece of trash. Will you be getting over there now, to where he's buried? Pay our respects?'

'I will. I promise. As soon as I can. They'll be keeping an eye on me but they can't stop me doing that. Look, I've got to ask this.'

Brendan glared at him. For the first time since Seamus had been shown into the room there was a fire in his father's eye which reminded him of the man he had known.

'I know what you're going to ask, son. Don't. Don't ever mention the subject, not until I tell you I want you to. And that will never be. It's nothing to do with you.'

'But how can I not mention it? I think about it all the time. Who was it? Who grassed you up?'

The door opened. Two uniformed officers entered.

'Time's up, please, gentlemen.'

Seamus stood up, went round to Brendan's side of the table and helped him to his feet. They embraced.

'I'll come and see you as often as I can, Da'.' Seamus was fighting back tears. 'I'll bring you tapes of the music you like. You can sing along, the way we used to. You know. *A Nation Once Again*. There'll be people like us in there. Maybe some you know already. You'll have friends. You can all get sentimental and nostalgic together. Maybe it won't be all bad.'

'Sure, I'll pass the time, son. Don't you be worrying about that. I've decided to learn Gaelic properly, if I can find someone to teach me. I tried before but never really got into it. But it'll be your visits I live for, son. And remember. Never mention it. Never even think about it. And you know what I'm talking about.'

# TWENTY-SIX

For the first few months after the police had interviewed him Seamus was followed everywhere by the second officer, the one who had stood behind him without saying a word. The officer made no attempt to conceal the fact that he was following him. Seamus finally lost patience one Sunday morning at the beginning of the holiday season, while out for a walk along the promenade. He turned round, walked up to him and invited him to join him for a coffee. To his surprise the officer smiled and accepted.

'I've been thinking myself it's about time we had a chat,' said the officer, once they had settled down at a table with their coffees. To Seamus's surprise he had a Belfast accent.

'Sergeant Davies. Ian. Yes, I'm from your part of the world. I'm seconded over here to help with the work on the mainland campaign. They seem to think that because I come from over there I'll understand the mentality. You thought I was the heavy one, didn't you?'

Seamus nodded. Sergeant Davies smiled, with an air of cheerful relief.

'You were wrong,' he continued. 'I've never done any heavy stuff. And I certainly don't understand the mentality.'

'What mentality?'

'The terrorist mentality.'

'Neither do I. If there is such a thing. And by the way, it's not my part of the world. I come from Merseyside. I didn't go to Belfast until I was fourteen. My father was from there originally. My mother is English.'

'It's not important now. We're calling off the dogs. The dogs being me. We searched your digs and the back garden, as I'm sure you noticed. We tested all the stuff from the cellar for your fingerprints.

Not a sausage. I haven't seen or heard anything remotely incriminating while I've been following you. We still believe you were involved. But we can't prove anything. They've better things for me to do. So you'll be pleased to know that from now on you'll have to do without the pleasure of my company. I'm having the rest of the day off now. I'm off to join those buggers on the beach having a good time. Thanks for the coffee.'

He rose and was about to leave.

'Sergeant Davies?'

'What is it?'

'Is it all right if I go over to Belfast for a short visit? I want to see my uncle's grave. Pay my respects, and my father's on his behalf.'

'As far as we're concerned, son, you can go to Timbuktu and never come back.'

# TWENTY-SEVEN

The grave was at the end of a row, separated from the road by a low fence. Linda had provided a modest headstone, recalling a loving husband who sought peace in the midst of conflict. Seamus laid two small wreaths, one on either side. He looked up, thinking he had spotted a movement behind some trees. A dog, perhaps. He heard the sound of leaves being crunched underfoot. This time the movement was to his right. A man stepped out from behind a tree into the pathway. Seamus registered his presence. Probably gone behind the tree for a piss. No loos about, and difficult to find somewhere in the open where one wouldn't be disrespectful to the dead.

Then he realised that the man was staring at him. He swivelled his eyes slowly. A bald man. Starting to walk towards him.

Seamus judged the distance towards the fence and its height. He remembered from his running days how before a sprint you had to load the energy into your lower legs and launch yourself out of the blocks. He sprang towards the fence and jumped it cleanly. Once on the pavement he ran, aware of the steps behind him, also running. He had not run for years and had momentarily forgotten that he had a limp. A spasm of agony in his right calf reminded him. But he knew the man was behind him. He could not afford to slow down. After a minute the pain eased and some of the fluency of his younger years returned. Only the heaving of his lungs and the rasping of his breath reminded him how unfit he had let himself become.

By the time he reached the church he could scarcely catch his breath. He turned. There was no sign of his pursuer.

He went round to the back of the presbytery and pounded on the door. The elderly housekeeper shuffled to the door with agonising slowness, tut-tutting and wiping flour off her apron.

'Now what in the name of…is that you now, Seamus? Bejaysus, you look as if the devil himself is after you. You'd better come in. Father Gerald is in his study. He left strict instructions he wasn't to be disturbed but I think he'll make an exception in your case. Come on in now, will you? I'll fetch you a glass of water while I'm getting him down.'

Father Gerald rushed into the lounge, where Seamus had collapsed into a chair.

'Seamus, I had no idea you had come back. What's up? Are you in some sort of trouble?'

Ignoring Father Gerald's greeting, Seamus jumped up suddenly and peered out of the window, glancing up and down the street, his chest heaving.

'For God's sake, man, what's the matter with you?' asked Father Gerald, coming up behind him.

Seamus turned to look at him as if he had only just become aware of his presence. He returned slowly to his chair. Father Gerald waited until his breathing had eased and he was ready to speak.

'I'm sorry, Father. I was going to ring you. See if we could get together for a drink. I'm only here for a flying visit. Been to see Uncle John's grave. First chance I've had. The police over there have been watching me for months. Now they say they've given up. But I'm not so sure. There was a man at the cemetery. I've seen him before. I know he's a Brit. On the military side. Special intelligence and security. And I think he knows who I am. He spotted me. I ran like a bat out of hell. I think I lost him.'

'Are you sure you're not being paranoid, Seamus? I know the feeling myself. After a while you get to think there's a spy round every corner.'

'Maybe. But I can't take any chances. Why was he there? Why was he keeping an eye on the grave? Why did he run after me? I was stupid enough to tell this policeman in England why I was coming. When I asked him if I could come over here to visit Uncle John's grave, he must have thought, we might still get him. We have one last chance. All we have to do is catch him making contact with someone suspicious.'

'Someone like me, you mean. Are you sure you were wise to come here?'

'I'm sure enough. They still don't know about you, do they? Pray to God they never will. The police in England must have tipped somebody off at this end. This chap gets to hear of it and volunteers to stake the place out.'

'But all you did was go to the grave. So why would he come after you?'

'No reason I can think of.'

Father Gerald stared at him. 'Seamus, are you telling me everything now? I can usually tell when you're holding something back and something tells me now that's what you're doing. Who is this man and what does he have on you?'

'Father, it's best for all of us that you don't know everything. That's the way it has always worked, hasn't it? Trust me. Or if not me, trust my instincts. I'm sure I'm in some danger.'

'Do you want to stay here for a few days? Or as long as you like. Sanctuary is what I'm here for.'

'No, Father, I can't stay. I want to get back. I wanted to put all this behind me. When that policeman told me they had given up on me, I thought I had. Put it behind me, I mean. Maybe I still can. If I can get safely back and into hiding, this might blow over. I know the face of the enemy now. And I always know when someone is following me. But there's one thing I must ask you.'

'What's that?'

'I must have the gun you keep here for me. And some ammo. The police took the one I had in London, along with all the other stuff. It was in the cellar. They never knew it was mine. We were always careful about prints.'

'All right. If you say you need it. But how will you get back? You can't get on a plane with a gun.'

'I'll hire a car. Drive to Dublin. Take a ferry to Holyhead. Get across the border tonight, a safe spot.'

'There are no really safe spots now. Tell you what. I'll drive you. See you off on the ferry. I've a young priest visiting here who can deputise for me. They won't search a priest's car. We'll make up some story if we're stopped. Remember, you're not officially wanted. Whoever this man is, whatever he wants, he's not working from any official wanted list, is he? He's not police. He's not mainstream British Army? That's what you believe, isn't it? Come on, Seamus. You must trust me if I'm to help you. You can tell me that much, can't you?'

'Yes. I believe that.'

'Right. I'll go and pack. Got any stuff here?'

'At a bed and breakfast place. I daren't go back there.'

'I'll send my housekeeper round to pick it up and pay the bill. We'll send it on when we know where to send it.'

'Thanks, Father. I'm sorry to impose like this.'

'Come on, Seamus. We're Volunteers, aren't we? And we're friends. We help each other. We don't impose. Are you sure about the gun?'

'I'm sure. They searched where I lived before. I'll find somewhere different now. I'll be able to hide it until I need it.'

'Just promise me you'll get rid of it as soon as you feel safe. You say you want to put all this behind you. But you'll never be able to do that until you get rid of the gun for good.'

'I promise.'

Seamus landed safely in Holyhead the following evening.

His contract in Brighton had expired. He found a job in a comprehensive school in Haringey and rented a room near Finsbury Park. Near the park was a disused railway line, by then a popular nature trail. One night he put the gun and ammunition in a box, took it to a spot he had selected the previous day and buried it.

He continued to visit his father each month. He worked diligently, earning the respect and admiration of his colleagues and pupils as well as their curiosity about his private life, about which he never spoke. He never joined in any social activities with his colleagues. Some were convinced he had worked for MI5, and perhaps still did. Not with that accent, others said. One was certain he had the explanation.

He had worked for MI5 undercover in Northern Ireland. His cover had been blown. He had barely escaped with his life. Now he had a new identity. He had probably changed his appearance. It would be wrong to ask too many questions. He was still a wanted man. They would all need to keep a lookout for anybody acting suspiciously near the school premises.

As time went by and he still never spoke about himself, the more sure they were.

# PART II

---

## THE FURIES

# TWENTY-EIGHT

He met Carlotta in Verona.

He had gone to Italy on impulse. He still called himself a Catholic though he had long since given up most of the required observances. Out of curiosity he wanted to visit a country where everybody was Catholic, where it wasn't a big thing, where it was taken for granted. He wanted to know what it was like to be a Catholic without it defining you as a member of a minority fated always to come second in the race of life.

He was sitting outside a café, drinking a cappuccino, in a narrow street near the Piazza Bra.

'Excuse me, Signor. Is this chair free?'

He had not noticed her approach. She must have glided on the warm afternoon air.

'Yes, the chair's free. But so is every other chair.'

'But only this one is opposite you. Only from here can I watch you scowl while everybody else is smiling, and wonder why.'

'That's not a scowl. I lived in Northern Ireland. Everybody scowls there, even when they're smiling. Why don't you sit down?'

The question was ironic. She had already sat down. Thirty, he thought, deeply tanned of course, English excellent, accent a mixture of Italian and American. The waiter hovered.

'What would you like?' he asked her.

'Sambucca.' He nodded to the waiter.

'I won't join you. Bit early in the day for me. What's your name?'

'Carlotta. Italian mother, American father. Parents divorced. Split childhood. Six months of the year here, six months in Philadelphia. Mother a fashion designer. I run a couple of her boutiques.

One here, one in Rome. Father a lawyer. Not married. In love now and then but not at present. That's it. My life story. What about you?'

'Even shorter. Seamus O'Hara. That's an Irish name in case you didn't know. Born in England. Moved to Belfast when I was fourteen. Back to England to go to university. Studied history. Teacher in a comprehensive school in North London. Unmarried. Never in love.'

'I'm sure there's much more to it than that, Seamus. "Seamus." Lovely name. So easy to pronounce. It just oozes out of the mouth. Not like Carlotta. You have to spit that out.'

Her drink arrived. She drank it down in one gulp, without even a cough or a grimace.

'Where are you staying, Seamus?'

'My hotel is that one, just over there. Do you want to know the room number?'

'Of course.'

'Room 203.'

'Is the key in reception?'

'No, I have it on me.'

'Give it to me. You haven't finished your coffee yet. Take your time. Say, half an hour?'

Her bright summer dress patterned with roses was a decorous knee length. But there was nothing decorous about her walk any more than there had been about her husky voice. Her hips swayed naturally and gracefully. She was not being provocative. She was just enjoying her body. As she entered the shadow of the hotel foyer the reflected light let him see through her dress. No underwear.

Not a prostitute then. If she had been, she would have worn a very short skirt and a low-cut top, with exotic black underwear. She would have been businesslike. She would already have negotiated a price. He knew, because he had met several already in Italy, in hotel bars, on street corners. Met them and paid for their services. Carlotta was different.

She was sitting on the balcony of his hotel room, sipping an elaborate cocktail she had ordered from room service. She asked him what he wanted to drink. He could have anything he wanted, she said, as he would be paying the bill. He picked up the phone and ordered a beer. They sat opposite each other, saying nothing. She smiled. Occasionally she laughed. Definitely not a prostitute. A prostitute had no time for doing or saying nothing, or for laughing. Time for a prostitute was money, a relentlessly ticking meter, laughter a waste of energy. But time for Carlotta was something she could make stand still, and laughter was as natural as breathing.

At last she went into the room and switched on the radio. She searched the channels until she found some band music, gentle, innocent, from an era long gone.

'Come and dance with me,' she called out.

He could not dance. He had never learned. He did not know how to hold a woman, just hold, not pull or grab. He did not know how to sway gently with a woman to music. Patiently, she taught him to hold his hands lightly against her back and to follow her steps without treading on her bare feet. Then she moved closer, found his hands and moved them down. Slowly, using only fingertips, encouraged by her, he explored what he could reach of her body, feeling muscle moving beneath skin beneath silk, layer on layer.

Why was she giving him so much attention? Perhaps he was wrong. He had never travelled much. He did not know the ways of the world. Certainly not the ways of every prostitute in Verona. Perhaps she really was one, just one of a sort he had never previously encountered. A very expensive one, who took her time with one client because she could earn more that way than with several spread over an afternoon with gaps inbetween. Did she think he was rich? Nobody had ever made that mistake about him before. He tried to remember how much money he had in his wallet. Would she take a credit card?

She pulled away from him and told him to close his eyes. He heard rustling noises. He opened his eyes. She was stepping out of her dress, her back to him. She moved to the window and stood there motionless.

He gasped. He had never seen a naked woman before. Not properly, not like that. Prostitutes were never naked. He had seen pictures in men's magazines but they were not real. Carlotta was real, sculpted like a statue, a prototype fashioned by the goddess of women, whoever that was. He knew that from that moment on all other women would be so many degrees minus Carlotta. Nobody would be plus. She was perfection. Art and sculpture fashioned by man had always left him unmoved. He could never see the beauty in something painted or shaped by human hand, however hard others tried to urge the appreciation on him. Now for the first time he knew what beauty was.

She turned round, laughed when she saw the look in his eyes.

'My God, you look as if you've never seen a woman before.'

'I haven't. Not like you.'

'Yes, you have. There's nothing special about me. You've seen but you've never really looked. I suppose you've never really touched either. Or heard. Or tasted. What a lot you have to learn.'

When he left the room a few hours later to get some fresh air he was still fully dressed while she was still naked, asleep on his bed. In the slant of the late afternoon sun her body was a landscape of golden curves and blue shadow.

His task had been to learn, not to possess. Under her direction he had watched, stroked, caressed, listened. He had learned all right. He thought he knew it all after his father had taken him to lose his virginity. But he had not even opened the book, did not know there was a book to be opened. Watching her respond to his touch had been like attending Mass, being part of the congregation but forbidden to pass through the Communion rail to the sacred places of the altar. At the moment of Consecration, the Host held aloft, he had held his breath as she held hers, time and consciousness suspended. The sacrilege of the image made him cringe with guilt.

What had happened? For twenty years he had lived quietly within the shell he had built to protect himself. Maybe the police had long since ceased to care. But there was at least one man for whom he suspected he was still a quarry. Over the years his sense of being hunted had receded but the shell remained, keeping out danger but also normal human contact. Now, in a place of warmth and laughter where nobody was a threat, he could at last drop his guard. He had done so. He had opened a door without realising it and Carlotta had walked through it. Just like that.

When he returned half an hour later she was dressed, sitting on the balcony, another drink in her hand. He took her by the arm. 'Let's walk outside.'

The season of open-air opera in the Arena was underway. Fragmented sounds of orchestra, chorus, some high soprano notes and rapturous applause reached them as they walked among the shadows of the ancient stones.

'Do you like opera, Seamus?'

'I don't know. I've never been to one. It's all sold out, anyway. I asked when I got here.'

'You asked at the hotel?'

'Yes.'

'Ah, but you didn't ask Carlotta. Because then you didn't know Carlotta. Now everything will be different because you have met Carlotta.'

'I don't think so. I think Carlotta will have moved on to her next conquest by tomorrow.'

She shrugged her shoulders and sighed with irritation.

'Tomorrow, tomorrow, tomorrow. All you English think about is tomorrow. This is Italy. We think about today.'

'I'm not English. All right, I'm half-English. My mother was English. But I was never close to her. I never felt English. English is so amorphous. So hard to pin down. Irish is better. Irish is clear and sharp-focussed. Irish is pride and passion. So I'm Irish. Do you teach all your lovers what you taught me today?'

'Of course not. Most of my lovers are Italian. Italians don't need to be taught.'

'That sounds like a national stereotype.'

'Like "Irish is pride and passion"?'

He laughed at her attempt at his accent. A strong flavour of Italian and American remained, adding an alien tunefulness.

'And you're not my lover,' she said, when he had recovered. 'Not yet. Good night.'

She slipped her hand out of his and disappeared into the crowds.

The next morning there was a knock on his door. Carlotta stood there, in tight blue jeans and a light brown blouse in shimmering silk. She was holding up an envelope.

'*Buon giorno, Signor O'Hara*,' she sang, in a very creditable soprano, to a Verdi tune well-known enough even for him to recognise it.

'*Buon giorno*,' he replied. It was her turn to laugh at his accent, which was drenched in Belfast. 'And what have you got there?'

'Guess.'

'I think you may be going to the opera.'

'Yes, and I know who is coming with me. Two tickets for *Aida*, tonight at nine o'clock. You and me. *Va bene?*'

'They must have cost a fortune. Let me pay.'

'I won't think of it.'

'Then at least let me buy you breakfast. And lunch. And dinner.'

Towards the end of the first act, they heard the distant throb of thunder. At first they thought it came from the orchestra. But within minutes the sky was black and heavy. When the first spatters of rain came the orchestra stopped in mid-bar and hurtled off the stage. Then the rain was cascading into the Arena in huge, warm, soaking drops. Apparently from nowhere dozens of local youths rushed in and along the aisles, shouting and offering umbrellas for sale. They ignored them and fought their way to the exit. By then the rain had plastered her thin white dress to her body so that she might as well have been naked. Laughing helplessly, they stumbled back to his room, peeled off their clothes and fell together into the shower.

The next day she took him to her boutique, outside which a small red sports car was parked. She spent a few minutes inside the shop, apparently arguing with an assistant. She came out and jumped into the car.

'Come on,' she shouted. 'We're going out for the day. To Lake Garda. I've just told Paolo he's in charge for today. He's not happy about it but that's too bad.'

It wasn't just the speed of her driving that impressed him. It was the way she paid more attention to him than to the road. She drove with one hand resting casually on the wheel, looking from the scenery to him and back again, keeping the conversation going without a break through hair-raising manoeuvres of overtaking on blind bends.

At Malcesine, where a mediaeval fairy castle overlooked the lake, they stopped for a drink and a meal near the landing stage. After the meal, at his insistence, they went down to the water's edge to feed the ducks. It was a strange Irish custom she could never hope to understand, he told her. Then he took off his shoes and paddled in the ice-cold water. She screeched with laughter.

'My God, the size of your feet!'

'I take after my father.'

Back in Verona they walked hand in hand through the narrow streets which were beginning to fill up, scurrying tourists mingling with strolling locals gathering for the *passeggiata*, mopeds scything through the crowds. He bought her a large cognac at a café in the Piazza Delle Erbe.

'What's this for?' she asked.

'I think you might need it. There's something I want to tell you.'

'I knew it. You're married. Goodbye.' She picked up her shawl.

'No, it's not that.'

'You're married and there's something even worse you want to tell me. Definitely goodbye.' She stood up.

'Carlotta, I'm not married. Honestly. It's about my father.'

'What about him? Apart from the fact that he has big feet. I think I could live with that.'

'He's in prison. And the worst thing is, I should be in there with him.'

'For having big feet as well?'

'He took all the blame.'

'For what? Were you murderers?'

'No. I mean, some people would call us that. I don't. He was…we both were… members of the IRA. You know about them?'

She stared at him, trying to work out if he was having a joke at her expense. Very slowly, she sat down again, fixing her eyes on his.

'My God, you're serious. Yes, I know about the IRA. Freedom fighters. My father told me about them. About how the British are still colonising parts of Ireland.'

'I wish it were that simple. Some of the things we did were wrong.'

'Don't tell me. I would try to understand but I probably wouldn't. How long is your father in prison for?'

'He got twenty years. He's served nearly all of it. They let him out on license last year because he's ill. He's gone back to Belfast. Says he wants to die there. I fly over to see him every month. I was the one who got him into it. I had met some people through a teacher at school and our parish priest. I introduced him to them. One thing led to another. We always thought we were doing the right thing. There was an Agreement earlier this year.'

'I know. I heard about it. The Good Friday Agreement.'

'It's not what we wanted, but it's a stage on the way. We would never have got that if we hadn't fought.'

'So there's peace now. It's all right. I don't care if you did wrong things in the past. I just want you…us…to be happy now. Will you try to do that?'

'Yes. Of course. I'll try. I promise.'

The next morning she spent an hour on the phone from his hotel room to her mother in Rome. The conversation was in Italian, but Seamus had picked up enough of the language to know she was discussing their wedding arrangements.

# TWENTY-NINE

Carlotta would not have called herself a good Catholic. She was not devout. She rarely went to church. She had not prayed since childhood. But the religion appealed to her because of the idea of the soul. For a Catholic, the body was only there to house the soul. So she had not expected to shock him when she first showed him her body, even though they had just met. But his reaction had startled her. He was intense about being a Catholic, and he worshipped her body as if it were a divine revelation. She was barely a Catholic, and she loved his complex, tortured soul. There was surely something wrong there. Italian mysticism for her, and Irish corporality for him? They were contradictions in terms.

She had tried to understand his version of Catholicism. They had talked endlessly about it. How in Northern Ireland it was a cause rather than a faith, a sign of defiance, a call to arms. In America she had heard politicians of Irish descent talk of the Troubles, eyes misty with nostalgia, voices trembling with anger. Her father had talked about it in much the same way. She had thought it was only a matter of getting the British out of the last few counties where they were still hanging on. Surely, in these post-colonial days, they could not stay forever. But they were still there. The Republicans had called a halt to the armed struggle for freedom. They had agreed to wait until the British were voted out, if that ever happened. Even more incredibly in her eyes, it seemed there were enough Unionists ready to share power. It was not what Seamus or his father had wanted. But at least the killing had stopped, or most of it.

And she and Seamus were married and living in Islington. Seamus was a surprising choice for her, when she thought about it. She had

had many lovers, mostly Italians, but also some French and Americans. But one with Northern Ireland roots? What was she thinking of? That was what her mother had asked her, though her father seemed to like the idea from the start. The fact was that she was tired of vain, spoilt charmers. What attracted her to Seamus was his sadness, his loneliness, his aura of being a little boy lost in a big, confusing, frightening world, of being someone nobody in their right mind could ever love. Maybe he was right. Maybe she was not in her right mind. In which case she was just what he needed.

She suspected from the start that his sexual experiences were confined to prostitutes. She had taught him to take his time, to step outside time. But she soon realised that when he did so he entered another world where she could not and would not wish to follow. For her, sex with Seamus was pleasant but no big deal, as with all her previous lovers. But Seamus seemed to be hammering desperately on the doors of Paradise, like a fallen angel. And, however much he beat, the doors never opened for him. She could always tell that from the expression on his face afterwards.

She was on the plane from London to Belfast, on her way to the funeral of Seamus's father, thinking these thoughts. Then she thought about the funeral itself. What would it be like? Would everybody be scowling? Would it be raining? She had heard that it always rained there.

She was pleasantly surprised on all counts. The sun shone the whole day. There were a lot of people at the funeral and most of them were smiling. It was also true that most were middle-aged men. It was not at all like an Italian funeral. The women there would certainly not miss out on the chance to laugh and cry and hug each other. Funerals there were for the women. Here it was the other way round. The few women kept their distance and their silence. She kept hers with them and watched while the men filed by the coffin and saluted. Even the priest saluted, which was yet another surprise.

She found it hard to read the faces of the women with whom she stood. They showed no emotion, or at least none she could read, used as she was to the animation of faces in Italy and America. Yet these were women who had suffered far more than she with her pampered life could possibly imagine. For them, being a Catholic wife had meant hardship and repression. But that was only the start. They had stood by their men when they went to war because they believed that only through war could their lives improve. Then a different reality had taken hold, one of families torn apart, of despairing visits to sons and husbands who would spend the best years of their lives behind bars, of standing by the graves of those who would never return, of realising that the better life which would surely come would not be for them but for future generations. She began to understand why these women were stoic and reserved at funerals. It was because they had stood by too many graves already. They had no more public tears to shed. The wells were dry. Only later, alone at home, would they sit and weep silent tears of the heart.

Afterwards she went up to introduce herself to the priest, while Seamus was talking to some people he later told her were old school-friends. She held out her hand, smiling.

'Hello, Father. I wanted to thank you for the service. It was lovely. I'm Carlotta. I'm Seamus's wife. My goodness, you do look shocked. Didn't he tell you?'

His broad smile had faded for a moment, before returning to its full splendour.

'His wife? No, he didn't tell me. Forgive me. I wasn't shocked. Just surprised. I always thought that somehow he would never let anyone pin him down. And now you've managed it. I'm absolutely delighted for both of you. I'm Father Gerald. I knew his father well. And I've known Seamus since he was a boy. So, you have an Italian name and an Italian accent with a touch of American. Am I right?'

'Totally. What a good ear you have. We met in Verona but we live in London.'

'Seamus, come over here,' he called out. 'Why didn't you tell me you had managed to acquire such a beautiful and charming wife?'

'I was keeping her as a surprise for you, Father,' said Seamus as he ran over. 'I would have told you sooner, but then with Brendan falling ill and dying and with all the arrangements to make…'

'I understand. Well, my warmest congratulations to you both.
I can't tell you how glad I am. Come over to stay with me, both
of you, when things have settled down. When you've got over this,
I mean. I know you and Brendan were very close.'

'That we were, Father. But we will come, and soon. Grief should
never stand in the way of friendship. On the contrary.' He and Seamus
embraced.

Before they turned to leave, she shook hands with Father Gerald
again. Only then did she notice his sadness. It was different from
Seamus's, whose eyes were still wet from tears shed at the side of
his father's grave. Seamus's sadness was something that could be
overcome in time and she was there to help him. But Father Gerald's
was different and he had nobody to help him. Time would never cure
it. She had thought nobody had loved Seamus before her. Now she
realised she was wrong. Someone had loved him and would always
suffer for it. And that love would be wasted if she chose to be jealous
or resentful. She had to acknowledge it and take it into herself, make
it part of the love she had sworn always to give to Seamus. She
realised she was still holding Father Gerald's hand as she tried to tell
him with her own eyes that she understood.

'Don't worry about him, Father,' she said, gently. 'I'll look after
him. For both of us.'

# THIRTY

---

She soon realised how mistaken she was in her belief that she could help Seamus overcome or at least learn to live with his grief.

She knew he had loved his father intensely. But the effect on him of his death shocked and enraged her. It was outrageous, out of all proportion. For weeks he sat at home, his face in his hands, silent, not even crying, though she was sure that would have helped him a great deal. She could not persuade him to talk about what he was going through. For long periods he would not talk to her at all.

Then, for the first time since she had known him, he went out drinking, at first once or twice a week, then every night. When he was drunk she refused to let him into their bed, but he did not seem to care. He had not touched her since the funeral. Until his father's death he had never been able to look at her enough. He would tell her he was filling his mind with images of her in case one day he lost his sight. Now he barely glanced at her.

Once, in the middle of the night, she thought she heard him talking. She crept silently down, through the hall and into the living-room, where he now usually slept. He was sitting on the edge of the sofa, fully dressed, his head in his hands. He pulled his hands away from his face so that at last she caught his words.

'No more killing. The killing's over, isn't it? Twenty years since the last. No more. Please, no more.'

Or that was what she thought he said. But if she was right, he must have been having a nightmare, remembering times long ago when the killing was still going on, when he was still part of it. But if he was having a nightmare, why was he sitting up, fully dressed, his eyes open?

He stopped going to the pub, but that brought no relief to either of them. He now drank at home, starting first thing in the morning before going to work, usually late. At first she tried her adopted English way, as far as she understood it, using stoic persistence and probing patience. Then the Italian way which was more natural to her, with volcanic upheavals of rage. She yelled at him, threw plates at him, yelled again, all to no avail. She made an appointment for him with the doctor, which he missed, as she always knew he would.

She left on the same day he lost his job. The headmaster summoned him before he could go to his first lesson to tell him he was being dismissed for being drunk in class. He went straight home, where he found a letter from her on the mantelpiece. He drank two tumblers of whisky before he opened it.

My darling Seamus
I am only a woman, not an angel. I cannot give you salvation. Nor can I share your guilt. That is between you and God. I am returning to Verona. Please do not try to get in touch. I love you and I always will.
Your Carlotta

He drank himself into unconsciousness and woke up on the bathroom floor, broken glass around him, a taste of vomit at the back of his throat and the smell of it in his nostrils.

It was the nightmares which had brought him so low, or rather the same nightmare night after night. Patrick coming through the door, his hair long and black and flowing as it had been when he was a boy, his eye-sockets empty, his bony finger pointing at him.

Now he could sink no further he had two choices. If he carried on as he had been doing, he would be dead within a month at most. Or he could do what he knew he had to do. Fulfil his oath to his dying father. Get himself back on his feet and go in search of Patrick, the traitor, the grass who had informed on his own father. Then, and only then, would he be rid of the nightmares.

He spent the morning throwing out all the bottles of drink in the house. He drank cup after cup of strong black coffee. Then he sat down to make a list of his options. After ten minutes the sheet was still blank. Where had Ruth and Patrick gone? Not back to Belfast, he could be sure of that. Ruth had always hated it there. Where then? He recalled the farewells in Liverpool before they and Linda had parted company. Had Linda kept in touch? Had she written to Ruth? Had she let it be known she could stay with her if things got too much? But she would have taken any such letters with her.

Where had Linda gone? To the address in Liverpool which John had given her. Where John's cousin, Dennis, lived. He thought he remembered it, or at least what the street and house looked like. It was John's base when he visited them. They had never gone to visit John there and Seamus had never met Dennis. But once, after a shopping trip in Liverpool, Brendan had driven past the house to show it to them. It was by a large park near the city centre. He searched his memory for the name. At last it came. Sefton Park.

# THIRTY-ONE

The man who answered the door was in his late sixties or early seventies with thin wispy white hair. About the right age. Could this be Dennis?

'Hello. I'm looking for Dennis. Dennis O'Shea. He's a relative of mine. I think he used to live here but I'm not sure.'

The man stared at him, then took off his glasses, wiped them and stared again.

'Ah yes, Dennis. Would you like to come in?'

The man shuffled inside. He wore loose, worn carpet slippers, over-long trousers that hung in folds and a shapeless beige cardigan which was unravelling in several places. Seamus followed him into a room on the left of a dark hallway. The room was a self-contained bedsit, one end of it screened off to form a small kitchen area.

'Sit down. Cup of tea?'

The tones were measured, slightly projected as if intended for an audience, no local accent. A teacher like himself perhaps, now retired, or an actor fallen on hard times.

'No. Nothing, thank you. I'm fine.'

The man sat down opposite him.

'Well now, let me see. Dennis. He owned the flat upstairs but he sold it a few years ago. After all that trouble. Unpleasant memories, you know. He moved away. I've no idea where.'

'Trouble? What sort of trouble?'

'It wasn't really anything to do with him. He had gone to Canada for several months. It was the ladies who had rented the flat in his absence.'

Seamus's heart jumped into his mouth.

'The ladies?'

'Yes. Two of them. They seemed to be very close, like sisters.
I only knew one of their names and that was later on. There was only
one at first. Then the other arrived. There was a boy as well. A young
man, I should say. Very good-looking. I suppose he was the son of
one of them.'

'Did he arrive with the second woman?'

'I really can't say. I didn't see them arrive. The boy might have
been here already. He was very quiet, you see. Very subdued. Not
what you would expect in a young man like that. I mean, you'd
expect him to be out with the girls a lot or having parties. But there
was none of that. I wondered if he had been ill, or maybe still was.'

'So what was this trouble you mentioned?'

'Well, one of the women left for a while. I think she took the boy
with her. When she came back she killed herself. The boy had gone
by then.'

Seamus tried to keep his voice from shaking.

'How? When?'

'Oh, it was a long time ago now. Going on for twenty years. I kept
a newspaper cutting about it. It was the only exciting thing ever to
happen in this house. I'm sorry to talk that way about such a tragic
thing, but you know what I mean.'

He rose out of his chair, opened a drawer in a sideboard and pulled
out a folder of papers. He sat down again and thumbed through it.

'Yes, here we are. September 1978.'

September 1978. When everything changed. When Brendan was
arrested.

'She drove down to that place near Crosby, by the beach. Sunset
Strip, the locals call it. She attached a hose to the exhaust and ran
it into the car. She put tape around the hose and along the top of
the window to stop any of the gas escaping. She knew what she
was doing. She had planned it all carefully, even though she was
very drunk. The police found an empty gin bottle in the car. And
her blood alcohol levels were off the scale. That's what the police
told me. They were amazed she had managed to drive there in one
piece. She must have been very depressed. There were a couple of

other cars on the strip that night but nobody noticed anything. It's traditionally a place for couples who want to be alone. She must have known that.'

'And she…you're sure it was the one who had gone away with the boy?'

'Yes. Read the article for yourself. There's a picture but I didn't think it was a very good likeness. But then I'm not good with faces.'

He passed it over. There was a photograph of Ruth, unmistakably her. The article said she had come to Liverpool as a refugee from the Troubles in Northern Ireland, bringing her only son with her. Tragically she and her son had quarrelled and the son had left. Now alone in the world she had taken her own life.

'You said the boy had left. What about the other woman?'

'She disappeared as well. Before the funeral. I couldn't understand why she would do that. The police asked me to identify the body because there was nobody else to do it. All I could say was that it was one of the two who had been in the flat. I couldn't put a name to her. I went to the funeral, just so there would be somebody there. I paid for it. There was nobody else to do it and she had been a neighbour. What's your interest, if I might ask?'

'I'm her son. Her other son.'

The man put his hand to his mouth.

'Oh, I'm so sorry. I must have sounded so callous before. What I said about it being the only exciting thing which had happened here. If only I had known…'

'It's all right. She left my father and myself when I was twenty-one. We lost touch. My name's Seamus.'

'Mine's Reginald Braddock.'

They shook hands.

'Nice to meet you, Reginald. Now I know your name I can write you a cheque.'

'What for?'

'The funeral.'

Reginald laughed. 'Forget it. It was a long time ago. I didn't mind. It was the least I could do.'

'Where is she buried?'

'St Anselm's. Just up the road from here. The police said there was stuff of hers in the car. That was how they knew her name, and that she was a Catholic. I remember some of the things they told me they'd found. Rosary beads, a Catholic missal, a copy of the New Testament open at St Matthew's account of the Passion. It must have been the last thing she ever read, sitting there in the car, waiting to die. Perhaps she was looking for consolation, or making a last desperate attempt to find a reason to go on living. If so, it didn't work. I can't remember exactly where the grave is. I'm sure the priest can tell you.'

The grave was heavily overgrown with weeds. There was a simple headstone with her name and dates of her birth and death. Ruth Gibson. She had reverted to her maiden name. No mention of being dearly beloved or remembered by those left behind.

'Your only son,' said Seamus, after the priest had left him there alone to collect his thoughts. 'That was what they thought. That Patrick was your only son. It must have seemed that way to you. Because that was the way it was. They were right. I was no son to you, God forgive me. I won't ask for your forgiveness. Because if you are up there watching and listening you will know what I intend to do next if I get the chance. And it's something you could never forgive. Goodbye, Ma.'

Except that he knew he would never get the chance. He had come to the end of the road. There were no more leads. Patrick had disappeared long ago.

He would return to London. Perhaps go back to the house and have a look round. See what had happened to the place where they had left the bodies of the two spies.

Then pick up the pieces of his life, if he could. He knew he would not get a reference which would let him go back to teaching. But he would need to find some sort of job, and somewhere cheaper to live.

The Islington flat would be beyond his means now, even if he were lucky enough to find work.

Whatever he did with his life, Carlotta would never again be part of it. Nor any other woman. She had wanted to look inside his soul and he had granted her wish. He had shown her his demons and she had fled to save her sanity. He knew he must never again let anybody see what she had seen.

# THIRTY-TWO

He had never been back to the house since Brendan's arrest. He wondered what sort of person lived there now. Did they have the slightest idea of what had gone on there? What about the bodies? Were they still resting in peace? Had dogs or foxes dug them up? Did children play with the skulls, thinking them animal?

He walked around the house several times. No lights on. No milk bottles outside. Abandoned, probably. The local press had covered the arrest and what was found inside in some detail. It wouldn't exactly make the place attractive to a prospective buyer or renter. He crossed over to the waste ground. There was a tattered poster attached to a fence. The local authority had put it there, announcing their plans to develop the site as an expansion of the nearby estate and inviting comments. The poster was over ten years old. Nothing had happened. Legal wrangles, probably. Planning blight would have put off any potential buyers. He walked over to the spot and moved the bricks away. The cellar entrance was still there, undisturbed. He replaced the bricks. Leave the dead to rest in peace.

He looked at his watch. Two o' clock in the morning. He had not expected to find anything and he hadn't. Just a pointless trip down memory lane. The end of his search. And the end of his nightmares, he hoped. Time to go away and forget.

From the corner of the street opposite the house he heard steps. A shape was approaching the house. He froze.

Got you, you bastard.

# THIRTY-THREE

He dozed on a park bench for the rest of that night. Early in the morning, his limbs stiff and bone-chilled, he caught the tube to Finsbury Park. He found the nature trail, and, eventually, the place where he had hidden the box. It was still early and he was alone. Slowly and carefully, he removed the gun. He wiped it clean, checked it was in working order and loaded it.

Later that day he was back in the street. He needed to find a place from where he could watch out for Patrick. There was a former Methodist chapel further up on the other side, now used as a centre for homeless people, vagrants, anybody down on their luck or just needing company, some hot food and perhaps a cheap bed for a few nights. Seamus looked the part. He mingled with the regulars, staying close to the window or by the front door so he could keep an eye on the house.

He saw Patrick emerge at eight o' clock in the evening. He followed him onto a tube train, not bothering to hide, confident that if Patrick turned round he would not recognise him or realise he was being followed. Patrick got out at Piccadilly Circus. Seamus followed him into a bar in Soho. Not like Patrick, going to a bar like that. Then he realised that he worked there. Seamus sat in a corner, watching him, unseen. Patrick did his work efficiently, but did not chat with the customers or the other staff. When he left to catch the night-bus home he was alone.

Seamus watched the house for a few more days but saw no callers. He was sure by then that nobody would miss Patrick except the bar and they would quickly replace him. They would certainly not send anybody round to the house. He made up his mind. He would make his move the next night.

# THIRTY-FOUR

Afterwards he returned to Liverpool. He found a tiny bedsit close to the cemetery where his mother was buried, so he could visit her grave regularly. He signed on and got night shift work as a security guard in a warehouse. During the day he stayed indoors and wrote and drew. After a week, he put what he had done into a desk drawer. He had written out a full confession of all the killings in which he and Brendan had been involved, as well as that of Patrick. He had drawn maps showing where the bodies were, very rough ones in the case of those near Belfast as they had always been at night in the countryside. If he died of natural causes his landlord or the next tenant would find the confession. If he decided to kill himself he would leave a note telling the police where to look.

He had hoped the nightmares about Patrick would stop, but they continued relentlessly. He never went to bed, letting himself fall asleep at his desk or on his sofa for a few minutes at a time. He became used to sleeping no more than two hours in twenty-four. But that only meant the nightmares were all the more intense.

One day he took a ferry across the Mersey to Birkenhead. He wanted to see the place where they had lived before the move to Belfast. It was a down-at-heel area of terraced houses and neglected parks, a desperate attempt at suburban respectability barely a few hundred yards from the riverside factories and warehouses.

It was there where Seamus first learned how to treat Patrick in a way that would please Brendan. The three of them were out walking in their local park. Seamus was ten and Patrick eight. There was a public toilet and Patrick wanted to go in on his own. He was old enough now, he said. He didn't need either of them to take him. Brendan nodded. He went in.

A group of boys were playing nearby. Four of them, bigger than Seamus, twelve or thirteen, were from the local secondary school. Brendan went up to them and whispered something in the ear of the one who seemed to be the leader. Brendan put his hand in his pocket, pulled out some coins and gave them to him. The boys went inside the toilet. Brendan winked at Seamus. They came out after five minutes, the leader smiling at Brendan who gave him some more money. There was no sign of Patrick. At last, Seamus told Brendan they should go in and see if he was all right. Brendan shrugged his shoulders. Seamus went in first. Patrick was lying on the floor, his hair soaked, his forehead bruised, blood pouring from his nose. The boys had obviously held him in one of the urinals while it flushed, then pushed his face against the wall. It's all right, son, said Brendan. We'll find out who they are and we'll see to them. He grinned at Seamus while he said it.

Seamus did find out who the boys were. His school building was next door to theirs, the playgrounds adjoining. He saw them there during a break and called them over. He knew how to get them to do what he wanted, now that he had seen what Brendan had done. All he needed was to 'borrow' some coins from the box on the mantelpiece where his mother kept the small change from the housekeeping. A few shillings a week were enough for them to come over into Seamus's playground during the break and give Patrick a few punches in the stomach. Patrick never said anything. The teachers supervising them at break never saw anything, or they pretended not to. His mother never noticed the missing money.

The area had changed little, becoming only a bit more run down and world-weary. A busy new through road had lured away the young and the socially ambitious to the more prosperous suburbs along the estuary towards the Irish Sea. The schools which Seamus and Patrick had attended had been demolished to make way for a shabby, litter-strewn shopping centre, most of the units of which seemed never to have been let. The park was still there, though the building which had housed the toilets was gone.

Why didn't you fight back, Patrick? Why didn't you tell Ma, or your teachers, or anyone? Why did you never tell me anything about yourself? Why did you never tell me who you really were?

He had started to drink heavily again, though with little effect in numbing his consciousness. He needed something a lot stronger. He had heard from a workmate about some estates in Bootle where drug-dealers could readily be found. He began to visit them each week.

One Saturday evening he was drinking in his local pub. There were several empty glasses on the table before him. They had contained beer and whisky. He was responsible for all of them and he had not even begun to feel drunk. A girl sat down opposite him. She was tall and thin, pale with a sharp nose and large green eyes. She stared at him.

'I'm sorry,' he said. 'I don't know what you charge but I can't afford it. And I'm not really in the mood. But you can buy yourself a drink if you like.'

He pushed some money over to her. She laughed, nervously.

'My God, if I were on the game, would I be shaking with nerves at the very idea of talking to a strange man? I suppose I should be flattered you noticed I'm a woman. I've seen you in here before but you never noticed me. You're always on your own so I thought you might be lonely. That's all. Thanks for the offer but you can keep the money. Goodnight.'

She rose to go. Something stirred inside him, a wish for company perhaps, however brief, however insignificant. Certainly nothing more than that.

'Sit down. I'm sorry. I didn't mean to offend you. I appreciate you coming over to talk.'

'If you only knew how long it has taken me to pluck up the courage.'

'What's your name?'

'Mandy.'

He could not help laughing out loud.

'Mandy! What sort of name is that for a grown woman?'

She laughed as well. 'Short for Amanda, I think. You're right. I'll stick to Amanda in future. Should have grown out of Mandy when I was five. What's yours?'

'Don't laugh. Promise me.'

'I promise. What is it?'

'Seamus.'

He was at last beginning to feel the effects of the drink. And there was something infectious about her laugh. Now they had started they knew they would find any name funny. So she laughed despite her promise and so did he.

'So, what do you do, Mandy…sorry, Amanda?'

'I'm a student. Ling…ling…oh, fuck! I can never say it after a few drinks. You need a degree in linguistics just to be able to say the word. There, I've managed to say it now. I can say it when it's in the middle of a sentence. What about you?'

'I used to be a historian. Then I was a teacher. Now I'm a security guard. Not much of a career, is it?'

'Not when you put it like that. It's like you've been going backwards.'

He leaned forward. 'Mand…sorry, Amanda. I want to tell you something. I want to tell you a secret. Come and sit round here, beside me.'

She giggled, rose and crammed her body into the space next to him, her hip and thigh in contact with his. Their arms were uncomfortably cramped, so she put hers around him.

'Okay,' she whispered. 'What's the secret?'

'I used to be in the IRA. So was my dad but they put him in prison. My kid brother grassed him up. So I killed him. I killed my brother. I shot him.'

She stared at him. 'Is that right, Seamus?' The mention of his name started them both giggling again. 'Well, I've got something to tell you. My brother poisoned my mother with arsenic.

So I killed him. With an ancient sword that's been in the family for generations. I buried him at the crossroads, like a highwayman. His ghost walks there every full moon. You know what this means, don't you?'

'Tell me. What does it mean?'

'We've a lot in common, that's what. We like to make up stories. You tell yours really well. I really thought for a moment you might be serious. Do you live nearby?'

He watched her undress. She was not like Carlotta. Of course she wasn't. Nobody could be. It was not that her body did not come up to Carlotta's standards. Mandy had different standards. She was built in a different way. Comparisons on a purely physical basis were not fair, not even possible. No, the real difference was to do with the way each woman undressed and how they behaved afterwards. Carlotta was only complete, only fully dressed, only really comfortable when naked. Frequently she was naked in the flat for hours at a time, doing housework, chatting on the phone. Sometimes she only just managed to remind herself in time to put something on before answering the door.

Mandy undressed nervously and clumsily, jamming the zip of her skirt and pulling several buttons off her blouse. When she had at last fumbled her way out of her clothes she stood awkwardly, her eyes looking down, then side to side, never directly at him. She used her arms and hands to cover as much of her private flesh as she could, as if her nakedness was not her idea but had been forced on her in some way. She was incomplete and vulnerable. This meant he could not be with her the way he was with Carlotta, the way she had taught him. Those lessons meant nothing now. They could only be applied to Carlotta and she had gone. With Mandy it could only be the way it was with those whores who could not be hurt. They could not be hurt because he had paid them. They could not show hurt because they had no living faces, only features set in stone. They had no bodies to hurt, only limbs that stayed frozen until it was over.

But Mandy could be hurt. Her face and mouth twisted. Her voice betrayed her fear and her body arched with pain. As he was hurting her he knew he was doing it and knew how she would despise him afterwards. But not more than he would despise himself.

'You know something?' she said, as she dressed. 'I believe you now. I think you really did kill your brother. There was me thinking I had found a lonely and sensitive soul I could spend some time with. And what do I get? A fucking psychopath.'

# THIRTY-FIVE

The years passed and his routine was unchanged. He worked his shifts, went to the pub in the evenings, never seeing Mandy there again, visited his mother's grave on Sundays. Weeks, months would go by without him speaking a word to another human being. Indoors, he often sat staring at the drawer in which he had placed the maps and the confession. He resisted the temptation to take them out in case he found himself driven by an impulse to burn them or tear them to shreds.

Why did nobody come for him? He had hoped that Mandy would tell the police about him. But if she had they must have dismissed her story as fantasy or the vindictive lies of a rejected woman.

He could not understand it. Surely they would have found at least Patrick's body by now. He had not pushed it out of sight. Anybody opening that trapdoor would see it right away. What was going on? He subscribed to the local paper for the area and had it sent to him weekly. He pored over every word. Nothing. Not even a mention of the site or any possible plans to develop it.

There was nothing for it. He had to go back and see for himself.

And if he hadn't? He would never have seen the notes which told him someone knew his secret, would never have known he had yet another quarry to hunt down, would never have stood in that room, his gun on the floor, staring at someone he knew to be dead.

'For fuck's sake, you're dead.'

'That's not a very nice way to greet your own mother, Seamus.'

# THIRTY-SIX

It was one of the local boys who told Ruth about the hiding-place.

He was about ten years old, very thin, his hands and face grimy. Despite the January cold he wore no jacket, only a dirty, grey open-neck shirt, and short trousers which were much too large for him and had, she supposed, been handed down to him by an older brother. She looked down when he tugged her sleeve outside the shops.

'Excuse me.'

She bent down. 'Hello. What's your name?'

'Secret.'

'That's a funny name. All right, Secret, what can I do for you?'

'Give me ten pounds.'

'Why aren't you at school?'

'Another secret.'

'Where do you live?'

'That's another.'

'Well, you do have a lot of secrets, don't you, Secret?'

'I've got another one. Worth ten pounds down. And much more later on.'

He coughed and wiped his running nose with his sleeve.

'What is it?'

'Ten pounds, please.'

'Well, as you're a very polite young man I'll give you a pound. Now, off you go back home, or school or wherever you should be.'

'Will you give me the rest if you like the secret?'

She sighed, realising she would never get rid of him unless she played along. 'I'll give you another pound. But only if I like it.'

'Five.'

'Two.'

'Deal. That's three pounds in part payment of the ten pounds down payment. You can give me the other seven later, plus my share of your share of the proceeds. This way.'

She followed him over to the waste ground, wondering how she could have been so stupid as to let herself be talked out of three pounds by this young fantasist. Brendan was not generous with housekeeping. She would have to raid the few pounds she kept by for emergencies. The boy looked round constantly to check they were alone. There was a pile of bricks on the ground. He pulled them away. Underneath was a trapdoor.

'What's this?' she asked.

'Cellar. The house was where we're standing.'

'Is this the secret?'

'No. What's inside.'

'What's that?' She was beginning to lose patience. He was about to lose the extra two pounds.

'Buried treasure.'

'Have you seen it?'

'No.'

'Then how do you know it's there?'

'This was our hiding-place. Me and my gang. I told the man about it. Like I told you. He came here, just like you. He said he wanted to take it over. For him and his gang. Needed somewhere to hide stuff he stole from banks. Gold and jewels. He gives us money to keep an eye on it.'

'I don't see anybody.'

'You wouldn't. We watch from the windows of the flats over there. You can't see this bit because there are pieces of wall still standing. But we know if anybody goes near. When he comes to take the treasure away he'll give us ten per cent. But if we look inside, even just the tiniest peep, he'll bury us alive down there. So we don't look. Ever.'

As he spoke her smile faded. She shivered.

'What man, Secret?'

'Big man. Lives in your house. I've seen both of you there. I thought you might not know. You didn't, did you? I thought you might like to know. I thought you might be prepared to pay to know. So you can get your share, and pay me mine.'

She gave him five pounds.

So why would they want a secret hiding-place outside the house? She knew they kept the operational stuff in the house cellar. If the cellar on the waste ground was only intended as a bolt-hole, why had they threatened its urchin guardians with burial alive if they dared to look inside? Then she understood. Some things you can't keep indoors. Because after a while they start to smell. She remembered those midnight trips in Belfast. When they returned they had the smell of death on them. They were up to the same thing here.

One night she followed them to the place the boy had shown her. It was the second time. She was curious to know what they had done with the first one, the one who never came back. Three had gone out for a drink. Only two had come back. Of course she knew that if any of them had seen her they would have killed her on the spot. But she no longer cared. She had to see for herself. They would have heard a man's footsteps behind them but not the light tread of a woman. She hid behind the remains of a brick wall. Let's take a short cut across the waste ground, Brendan had said. He stopped by the trapdoor. Said he had to have a pee. Should have gone before they set out. They all laughed. Your bladder's getting weak in your old age, Seamus said. The stranger was polite. He looked away. Then Brendan was pressing the gun against the back of his neck, telling him to kneel down while Seamus opened the door.

That was the moment when she decided she and Patrick had to leave. She was used to furtive activities involving the moving of mysterious consignments in and out of the house cellar, the comings and goings of strangers in her own home to whom she was not allowed to speak. That was just about bearable, slow poison though it was to her heart. But this was different. This was cold-blooded execution, carried out before her own eyes by her own husband and son.

She kept the secret for years, long after she and Patrick had parted company. She had spent many of those years in a fruitless search for him. At last she decided to kill herself. She had had enough of living like a shadow. But first she wanted to do some good with what she knew. She would tell the police about the bodies. Maybe those men had families. Of course she would need to check the bodies were still there, or the police would dismiss her as a crazy woman.

She was on her way to the waste ground when she saw Patrick walk up to the house and let himself in. As simple as that. She cursed herself for her stupidity. Why hadn't she thought of it? He had gone back home, that was all. He had never had another home since they had left together. Where else could he have gone? He had planned it that way. He had taken her key from her handbag when he left, and she had not noticed. Now at last she had found him. Now she would watch and wait, see what she could find out about his life. But there was one thing she could not do. She could not let him know or even suspect she was there. That would be too painful for both of them.

The house opposite was empty. From its condition it had been that way for years. She broke in through a back window. An upstairs room at the front gave a clear view across the street. There was a damp, mouldy mattress on the floor, the only furniture left in the entire house. The house was not completely unoccupied. A large tabby cat and several mice lived there in a peaceful co-existence.

After a few days she knew his routines. He stayed indoors all day. He left every evening at eight, returning about two in the morning. She always watched him leave the house. Sometimes she missed his return because she had fallen asleep. One evening she watched as usual, but did not see him leave the house. She remembered she had missed his return the previous night. She waited until the next evening. Again he did not emerge. Nine o'clock came, an hour past the time he should have come out. She had to knock on the door, to find out if he was ill and unable to ring for help. If she heard him come to the door she would run back to her hiding-place and watch from there.

No reply, after several minutes of repeated knocking. She went round to the back door. It was unlocked. She let herself quietly into the yard and looked up at the windows. No lights on anywhere in the house. Was he lying in there somewhere, hurt or sick and unable to get to the door?

In the morning she decided to call the police. She would say she was a neighbour and was concerned because she had not seen him for several days. Well, it was true, wasn't it? The police could break down the front door. Unless…

She realised the thought had already occurred to her. She had just not acknowledged it. Now she had to. Seamus had come for him. She had missed it. She had been asleep. Like Christ's disciples, during His agony in the garden. *Could ye not watch with me one hour?*

She crossed the road to the waste ground and eased herself through a gap in the fence. She walked over to the spot. She imagined the scene, just as she had witnessed, the night she had spied on them. Seamus's gun in the back of his neck, the command to kneel down while Seamus opened the trapdoor. One shot, muffled, like the blow-out of a car tyre. She pulled away the top layer of bricks. The rotting wood of the trapdoor came up easily. She let herself gently down into the hole, white dust clinging to her torn coat, the stench of decay in her nostrils. Sounds of rats squeaking and running. Away from her, thank goodness.

There was just enough light from the opening to see by. She could not see what was left of the other bodies. Seamus and Brendan must have moved them away from the entrance. But Seamus had not moved Patrick's body. He had made no attempt to hide or cover it in any way. It lay there, limp and awkward, where it had fallen, one arm underneath, the other splayed out to the left.

She tried to remember the words of the funeral service. *So we commit his body to the grave. Dust to dust, ashes to ashes.* Would it be a sacrilege to make the Sign of the Cross over him? She had not a priest's power to bless and no priest would ever stand by this grave. She made the sign hastily, clambered out, replaced the trapdoor and walked away.

The house was empty and Seamus had gone. Too late to tell him to his face what she knew. She wrote out a note and pushed it through the letter box.

She stayed in the house opposite, leaving only when she needed to find some casual work or borrow money off a friend. Always she came back. Sometimes she returned to the waste ground, picking her unsteady way like a ghost through the rubble. An infection seemed to hang in the air, as if a miasma were seeping up from the rotting bodies below.

The blight spread to the surrounding houses and blocks. Nobody bought or sold. Nobody moved in. The remaining inhabitants left or died. The bulldozers never came to clear it all away and make a fresh start. Even her sole companions, the cat and the mice, had gone.

So she watched and waited, never expecting Seamus to return, hoping against hope that one day he would. So he would see her note. So he would know someone knew what he had done.

# THIRTY-SEVEN

'I don't suppose you're going to give me a kiss, Seamus.'

'That would be like kissing a corpse. You look and smell like one.'

He barely recognised her. Her face was thin, dirty and deeply lined, her remaining strands of white hair trailing close to her skull. Her coat, buttonless and open at the neck, was torn and threadbare. Her voice was hoarse and deep, mistakable for a man's.

'Thanks. You're not exactly looking yourself these days, either. Have you been living rough like me?'

'Living rough? I've seen your grave. I've been looking after it. Climbing out of there is a bit more than living rough. So who's in there? Who's been getting the benefit of the flowers I've been putting there like a dutiful son?'

Her eyes widened so that the creases on her forehead deepened and formed waves. For a few moments her expression of surprise was frozen as if by a clown's make-up.

'You've been putting flowers on my grave? Oh Seamus, how touching! I didn't know you cared. If I'd known you'd be so nice to me once I was dead I would have died much sooner. I'll tell you everything you want to know. And quite a lot you don't. But you mustn't press me. It'll take time. We'll need to go on a little journey. I've got a car outside. Friend of mine who died recently gave it to me. Bit of an old banger but it'll get us there.'

'And when you've finished your story you plan to kill me, is that it?'

'Oh no, Seamus. You're the killer round here.'

'Why did you come back here?'

'Why did you? That time you killed him, I mean. How could you have known he was here?'

'I didn't. I'd given up searching. I just wanted a last look at the place.'

'Or maybe to see if anything had happened to the hole where the bodies are? Maybe you couldn't understand why they still hadn't been found.'

Seamus ran up to her, grabbed both her shoulders and shook her, then slapped her hard across the face. Tears streamed down her cheeks. His voice was raw with anger.

'How in God's name did you know about those?'

She pulled out a torn handkerchief and wiped her face.

'I suppose I deserved that. But if you ever hit me again I swear I will kill you. One of the children you paid was open to another offer in return for letting me in on the secret. I suppose he thought I would blackmail Brendan for a share and then pay him out of that. So he would get paid twice over. Greed will be that young man's undoing if it hasn't already. It never occurred to him that you two would have killed him without a second thought if you knew he had snitched on you. I followed you and watched you. So, why did you come back again?'

He retreated to a corner of the room and sat down.

'You're right,' he whispered at last. 'I wondered why they hadn't found them. I'd decided to give myself up. Tell the police where they were. Then I saw the notes. I had to wait until I knew who had discovered my secret.'

'And killed them too.'

'That was the general idea.'

'I found Patrick by chance as well. I had no idea where he was. I thought I would tell the police about the bodies. I came back here to see if I could remember the exact place and check they were still here. Then I saw him. You came for him. I missed you. I found him in that hole with the others.'

'You watched him? You were watching him right up to the end? You sick bastard. Even when he finally got away from you, you still came after him and watched. But you failed, didn't you? You couldn't protect him. You didn't see me come for him.'

'That's right. I failed. You came for Patrick like some great avenging angel. And I missed you.'

'And you're my avenging angel? Or the Furies? Father Gerald told me about them.'

'Not me. I'm only an agent. You have the gun but I have what I know. And that will set the Furies onto you. I won't. You'll set them on yourself.'

'So I'd be mad to listen to you.'

'If you don't you'll go mad soon enough, wondering what it is I know. Until the day comes when you realise the truth for yourself, and by then it will be too late.'

'Too late for what?'

'Redemption. I know my mythology as well. We did it at school. Orestes was pursued by the Furies but he finally found Redemption.'

Seamus felt the weight of his body sinking into the chair. By then he should have found the release either of his own death or that of the one person who knew his secret. He had expected to feel relief, even elation. Instead he felt a cold chill taking possession of him, limb by limb. This visitor from beyond the grave in the form of his own mother was teaching him the real meaning of fear. He had known panic and terror, remembered times when they lent wings to his feet to carry him out of danger. But real fear was a slow, creeping paralysis. He looked up at the woman sitting motionless opposite him. She was old, older than her years. She looked very frail. She could not jump out of her chair and run for it. He could try to pick up his gun and kill her and then himself. Then it really would be all over. No more nightmares, no more pursuing and being pursued by shadows. He could not kill his own mother of course. But surely this apparition could not be his mother? The whole idea was ridiculous. He had heard and read in detail how she had died, talked to the priest who had buried her and entered her name in the parish records, seen her grave, visited it regularly, placed flowers on it. This was some creature from Hell disguised as her, sent to torment him. So his gun was no use to him because no earthly bullet could kill her. In any case his legs were now too heavy to move and he knew his hand would never be able to control the gun.

'So you're my Redeemer,' he said. 'You don't exactly look as if you've come down from Heaven, more like up from the other place. Even if you're real I can't kill you. That would set the Furies onto me for an unnatural crime and I would never know what you have to tell me. So I have to listen to you. But what you tell me will set them onto me anyway. The difference is that you'll be there to save me. This is like one of those riddles of Ancient Greece. It's a trap and I have no choice but to fall into it. It's my destiny.'

'That's right.'

'All right. Go ahead.'

'Not here. I told you. We have to go on a little journey.'

# THIRTY-EIGHT

He climbed into the passenger seat as she switched on the engine. He turned towards her.

'When did you learn to drive?'

'It's all right. I have got a license.'

'Turn it off.'

She obeyed, an unspoken question forming on her lips.

'Wait here.'

He got out of the car and paced up and down outside the house for a few minutes. Then glancing round several times he returned to the front door and let himself in. She stared after him, shaking her head. He came out after a few minutes.

'So what was that all about?' she asked, as he sat down again beside her.

'I have a sixth sense about being followed. I had it last night.'

'That's right. Because I was following you.'

'Then why have I still got it?'

'Because you're paranoid. Why did you go back into the house?'

'I remembered the gun. It was still on the floor.'

'What did you do with it?'

'Hid it.'

'Where?'

'Somewhere safe. Let's go.'

They stopped at a service station on the M6. He ordered food for them while she went to have a shower. When she returned she looked a little younger and fresher, though she still wore the same old clothes.

'Have you got any money, Ma?' he asked, when they had finished eating. The food had left a taste like cardboard in his mouth.

'A few hundred my friend left me, as well as the car. What about you?'

'The same.'

'Why do you ask?'

'I wondered if we had enough to get you some new clothes in the next town.'

'Maybe. If we can find a charity shop somewhere. In the meantime we need to know if we're going any further.'

'Why shouldn't we?'

'It depends on whether you're going to tell me the truth, Seamus.'

'About what?'

'It wasn't all bad over in Belfast, was it? Not even for me. I had Linda. We were great friends. Like sisters. But it was much better for you. You had a whale of a time. You had your dad. I had lost him but you and he were as close as that.' She held up two fingers, one crossed over the other. 'And then there was John. I never much liked him. Bit too fond of the sound of his own voice. All mouth and trousers. But a good man at heart. You doted on him, didn't you? What's the matter, Seamus? Am I making you uncomfortable? Am I embarrassing you, reminding you of your wild young days? Can't you look at me? I'm your mother. Surely you can look at me. He was fun, wasn't he, your Uncle John? Remember those firework parties? You looked forward to them so much.'

'All right. Yes, we had some good times. John was good to all of us, until he just walked out like that. So why do you want to talk about him now?'

'Because I want to know how you can live with yourself, that's why. I'm not talking about Patrick. Because I don't think you can live with yourself for that. I think you've been dying slowly ever since you did that. But you did live with the other thing, didn't you? It was family but you lived with it. Did it never bother you at all? Never give you a sleepless night, or even a pang of conscience? Tell me or I leave you here.'

'Tell you what? I don't know what happened to him. He just left, the bastard. Got out just before things got really dangerous for us. I don't suppose Linda ever found him.'

'Of course she didn't. Because he wasn't there to be found, was he? When did you realise?'

He looked around at the other customers, children fractious after hours of boredom cooped up in cars, parents tired and irritable, wondering why they had decided to come out in the first place. He heard the sounds of their voices rising to be heard above the clatter of knives, forks and tea-cups, envied the trivia of their conversations, the pettiness of their quarrels. All would be forgotten when they reached their destinations. What was it like to be like them, to live and talk in the moment and then move on? Carlotta had tried to teach him to live in the moment. She had failed, because she did not know why he could never do that. He squirmed under his mother's steady stare. She was waiting for him to speak. He knew she would wait for hours if necessary. Over the years of loneliness, of betrayal, of living the life of another, she had learned patience above all else. He had to ask. He had to know what she knew.

'Realise what, Ma?'

'That he was on their side. It must have occurred to you. Why did we have such a charmed life out there? How did he manage to get work at the factory for himself and then for Brendan? How come the local gangs left you alone? How come our houses were never attacked while he was still there? No lies, Seamus. Or this goes no further. I know you and Brendan were a two-man execution squad. I've seen you in operation, don't forget. So when and how did you kill him?'

# THIRTY-NINE

Badger handed Brendan an envelope.

'Burn that when the two of you's have seen it.'

'What's this?'

'You've been doing a good job for us, both of you's. Very efficient, very clean. This one's different. You have to know who it is.'

'Why different?'

'I was all for someone else doing it. But they want you two. You're the best we have. So this is yours. It's important. A big one. He has connections. But that's not all. You know him. And he knows you. You're close. I'd say you were as close as family, if you weren't family already.'

Brendan opened the envelope. There was a photograph inside of two men coming out of a bar in the city centre. He whistled and handed the photograph to Seamus.

'Fucking hell,' said Seamus.

'Who's the other man?' asked Brendan.

'We don't have a name for him, code or otherwise. All we know is he belongs to a special intelligence and security unit of the British Army. So special it doesn't exist. A unit that runs informers.'

'I've seen him with John,' said Seamus. 'At the youth club. At first I thought he was from the estate, just someone wanting company. But there was something strange about him. As if he wouldn't hesitate to kill with his bare hands if he suspected the slightest danger. John never introduced him or told me anything about him. Now I know why.'

'You were right about him,' said Badger. 'He's trained to kill, quickly and quietly, and he's done it all over the world. In city streets at night, in jungles, deserts, anywhere there's fighting and people prepared to pay for his services.'

'Is he a target as well?' asked Seamus.

'Not yet. We're watching him to see who else he leads us to.'

'But if John is an informer he may have shopped us already,' said Brendan. 'This is too dangerous for us. We have to get out.'

'I wouldn't be so sure of that,' said Badger. 'He'll know you're sympathisers of course. He would expect you to get your hands a bit dirty from time to time. But even if he had suspicions that you were Volunteers you wouldn't be a priority. It's the big fish he's after. You haven't killed any high profile enemy. You haven't been involved in planting bombs. He doesn't know what you do. You keep your mouths shut. You don't keep any of your stuff in the house. The last place he'd think of looking for names to pass on would be his own home.'

'Okay, so he's been seen with this chap. Is there any other evidence against him? Do we know if he has shopped anybody, any big fish as you put it?'

'I can't tell you that. You should know better than to ask. This should be enough for you.'

'It is enough,' said Seamus, his voice shaking. 'The treacherous bastard. I'll take him out, Da', even if you don't have the nerve.'

'Shut up, son, for God's sake. Of course I've got the nerve. Only it's my brother we're talking about. I've got the right to ask questions.' He turned to Badger. 'All right. It's agreed. We take him out. But not in the same way as the others.'

'What do you mean?'

'We decide when and where. We let you know when the body's ready for collection and where to find it. You arrange disposal. We never know where you take it. And this is our last job over here. We get out as soon as it's done.'

'Where do you want to go?'

'Back to England. I'm not sure where yet.'

Badger smiled. 'What about London?'

'Why?'

'There's an ASU moving there. We're taking the campaign to the mainland. You two can help. I can arrange that.'

Brendan looked at Seamus who nodded.

'All right,' said Brendan to Badger. 'Is it a deal? You leave it to us to take him out in our way. Then we go to London.'

'It's a deal. When it's done go to a call box. Call this number.' He wrote on a piece of paper and handed it to him. 'Someone will pick up after five rings. They won't speak. Just give the place. Then the codeword. I've written that down. Burn the paper when you've memorised what's on it. When you've given the codeword don't wait for confirmation. Just hang up and get away.'

Badger got out of the car and walked off, as slowly as ever, whistling tunelessly.

Seamus shook his head. 'What the fuck was all that about? Why don't we just take him out in the normal way?'

'Because I want him to know who is doing it and why. And before I kill my own brother I want to hear him confess.'

'He won't.'

'I think he will. I know I couldn't beat it out of him. Neither could they. That's why I said I wanted to handle it myself. Because I think I can find a way.'

The noise in the factory yard was deafening, the heat stifling. Sparks flew from welding tools. The whining sound from oxyacetylene cutters bore into the ears of the men in blue overalls and protective goggles who worked them, setting their teeth on edge. There was an all-pervading smell of oil, tar and red hot metal.

Brendan found John in a corner, having a quiet smoke during his break.

'Brendan, what is it? Don't normally see you over here. You look worried. Is it Ruth? Or Patrick? Are they unwell?'

Brendan looked around. 'John, I need to talk to you. Can we go in here?'

There was a disused paint shed nearby. They went inside. Rusting cans and oil-drums strewed the floor. There was a strong stench of dried paint and turpentine. They huddled together in a corner. Brendan whispered into his ear.

'John, I've got to warn you about something. There's some people asking after you, over our side of the yard. Heavy types. Real muscle. They don't work here, I'm sure of that. I didn't know them but one of the guys on our shift said he thought they were IRA enforcers, punishment beatings, things like that. Said he'd seen them before. I said I thought you were off sick today. I promised to find out. That's what they think I'm doing now. They're waiting for me. Shit, John, what the hell have you been up to? You're going to get yourself killed. And me. And we have families we're responsible for.'

John sucked in his breath. 'All right, Brendan. Thanks for telling me. Get back now, before they come looking for you. Tell them I really am off sick. I knew it would come to this one day.'

'Come to what?'

'Come to me having to get away, that's what. I keep a bag packed here. I'll get out the side gate. I'll ring Linda later. I'll tell her I've gone to Liverpool. But I won't be there.'

'Where will you be?'

'I can't tell you.'

'For fuck's sake, John, I need to know what's going on. If I'm to cover for you here and at home and with those thugs you owe me an explanation.'

John looked round frantically.

'There's no time. They could be here any moment. And seeing you here with me they'll go for you as well.'

'John, if you don't come clean I'm going to go and tell them where you are right now.'

'All right, all right. We can meet tonight. Just you and me. Midnight at the youth club. Nobody ever goes there now. I'll hide out till then. I'll tell you everything. Now get back and let me get out of here. You go out the front door. There's one at the back here. I'll get out that way.'

John threw his arms around Brendan, pushed him away and darted behind a rack of empty shelves.

They searched the streets and the waste ground around the club carefully before going in, to make sure John had not brought anybody with him. They checked their guns for the final time.

'All right, son,' whispered Brendan. 'I'm going in now. You come in the back way in twenty minutes.'

Brendan had seen John go in alone but could find no trace of him inside. He picked up a chair which lay on the floor and sat down. He was aware of steps behind him, and a sound of heavy breathing.

'John?'

'Don't look round, Brendan.'

'Linda got your call. She thinks you've gone to Liverpool. What's going on?'

Brendan heard a click and felt something cold and hard against the back of his neck.

'I didn't know you had a gun, John. I thought you were a man of peace.'

'I was. I still am. For years I've worked for peace between the communities. I raised the funds to get this place built and done up. Now look at it. Some people just don't want peace. People like you.'

'Like me? Come on, John. You know where my sympathies lie, but I'm not a man of violence.'

'No? Not like those thugs who came to the yard today?'

'That's right.'

'Only there weren't any thugs, were there? You made all that up. I made a few other phone calls after I left. There was somebody coming after me. But it was you all the time.'

'So you're going to kill me, John. Your own brother.'

'No. I'm not an executioner. I won't kill you unless I have to. I'll knock you out. Then I'll make a phone call and some people will come to collect you. I'd advise you to cooperate with them. They can get very upset with people who don't cooperate.'

'All right, I'll cooperate. No need to knock me out, John. You're a man of peace, you said so yourself. Just leave me tied to this chair while you make your call. I'll let you. Put the gun down.'

The pressure in the back of his neck eased, then ceased. Brendan could still feel the impression on his skin. He rubbed the spot with his fingers.

'I've still got the gun in my hand, Brendan. Don't get any silly ideas about trying to run for it.'

'I won't. So you haven't shopped me yet?'

'No. I wanted to be sure. Now I am. I wanted to warn you. Give you time to think. I wanted to arrange for you to be found here. I didn't want you being picked up by the Brits or the RUC at the house and being beaten half to death in front of our families.'

'That's big of you, John. I appreciate it. So who have you shopped?'

'I told you, Brendan. I'm a man of peace and I work for peace. Only now I have to do it in different ways. I don't like being deceitful but those are the times we live in. You have your contacts. I have mine, on both sides.'

'Informers?'

'If you like. I prefer to think of them as people like me who want to stop the bombings and the shootings and the ambushes. They tell me where, when and who. I pass the information on.'

'To the Brits. To the enemy.'

'To people who have something to offer me in return. Me and my family. And that includes you.'

'Protection, you mean?'

'It works, doesn't it? Or it did until today. I hope you realise what you've done. Stupid of me, not realising what was going on under my own roof. But I'm no spy. I'm no good at keeping my eyes and ears open. That's more your line, isn't it? I'm blind, deaf, naive, trusting, not the qualities of a good spy. I'm a liaison man, a networker. I trust people because I'm told I can trust them, not because I can see into their hearts. I trust my contacts, my friends, and above all, my family. I knew you were up to something. When you got those wheels. I never believed you were helping out some farmer just for the fun of it. I assumed you were moving weapons and stuff around. I didn't mind so long as you didn't hide it in my house. Which I knew you didn't.

I would never have dreamt you were a killer, or that when my number was up it would be my own brother who would come for me. Did you think how it would be for your family once I had gone?'

'My family? Yes, John, I thought about them. I'm thinking about them right now.'

There was another clicking sound, a different tone, dry and short.

'Your number really is up, John,' said Brendan. 'And you're still too trusting. All right, son. I think we've heard enough. Go ahead.'

# FORTY

'I've never been here,' said Ruth. 'Pretty weird, looking down on your own grave. Come on. Let's walk.'

They had spent the morning in the city centre buying second-hand clothes for both of them. She wore a dark green overcoat with no buttons, several sizes too large. He wore a leather jacket which looked as if it had been pulled through yards of bramble thicket. They strolled slowly along the grassy paths between the lines of gravestones, side by side, always with a few inches of space between them.

'What happened after you left?' asked Seamus.

'I had no idea where to go. We drifted around, got cheap lodgings and casual work here and there.'

'Did you ever talk of splitting up?'

'Never. Patrick wasn't ready to go out into the world on his own.'

'He was nineteen when you left. When was he ever going to be ready? Never, if you had your way.'

'I had sheltered him. I admit it. Can you blame me, with the life we had led, the violence, the threats, the stuff you and Brendan were up to, spending every day waiting for the knock of the police on the door?'

'Maybe it was you who couldn't face the world on your own. He knew that. He was protecting you.'

'All right. We were protecting each other. What's wrong with that, for God's sake? But I couldn't go on. The burden was too much. We had no friends. I worried constantly in case he might just go off one day, fall in with a bad crowd, maybe get into drugs and stuff like that.'

'Or meet a girl and fall in love. You couldn't bear that thought, could you? You needn't have worried. You'd already made sure that couldn't happen.'

She stopped and stared at him, searching his eyes for clues. He couldn't know, not everything. Was he bluffing, hoping to provoke her into some sort of confession, retaliating for the way she had forced him to confess to killing John? Seamus's expression was impassive. After a few moments she looked away and walked on. He followed her, remaining a couple of steps behind.

'Yes,' she said. 'I was afraid of that too. What did he know of the world? How could he judge people? How could he stop himself being taken advantage of? I had to find somewhere safe for us. I had no family to go to. They cut me out of their lives when I converted to marry Brendan. We couldn't save any money and what we had was running out. Then I thought of the address John had given to Linda. Linda had begged me to keep in touch but I hadn't had the heart. She had never written to me because she didn't know our address. I remembered hers and we went there. I was hoping against hope. It could have been the wildest of wild goose chases. Imagine my relief when she answered the door. We hugged each other for ages. She hugged Patrick as well. I was crying, for the first time in years. It flooded out, everything I had bottled up for so long. Now I had found my best friend again. Now I wasn't alone any more. With Linda to help me I could face the world again, find my place in it.

'She told us she had found the place empty. No sign of John, and Dennis was away. A local agent was advertising it for rent. She went to the agent and told him she knew the owner. The agent phoned Dennis in Canada. He said she could have the place rent-free until he got back in return for looking after it. She had been very lonely there. She had found neither sight nor sound of John of course. Then the Belfast police contacted her. They had found John's body. She went over to arrange the funeral. They told her he had probably been killed by a paramilitary group but they had no idea which one.

'We were there for about a year. We got jobs in the supermarket where Linda worked. I used to borrow Linda's car for shopping and trips out. I had never learned to drive. She taught me. She was good. I passed my test first time.'

'So what happened to break up this happy home?'

'I was returning one evening with Patrick. We had been out for a drive, just the two of us. I saw this man outside the front door, sitting on the step, smoking a cigarette.'

'What sort of man?'

'Big, very strong, shaven head. Army type, perhaps. But normal clothes. Respectable. Suit and tie. I was about to turn into the space in front of the building where we parked the car. I saw him just in time. I sensed danger so I drove on, racking my brains, trying to think where I'd seen him before. Then I remembered. I'd seen him outside the house in Belfast, just after John disappeared. He vanished when he saw I'd noticed him. This time he didn't see me.'

Seamus nodded. 'The bald man. John's contact. The other man in the photograph. When John disappeared he tried to find him. He watched the house in Belfast. Then he came over to Liverpool. The only lead he had on him was Dennis's address. Probably had that on file when he was setting John up as an informer, somewhere John would go if he had to leave in a hurry without telling him.'

'I realised at once he was waiting for us. I always wondered if you two had been involved in John's death, from the moment Linda told me what the police had told her. I had a sort of sixth sense that this man had made the same connection. He obviously wasn't police. He wasn't going to ask me politely where Brendan was. I got the hell out of there.'

'Where did you go?'

'Where we're going next. Shit, what the hell are you doing?'

Without warning he had grabbed her arm and pulled her behind a large gravestone.

'Shut up, Ma. I thought I heard footsteps.'

'Don't be so ridiculous. Of course there are footsteps. This is a cemetery. There are always visitors.'

'I thought I heard footsteps close behind us just now. They must have hidden when they realised I'd heard. I'm going to have a look.'

'Now I know you're paranoid.'

He returned after a few minutes, shaking his head.

'All right, you're right. I'm paranoid.'

'Let's go.'

# FORTY-ONE

They turned off the dual carriageway onto an unmarked side road. After half a mile they came to a deserted village, the few shops boarded up, the pavements sprinkled with dustings of sand scurrying before the wind. They drove on until the road became a track between sand dunes.

'We used to come here for holidays when I was a child,' she said. 'There's a holiday camp a bit further on. Or there was. Not a good place for it. Everywhere round here is subject to coastal erosion. The sea retreats further and further. More and more sand is blown in until it covers everything. There are whole villages buried out here. We'll have to get out and walk.'

They left the car and trudged through a desolate landscape of low dunes. The wind drove scouring particles into their faces. The reflected light off the sand dazzled their eyes. High light clouds fluttered across the sky in shades of white flecked with grey, with here and there a red under-glow from the late afternoon sun. The distant, invisible sea swished faintly in their ears.

'So you and Patrick came here to hide,' said Seamus.

'Yes. I never thought anybody would find us here. There's the entrance to the camp, over there. You can still see some of the buildings. Most of them are half-buried now. It was late September when we got here. The owners were about to close it down for good. It was empty. Nobody here but a caretaker. But some of the chalets had been in use during the summer months, the ones at the back which had not yet been invaded by sand. I had planned to climb over the fence and find a chalet where we could hide. But the front entrance was open. The caretaker told us we could stay for nothing for a few nights, after I explained we were running away from my violent husband. He found us a chalet which was still clean and comfortable, with a double bed and bathroom. He gave us clean bedding. Invited us to share his dinner. It brought back all my favourite childhood memories. I told Patrick about them. About making sandcastles on the beach, swimming in the freezing sea, much closer then, rides on the donkeys. Let's see if I can find it.'

The fence had long since gone. They scrambled over hillocks between the collapsed chalet roofs until they found some that were still intact though covered up to the doorsteps in sand.

'That one. Over there. We can get in if we just shovel some of this sand out of the way. Help me, Seamus, will you?'

He did not move. She turned back towards him.

'Come on, help me, please.'

'Look, we don't need to do it like this, Ma. You can just tell me.'

'I want to get it right. I want to remember the detail. Being here helps me to do that. There. The door will open now. In here.'

He shrugged his shoulders and followed her. The floor was covered in a layer of sand which had blown in through the broken window. She stood in the middle of the room. She was shivering. When she spoke she struggled to control her voice.

'This was the bedroom. They came early on the second morning. They just burst through the door. There were three of them. The bald man and two others. They weren't masked. I can see their faces to this day. They must have forced the caretaker to tell them which chalet we were in and then told him to get lost. One of them brought in two cane chairs from the kitchen. They tied us to them, opposite each other.

'So the British Army is torturing women and children now, I said to the bald man. Hardly a child, he said, he looks more like a man to me. While he spoke he was looking Patrick up and down, smiling. Then he stepped up to Patrick's chair and ruffled his hair, still smiling. I remember he was quietly spoken, with a sort of public school drawl, like an officer. I was surprised. Surprised and sick with terror. His accent was so totally out of character with his appearance. When someone speaks like that, they usually mean to sound reassuring, as if they have authority, they're in control, they're going to protect you from any threats. I expected his speech to be rough, crude and angry, and his actions to be the same. That would have been bad enough. But I was ready. Ready to be punched and beaten. But when he spoke, it made my skin crawl. Now I knew it would be much worse than any beating. He would be methodical, scientific, patient.

'And we're not army or SAS or police or secret service, he went on. We're freelance. We were army. We were discharged months ago. Conduct unbecoming. Our methods were unorthodox, you might say. We were becoming an embarrassment to the powers that be. According to the records we went to Africa as mercenaries. And when we've told the police where to find that bastard husband of yours, when he's well and truly banged up, that's where we'll be. Africa. Only we don't want to leave unfinished business behind us. We want to tidy things up. That's why we're here. This is personal. John was a good man. He was a great help to us. He took a lot of risks. He didn't deserve to die like that. Shot in the back of the head like an animal at the slaughterhouse.

'He said the body had been left in one of the bins at the back of the youth club. All Linda had told me was that the body was found on the premises. Nobody went there anymore. It was only noticed when it started to stink. That was disgusting, Seamus. Yes, I know the business you're in. You kill people you see as traitors. Uncle, brother, it makes no difference to you. But how could you have dumped him there, like so much rubbish? Didn't you owe him more respect than that?'

Seamus walked up to her, spreading his arms, hoping the gesture would show her he had nothing more to hide, that he was speaking the truth.

'I never knew about that until the police in Brighton told me. Honest to God, Ma. It wasn't meant to be like that. It wasn't the usual way. We never disposed of the bodies. We told them when it was ready. They were supposed to bury it somewhere it would never be found. They must have been disturbed and panicked. Or they put some new people onto the job who didn't know the ropes.'

181

She shrugged her shoulders and turned away. She spoke quietly as if to a third person who was standing in the empty space before her. Seamus strained to hear her.

'He, the bald man, I mean, said John had once been sympathetic to the Republican cause but became sickened by the violence. He thought that if the IRA lost some of their key people they would lose faith in the armed struggle and try to further their cause through peaceful means. If they did that the violence on the loyalist side would cease as well. Maybe he was misguided, Seamus. But that was what he believed.'

Seamus made a sudden movement towards the door.

'For Christ's sake, let's get out of here,' he said. 'I don't want to know any more about what happened here.'

He stopped outside, holding his breath. Slowly he reached into the inside pocket of his jacket. She came up behind him and stood in the doorway.

'What's the matter?'

'That's the matter.' He pointed to the sand in front of the chalet.

'I can't see anything.'

'Footprints.'

'Ours, you idiot.'

'Are you blind or something? There are three sets. A man's set as well as ours. There were none before we arrived. Who else knows about this place?'

'Nobody. Apart from the men who came after us. If they are still alive after all these years. But why would they follow us now? And how did they pick up the trail? They got what they wanted. They could have killed me at the time.'

He glared at her.

'But it's not you they want, is it? It's me. Patrick gave them Brendan so you made a deal with them. The police told them I wasn't there. They would find me but they couldn't be sure they could pin anything on me. Brendan was telling them he was a one man operation, that I knew nothing about what they had found in the cellar. So their price for not killing you was that you would let them know when you had found me and got me to confess to being in on killing John.'

She shook her head violently.

'What are you talking about, for God's sake?'

'The bald man was lying to you. He never went to Africa. Maybe he had been officially discharged but he was still working for the Brits. People like that were useful to them, people with no scruples I mean. He was experienced. He had a lot of contacts. He knew me by sight. He knew I was John's nephew. He saw me in Belfast when I went to visit John's grave. That was after the police had told me what happened to John. The police must have tipped him off so he could follow me and see if I made contact with anybody. It was their last chance to pin something on me. He was waiting in the cemetery. I spotted him and ran for it. He came after me but I lost him. I got over the border in secret and came back the soft route by Dublin.'

'How come he didn't find you afterwards?'

'I changed my job and moved into a new flat. The police had stopped keeping tabs on me. He had no way of finding me. And even if he had he couldn't connect me to John's death unless I confessed. Which I would never have done to him. But what if I told someone else? And like the fool that I am that's what I just did a few hours ago. I told you. In the interests of honesty. Honesty! I was signing my fucking death warrant. Did you have a fucking tape recorder on you? While I was in the gents you made a telephone call, didn't you? No wonder I knew we were being followed.'

'You felt that before we left London.'

'Of course. The arrangement was he would hold back until you had my confession in the bag. And he was never going to kill me in the cemetery, was he? But this place is ideal. Nobody comes here. A body could lie here forever. It's been a long time coming, hasn't it? I just hope it was worth the wait, for both of you. Of course you had no intention of keeping your side of the bargain if you could avoid it. But all that changed when you knew I had killed Patrick. Now you wanted revenge too. You and the bald man were both on the same side.' He slapped the side of his head. 'Christ, I've been so stupid!

So bloody careless. And you've been bloody clever, I have to admit that. Cleverer than I would ever have expected of you. Except you didn't plan for me having my gun with me.'

She caught her breath.

'You don't, do you? You told me you hid it at the house.'

'I lied.'

'You're totally paranoid.'

'Just taking precautions. Very reasonable ones as it turned out.'

She took him by the arm.

'Seamus, this is ridiculous. You really are being blind and stupid. Do you still not have the slightest idea what this is all about? Have you really no idea why we are here? I never had a tape recorder. I never made a phone call. I'm not a spy or an informer. I don't want you dead. Of course I don't. That's the last thing on God's earth I want. I asked you to tell me about John so we could be honest with each other. That's God's truth. There's nobody else here now. Anybody can walk across here. It was just a passer-by.'

Before she realised what was happening he had stepped behind her and pressed the muzzle of the gun into the nape of her neck.

'Seamus, please, you've got this all wrong.'

'Shut up. Walk forward, slowly. If he's waiting to take me out he'll have to shoot you first. I don't suppose he'll mind that but it might make him pause for long enough for me to get him first.'

'Seamus, you're crazy.'

'Walk.'

They turned a corner into a sharp wind which had blown sand across all the footprints. Slowly, the gun still pressing into her neck, Seamus constantly darting glances around him, they stumbled across the sand until they reached the car.

'Now do you believe me?'

'I believe he backed off for the time being, that's all. Get in the car.'

# FORTY-TWO

When they were both in the car he told her to start the engine.

'Not yet,' she said. 'Don't you want to know what they did to me? You know about torture, don't you? You did it to those poor bastards before you shot them.'

'I never tortured anybody.'

'You're lying. I can tell. That's one thing you must never lie to me about. Not that. Because I know much more about that than you ever will. I've been tortured in body, mind and heart and it's still going on. All because of you and Brendan and that wretched cause of yours. So tell me about the torturing you did.'

'Never after I joined.'

'But before?'

'A long time before. There was this boy at school, snitched on me and a friend. My friend's father was a Volunteer. He must have done interrogations, or knew those who did. He had this machine. My friend…we…borrowed it. To teach the snitch a lesson.'

'And did he learn his lesson? Did the others learn? Did they look up to you and respect you? Or did they hate and fear you? You never understood the difference, did you? Not then, not all those years you lived by the gun, not now. Particularly not now. When the others put their guns down, you kept yours, to use on Patrick. Even after that, all scores settled as you thought, you kept your gun, ready for use. When you realised someone knew what you had done, you came after them, prepared to kill again. You only dropped the gun when you saw me because you thought I was already dead. Yes, you always chose to be hated and feared. So, you used a machine, did you? They didn't have a machine. They used lighted cigarettes on my breasts. You're looking very pale, Seamus. What's the matter? Are you suddenly squeamish after all these years?'

'I'm sorry, Ma,' he whispered. 'So sorry.'

'The worst is waiting for it to start. Then you just try to scream the pain out of your skull. But all that does is make room for the next pain. And so on. Until you think your head will explode. I screamed so much my voice has been hoarse ever since. I still have nightmares about it, thinking I'm back there with them and it's going to start again. But of course you don't know anything about it. You never tortured anybody, after you joined. I suppose they had other people to do that. Specialists. Your speciality was execution.'

'Execution of traitors.'

She clapped her hands.

'Of course. I forgot. You did the honourable stuff. Including disposing of your own uncle and brother.'

'All right, you've suffered. I accept that gives you a right to say these things. So go on, if you have to.'

'They got bored with me after a while.'

'Go on. Finish the story. They were going to start on him next. So he told them where to find Brendan. So why did he hide? He could have come clean. Gone to see him in prison to explain. Asked for his forgiveness. I suppose he was too ashamed. You had defied them but he was too weak. He was a coward. I still don't see why you're telling me this. It doesn't change anything.'

She turned the engine over. It chugged, gasped, then expired.

'Sand's blown into it,' she said. 'We'll have to walk back to the village and ring for a garage to tow it in. If we can even find a working telephone there.'

'Before we go anywhere, tell me how they found you here. How did they know about this place?'

'Only one person knew.'

'Linda?'

'That's right.'

'Your best friend. Did they torture her as well?'

'Oh no. They didn't need to. She was very helpful. They didn't even need to ask. She knew about your comings and goings, knew the sort of company you and Brendan had fallen into, the same way I did. She couldn't be sure Brendan had killed him. Maybe she thought he had just tipped somebody off. But she told the bald man of her suspicions. He may have had other informers, may have already had Brendan down as a suspect. After talking to Linda he was sure Brendan was his man.'

'She never asked you for the address directly?'

'No. What reason could she give for wanting to know? I would have got suspicious right away. She must have searched our rooms when we were out. She wouldn't have found anything. No, the only way was to contact the bald man and put him onto us. She waited. She had a lot to lose. She would lose the life we had together. She would be on her own again. But if she betrayed me there was a chance she might get Brendan put away. In the end she made her choice.'

Seamus punched the dashboard hard with his fist.

'Be careful. That's my car you're wrecking.'

Gently he massaged his bruised knuckles with the fingers of his other hand.

'Sorry. Of all the fucking treacherous...So how did he know where to look?'

'I had told Linda about this place. We were looking over some old photographs, back in Belfast. I told her about the happy times I had here when I was a child. I said if I had the chance I would come back here for old times' sake. She must have remembered and told him. She would also have given him the number and description of the car.'

'So she got her revenge. And you made her pay for it, didn't you?'

'Once they had the information they wanted they left us there, tied to the chairs. I was in agony. I passed out a few times. The local police came for us hours later. They took us to the nearest hospital. They treated me for the burns, and both of us for shock. When we were discharged we went back to Liverpool. Linda gaped when she opened the door. What's the matter, I said. You look as if you've seen a ghost. Just surprised to see you back so soon, she said. She must have assumed they would kill us once they had what they needed. I apologised for taking the car without telling her. I told her some story about Patrick being taken ill suddenly while we were out so I had taken him to the nearest casualty, miles away. They had detained him for a few days. I had been so worried I had forgotten to phone her. The story fitted our appearances. We both looked ill and in shock. Patrick went straight to his room and refused to talk to either of us or to take any food. That night we heard on the news that Brendan had been arrested. Patrick was listening to the radio with us. He went to his room, packed a bag and left. Didn't say a word. I kept asking him where he was going to go. He didn't reply.'

He turned towards her. 'You let him go, knowing he'd be a target if the word was out he was the one who shopped Brendan? So what happened between you? You were really prepared to put him in that danger? If you were angry with him because of the betrayal, why are you so angry with me for killing him? You helped me by letting him go. You're as responsible as I am.'

'I had to let him go. You'll see why. I was telling you about Linda. That evening, after Patrick had left, I sat her down in the kitchen. I sat opposite her. She was shaking. She wouldn't look at me.'

# FORTY-THREE

'Now it's just the two of us, Linda. There are some things we need to sort out. I know what you did. You set those thugs on to us so you could get revenge for John. You remembered that place I told you about. The holiday camp. When we were drunk and looking at my old photos. You were so drunk you couldn't distinguish between puddles and poodles.'

Linda looked up and laughed.

'Yes, I remember. Me and my puddles. We had some good times together, didn't we? We could get drunk again, you know. I've got a bottle here. Talk about the old times.'

'Maybe some other time. Remember what you said? About us always being there for each other? It was after that time you rescued me when I got lost.'

'I remember. Are you sure you don't want a drink?'

'Quite sure.'

'Do you mind if I do?'

'Go ahead. You live here.'

'Thanks.'

Linda staggered out of her chair as if already drunk, opened a cupboard and took out a bottle of gin. She pulled out the stopper and drank straight from the bottle.

'So now you've got your drink, tell me,' said Ruth. 'Why did you send those men after me?'

Linda spat and put the bottle to her lips again.

'You know why. That bastard husband of yours killed John. His own brother. And that creep of a son of yours. They were in it together, weren't they? It had to be them. Somebody lured him to the club. John would never have let anybody else get that close to him without protection. I suppose Brendan set up a secret meeting, to warn him of danger. John was always far too trusting. Pity they didn't get Seamus as well. But it'll be a sentence on him, seeing his beloved dad locked up. I didn't know you would be that bothered about Brendan being caught.'

'Of course I am. He's my husband.'

'And John was mine. We took them both down a strip, didn't we, that time we talked about what they did for sex, now they were no longer interested in us. You wouldn't have thought we cared. But when that man told me about finding his body, dumped in the bin like so much garbage...I suppose women can only be friends up to a point. When your husband kills mine then it gets difficult, you have to admit. It would have been easier if you hadn't run away. If you had just come in when he was here and told him where Brendan was.'

'You thought I would do that? You thought they only had to ask and I would have told them? This is what they did to me to try to get me to tell. Look.'

Ruth tore off her blouse and bra. Linda shook her head and closed her eyes. Ruth grabbed her by the hair until she opened them again.

'Look, for God's sake! This is your doing. Well, now you have your revenge. And you have to pay for what you did to get it.'

Linda put her hand to her mouth. Then she rushed into the bathroom. Ruth heard retching sounds. Linda returned after a few minutes, wiping her mouth with a flannel. She sat down again and took another swig from the bottle. Ruth waited, staring at her.

'I'm sorry,' Linda gasped at last. 'I didn't know they would do anything like that. But it worked, didn't it? You did tell them. You or that other weird son of yours. Thank God I never had kids if yours are anything to go by. It doesn't matter. They got him. And I'm glad. Go ahead. Kill me. I don't care. Take one of the knives from the drawer and kill me. It's what you've been waiting for, isn't it? Now that creep Patrick's gone, you have your chance. I've nothing left to live for.'

Ruth shook her head.

'No, not like that, Linda. I'm the one who's going to die. You're going to live. In a manner of speaking. I tell you what. It's a lovely evening. Why don't we go for a little drive? Are there any garages or sheds around here?'

Linda stared at her, then giggled.

'Yes,' she said. 'Round the back of the building. Are we going to do some gardening first? Oh, what fun! I didn't know you were interested. Only I'm afraid we haven't got a garden.'

'Come on. Let's go. We're wasting time.'

'Can I bring the bottle with me?'

'Of course. I need to get some stuff first.'

Ruth went to her room, put on a new bra and blouse and gathered all her personal papers together. She put them in her handbag. When she returned, Linda was still on the same kitchen chair but swaying slightly, humming to herself.

'Remember this one?' asked Linda, her voice heavily slurred. 'From "Carousel"? We used to sing it together. You and me. With Patrick listening, all wide-eyed. Something about...How did it go? Oh yes. "What's the use of wondering if your fella's good or bad, he's your fella and you love him, that's all you need to know."' Her voice wavered and croaked as she tried vainly to find the pitch of the notes. 'I always thought that was daft. But it turned out to be true with us, didn't it?'

'You always did like the sentimental songs, didn't you?' said Ruth. 'Only I'm not in a sentimental mood at the moment, so you'll understand if I don't join in. Give me your keys.'

'On the hook on the back of the door.'

Ruth picked up the keys and put them in her handbag. She pushed Linda towards the door, supporting her under the armpits as she staggered down the stairs and over to the car. She left her slumped in the passenger seat while she rummaged inside one of the garages. After a few minutes she returned carrying a length of hose and a roll of duct tape. She put them in the back of the car and climbed into the driver's seat.

'I thought we'd go to Sunset Strip. Do you know it? It's just north of Crosby along the estuary. Lovely sunset on an evening like this. Good views of the Welsh hills.'

After a few miles Linda's eyes had closed. She began to snore gently. Half an hour later Ruth turned off the road and drove along a gravel way. She stopped and turned off the engine.

'Well, here we are. Just in time for the sunset. Look, Linda. All that lovely red fire on the water. The Welsh hills lining the horizon. You've never been here, you say? Look at what you've been missing. Come on, wake up.'

Linda stirred and groaned.

'What time is it?'

'Time to go to sleep again. I would have let you sleep on but I didn't want you to miss the view. Close your eyes again, Linda. That's it.'

Ruth put her arm around her.

'Linda? Do you remember what we agreed, that time after you rescued me? We promised each other we would always be friends. You asked me if I had done anything like that at school. I said I had but we had drifted apart. But look at us, Linda. We found each other again. Despite everything. And here we are. Linda?'

Linda stirred again but did not open her eyes.

Ruth got out of the car. After checking nobody was watching she opened the rear door, took out the hose and fixed one end of it to the exhaust pipe. She climbed back into the driver's seat, the other end of the hose in her hand. She opened the window slightly, then closed the door, checking that there was enough of a gap for the hose to snake through the window into the interior of the car. She picked up the duct tape from the back seat and put it in her handbag. She put her arms round Linda again and kissed her.

'Ruth?' murmured Linda, still keeping her eyes closed.

'Yes, darling?'

'I love you.'

'I love you too, Linda.'

'I've been wondering. If we had been lovers perhaps we wouldn't have been so cut up about our husbands. I mean, those bastards didn't care about us, did they? If we'd had somewhere else to put our feelings, we wouldn't have cared so much about what happened to them, would we?'

'No. I suppose not.'

'It's too late now. And we could never have done anything like that, could we? Be lovers, I mean. Not there, not then. That sort of thing wasn't done, was it?'

'No. Not done. We have to say goodbye now, Linda.'

'I know. Goodnight, Ruth. God bless. Sleep tight. Watch the bed bugs don't bite.' She half-chanted the little childhood rhyme, the sound barely falling from her lips.

'Goodnight, Linda.'

Ruth took out of her handbag the papers she had collected from the flat and strewed them over the back seat. She switched on the engine. She checked the gauge. Enough petrol. She got out of the car, closed the door, took out the tape and sealed the gap carefully, making sure the hose was secure. She walked to the top of the nearest dune, took out a cigarette and lighter from her bag, lit up and watched the final traces of the sunset. The crimson turned to orange, then pink. The breeze off the estuary was blowing strongly now, buffeting her cheeks. She stood up and breathed in deeply.

She walked slowly back to the car and peered through the window. The engine was still running, a slow, effortful churn. She could feel the heat off the bonnet as she passed in front of the car.

She began to walk back towards the road. It was late and she had to find a bus-stop.

# FORTY-FOUR

'You said I was the killer, Ma. But you killed her.'

'Don't you dare to compare us, Seamus.' She spat the words out of the corner of her mouth. 'I'm not like you. I could never kill in cold blood. She wanted to die. I just helped her on her way.'

'And you became her.'

'That's right. I'd put all the papers that identified me by name in the car. Gibson, that is. No mention of O'Hara. I'd reverted to my maiden name. My driving license was in the name of Gibson. There were no photographs in the car. I had one but I kept it, to send to the press later on. I got the bus back to her flat. I had taken her key and I let myself in. I found her personal papers in a drawer in the kitchen, along with a huge wad of cash. Blood money from the bald man, I expect. Thirty fucking pieces of silver. I took it all and left. The last thing I did was post my picture to the paper with my name written on the back, once I knew the body had been discovered. The police would have identified her as me from the stuff in the car. I assume they went round to the flat to try to find someone to identify her in person. But they had no reason to suspect anybody else was involved in her death. They wouldn't have noticed any discrepancy between her appearance and the photograph in the paper. If they had they would have assumed the paper had made a mistake.'

Seamus laughed and clapped his hands.

'Well done, Ma! You certainly fooled me. So you left with a new identity. Good for you. What did you do?'

'Got jobs here and there. Cleaning, waiting at tables. I stayed with this man sometimes. I told you about him. He helped me out with money and a place to sleep when I needed it. He never asked about the past. I think he suspected I was a recovering addict. Drugs or alcohol. It was true enough. I've done plenty of both in my time. It was as if I had been sleepwalking. I didn't wake up until I saw that man outside Linda's flat. Until I knew we were in real danger.'

He put his hand gently on her shoulder.

'That changed you, Ma. You were never brave during the Troubles, were you? You took refuge in booze and pills. I knew that. I'm not blaming you. I've done that too. But the way you resisted those men. That was very brave. And the way you made Linda pay. I admire that too. You should have joined with us. You'd have been a credit to the cause.'

'You're forgetting something, son. I wasn't Irish. I studied the Bible and I love the Gospels but I was never really a Catholic. And worst of all I was a woman. No, your war was all yours. Mine started much later. When I knew we were targets. Then I knew I had to find some courage from somewhere.'

'We had women. The best and the bravest of us were women. And non-Catholics. I was never much of a Catholic. And it wasn't compulsory to be Irish. It was belief in the cause that mattered. If you'd had something to believe in, to take part in, maybe you and Patrick...'

'Maybe what, me and Patrick?'

'You know what I mean.'

'Not really. Come on, Seamus. Spit it out.'

'Maybe your obsession with Patrick...I'm trying to understand, Ma. All right, maybe it wasn't a cause you needed. Perhaps if Brendan...you must still have loved him, even though he didn't have time for you.'

She opened the glove compartment, took out a crumpled tissue and dabbed the corner of her eye. She stared out of the side-window. Seamus shook his head and sighed. He had gone too far. He had opened an old wound, a hurt far deeper than anything she had suffered at the hands of the bald man. Stupid of him. He had sensed something opening up between them in the last few minutes. The possibility of an understanding, even of a little warmth, despite everything he had done. Now she had clammed up again and it was his fault. She would say nothing more until…maybe never. Perhaps it was all over. She would take him to a train or bus station the next day, drop him off and drive away. That might be the best thing for both of them. It was too painful for her. And he would be better off on his own. She had offered him Redemption but he no longer believed in the possibility. He would decide his own fate.

He was startled when she spoke at last, interrupting his thoughts.

'Yes, I loved him. I never stopped. I had given myself to him before, my nakedness, the sounds and movements of my body, all out of love. He was the only one. I had never forgotten, even if he had. So when those men were hurting me I gave my body to him again, this time in pain, not pleasure. Only he never knew. I was the centre of his world once.' She turned back to face him, forcing a smile. 'Then you arrived. And you became the centre of his world. I didn't blame him. Or you. But I still loved him. Of course I did.'

'Did you hate Patrick for betraying him? Was that why you let him go? Couldn't you forgive him? Do you really want to go to your grave hating both your sons?'

'My grave? Oh yes, you're right to remind me about that. I'll be there soon enough. No more for now, Seamus, please. Let's go. And for God's sake put that gun away.'

# FORTY-FIVE

In the main street of the village they were surprised to see a bent and rusty sign advertising a hotel. It pointed down a side path. The path led past a former golf course sheltered by pine trees from the sea winds. The bunker sand was tainted with patches of soil and small tufts of grass. Clover and daisy had invaded the now luxuriously overgrown greens and fairways. They had met not a soul either in the village or on the path. There would surely be no hotel, only yet another building crumbling into disrepair. After half a mile, turning a corner, they were surprised to come across a large redbrick house, a hotel sign above the door. A dirty estate car stood in a small car park, its tyres encrusted with sand. They were even more surprised when the door opened to their knock and a gentleman told them that, yes, they were open and they did have a couple of rooms free. From the hotel reception desk Seamus rang a garage they had passed on the dual carriageway. He told them where they could pick up the car.

After a silent dinner served by the owner in person, at which they were the only guests, they walked back down to the sand dunes. She took his arm. Behind them the sky had darkened to purple, while ahead a strip of blood red hung low over the horizon.

'Did you bring the gun with you, Seamus?'

'No, I left it in my bag in my room.'

'You must feel naked without it. You don't think we're being followed anymore?'

'No. Whoever it was has gone.'

'If there was anybody. So it's just the two of us now.'

'Yes. "Just the two of us." That's what you said to Linda. Before you killed her.'

She stopped suddenly, released his arm and stepped away from him.
'Go on, Seamus. What are you thinking? You can tell me.'

'I was just wondering…is this where you kill me, now you know I'm unarmed? We're all alone here. Nobody will see or hear. Do you have a gun? Do you want me to go and fetch mine for you? Do you have it already? Did you pick it up from my room before we left? Were you checking just now that I don't have another? Go ahead if you want to. Kill me. I won't try to get away. I'll just kneel here in the sand. Go on. Do it. We have finished, haven't we? We've told each other everything. So go ahead.'

She shook her head. 'No, Seamus. Of course I don't have a gun. I'm terrified of the sight of them. And we certainly haven't finished. Not by a long chalk.'

'Haven't we? I think I have.'

'Well, I haven't. But I can't talk with you over there, suspecting me of having a gun. Let's walk on as before. Let me take your arm. Is that all right?'

He paused and nodded. She walked over to him and took his arm again.

'You asked me earlier if I wanted to go to my grave hating both my sons. Remember?'

'I remember.'

'It won't be like that, I promise you. I could never stop loving Patrick. He left because he couldn't bear to be with me a moment longer.'

'When those men came for you, did they find you together? Were you sharing the bed?'

He expected her to pull away again, but she continued to hold his arm and walk slowly beside him.

'It wasn't like that, not the way you think. When we were on the run we were together all the time. Day and night. It had to be that way. We didn't dare let each other out of our sight. We slept together in that chalet because it was the safest way. We were alone and frightened so we comforted each other. There was nothing dirty about it.'

'What was dirty was the way you made it happen like that. You persuaded him you had to stay together. Do you really think he didn't realise it was more dangerous that way? He stayed with you to protect you. He failed. They found you. But that was why he was with you. Not because he loved you, not in the sick way you wanted him to. Not in the sick way you loved him.'

'Sick? No, Seamus. Special, but not sick. Not that. I talked to the priest about it. I thought he would understand but he didn't. It was a burden and a duty, like the stigmata suffered by those saints. An agony but still a gift from God. It was always my destiny to love, however much pain it would cause me. Brendan was the first. I thought we would love each other forever. Then you. But neither of you were interested. You had your own destinies. You lived in your own world of hatred and revenge, shootings and beatings, all in the name of making the world a better place. But how could it be a better place if the love of women had no part in it? My love had to go somewhere. There was only Patrick left.'

'He was beautiful. That was why you loved him. If you dare to call it love.'

'It was his soul that was beautiful. I was the only one who would ever appreciate that. If only he had been ugly so nobody else would want him. He would have had to stay with me. But he had been cursed with physical beauty as well. So they would try to take him from me. Those bitches, those whores out there. They would see the beauty of his face and body but not of his soul. They would destroy him. It was my duty to protect him because he was so special. And instead he died protecting me. I knew where you had dumped him. I opened the trapdoor and looked down at him. He was still beautiful, even there in that hole, a crumpled, broken corpse. Beautiful because he had died for me.'

'Died for you? Died to protect you? What are you talking about? He died because I killed him and I killed him because he shopped Brendan. Simple as that. Nothing to do with you, except you were there to see it. So go on, tell me. Tell me I was right. You haven't yet said it in so many words. Tell me he shopped him and you heard him do it.'

She let go of his arm, turned away and clambered up to the crest of a nearby dune, the sand clinging around her ankles with each step. He followed her, remaining several paces behind. She turned round. Her expression was unfocussed, her words spoken as if to the surrounding air. He struggled to catch them.

'If only they hadn't made me choose…'

# FORTY-SIX

Seamus stared at her, his mouth open. Her eyes focussed at last on his.

'What could I do, Seamus? What could I do, for God's sake? If it had only been between me and them…Brendan would never have gone to prison. I would have died first. Only they made me choose. What could I do?'

'Go on.' His voice croaked.

'When they had finished with me the other two men took him into the next room. I shouted after them, begging them not to hurt him. The bald man said they had no intention of hurting him. On the contrary. They liked the look of him so much they were going to take him with them. To train as a mercenary. They always needed new recruits. They would take him with them to Africa. They would need to lick him into shape first. They guessed he was still a virgin so they would need to do something about that. If he was lucky he would survive six months in Africa. He might even come back alive but he would be very different. He would be a man like them. I wouldn't recognise him. Surely I wouldn't want to stand in his way. The only problem was that I wouldn't be able to say goodbye. He was already on his way. I screamed for them to stop, to bring him back. Tell us where we can find Brendan and we will, he said. The bastard knew my weak spot, the one way to get me to cooperate with him. Linda must have told him. So I did. That's right. I told him where to find Brendan. I did it for Patrick. They made me choose. So I chose.'

Seamus ran up to her, his hand raised, his chest heaving.

'That's right,' she shouted. 'Go on. Hit me. Hit me first. Then kill me.'

He shook his head slowly and lowered his hand.

'No. No, you're lying. You're making this up for some sick reason of your own. So I'll hate you instead of him. All right. Okay.

Let's play the game your way. Let's assume it happened the way you said. You didn't do it for him. You did it for yourself. Because he was your possession, as you thought. Your only possession. You condemned my father to rot in prison for twenty years because you couldn't bear to be parted from your precious Patrick.'

'All right,' she screamed. 'For myself. So he would be grateful. So he could start to love me just a little. Instead of always hating me.'

She turned round and ran past him down the slope. When he caught up with her, she stopped, her back to him, her breath rasping. He waited until her breathing eased. Sensing she was about to speak again he moved round to face her. She looked up at him, her eyes brimming.

'It was all I ever wanted, Seamus. Just one look or word or sign from him, in return for the love that never stopped pouring out of me towards him. One drop in return for an ocean. Was that too much to ask? But it never happened. It could never have happened. Not because of fate or God, but because of me. I couldn't see it then. Now I can. Can you see it, Seamus? Is this why I brought us here, so we could both see it? Here, where there is nothing but sand and the sky and our own memories and consciences? Look, I can see it in the sky, a huge finger, pointing at me, accusing me, condemning me. I brought you here to accuse you and now I stand accused.'

She covered her face with her hands and sank to her knees in an attitude of prayer. After a few minutes she spoke again, so quietly that Seamus had to kneel beside her to catch her words.

'He always hated me. Because I would never let him grow up and find his own way. Do you know why he barely spoke? It wasn't because he was backward. It all started when he was very young. I wouldn't let him speak, especially when he started to ask difficult questions or put forward ideas of his own. I told him his voice was coarse and unpleasant and grated on my ears. That wasn't true. His voice was as beautiful as everything else about him. It was the whole idea of his having something of his own to say, something that showed he was separate from me. So I shut him up. Sometimes I slapped him if he tried to keep on speaking. But later, when he started to learn the guitar, I smiled to encourage him. I praised him when he progressed. Because there were no words to offend me. We could share the sounds as if they came from both of us, from one mind and soul and body. I made him afraid, desperate to please. So he spoke as little as possible and then only quietly. He took to writing in secret. What I'd give now to hear him speak, even words of hate. I thought I was protecting him. Now I know I was killing him.'

'I'm still trying to understand, Ma,' he said, gently. 'You were lonely. Maybe Brendan and I were a bit to blame for that. All right, maybe more than a bit. But the way you talk about love…Christ, what do I know about love, for God's sake? Between a man and a woman, I mean. There was somebody, once. She tried to teach me. Until she saw into my soul. No beauty there. She fled when she saw it, a corpse rotted from within by the poison of hate and revenge, scavenged from without by the ghosts of the men I had killed. But there's only one way we can reach out to find someone's soul, to love it, protect it, keep it safe. We're not like God. We can't go straight in there. We have to use our bodies, our senses. We can only do it with a certain look in our eyes and a certain touch and a certain music in our voice. That wasn't your right, Ma. To go that way with Patrick in search of his soul. That was another's right. The right of someone he never met, never could meet. Because you taught him to recoil from those looks and those touches and that music.'

'I know,' she whispered.

'I always wondered… was he good? With the guitar, I mean. I wouldn't know. I don't know enough about that sort of music.'

For a few moments he was not sure she had heard him.

'Was he good? You really don't know? His teacher wrote to me, suggesting I let him audition for music college.'

'So why didn't he?'

'I never told him about the letter. I tore it up. He never knew how good he was. He had nobody to compare himself with. I wonder what became of the guitar. We couldn't take it with us when we left.'

'I can tell you, Ma. I can tell you a lot of things about him even you don't know.'

'Don't be ridiculous. You never knew the slightest thing about him. You were never interested.'

'You're right, when he was alive. But after I killed him I began to discover him. Shall I tell you about it?'

Yes, I discovered him. And I discovered you too, Ma.

# FORTY-SEVEN

After he had closed the trapdoor and replaced the bricks, he picked his way slowly and silently back to the gap in the fence through which they had come. He was sure nobody had followed them. He put his head through and glanced up and down the street. All clear. All he had to do was melt away into the night. It was over. Nobody would know what he had done. The traitor was dead. Seamus was free. He had fulfilled his oath. In death he had at last given Brendan the justice denied him in life.

As he passed in front of the house he paused. The key was still there on the front step, where he had told Patrick to leave it. He could go in. Nobody would see or hear him. He could rest for a while. Wash the dirt and the residue of gunpowder from himself, turn himself from a man who had just executed his brother in cold blood into someone no different from anybody else, who would attract no notice or suspicion when he came out again to find his way home.

Home? Where was that? Belfast was where he had felt most at home. He could go back there. He could be near his father. He could pick up the threads of his friendship with Father Gerald. But could Belfast be home to him now? When he had lived there he had been at war. He had loved the excitement and the danger. What could an ex-soldier like him offer to those who were now trying to build peace? Father Gerald apart, would anybody know him there? Would he even recognise the place? Perhaps he could find a sort of home there. There would be clubs and pubs and other places where former soldiers would come together to relive their past glories. They could tell visitors about their street battles with the Brits and their sufferings in prison, show them the places where their comrades had fallen. They could walk those streets together, looking around in bewilderment and resignation to see the world they had known changing and passing on to a generation who had known nothing of their dreams and hopes and sacrifices. But was that what he wanted for himself? He could do worse. But there was something else, something he already knew would make it impossible. Those former soldiers had acted with courage and honour in their own eyes. They could hold their heads up. They had done nothing of which they would ever be ashamed. They could even be proud of the way they had accepted the Agreement when their objectives were still so far from being achieved. They saw honour in the way they had lain down their arms as in the way they had taken them up in the first place. But could the same now be said of him? How would they react if he told them what he had just done, a few moments ago, on that waste ground? How could he now go back to claim a place of honour among them?

What about the gun? He could feel the hard metal shape in his pocket, still warm. He would not need it again. He could take it to the same place to hide it. Or...perhaps he would need it one day. Not that he was in any danger. But for some reason he found its presence a comfort. He had no wife or family. His one remaining friend was out of reach. He had lost everything, except the thing which had once transformed his life and given it meaning and purpose. He had found his gun and he had used it. It was part of him and always would be. He would keep it by him now for what was left of his life.

He opened the front door and stepped inside. The hall was clean and tidy. So too was the front room, which had been their council chamber and library, with a view onto the street clear enough to give notice of approaching visitors. If the police came, there might be time enough to get down into the cellar and out through the small metal door at the side of the house. But the police had never come. Not until they came for Brendan and by then he had no thought of escape. He had opened the door and invited them in, offering them a cup of tea. When they declined the tea he had let them take him quietly away.

Patrick had changed nothing. The books were still on the shelves. The police had searched everywhere but had not taken any of them away. They had been heavy-going for Brendan. Night after night he had struggled with Marx, Engels and Trotsky, ground his way through volumes about Castro and Cuba, wrestled with studies of political and social philosophy. Seamus had done his best to be patient, to lead him through the dense tangle of intellectual argument. You need to understand, Da', he had explained. You need to see where we stand on the stage of world history. This isn't just a local struggle. In the end it was enough that Brendan understood that much and let that understanding light the fire in his eye. He needed to believe that everything, even those furtive trips to the waste ground, his gun concealed in his coat pocket, was part of a universal revolution. When the intellectual justifications proved too much for him in their complexity and too little in their power, he fell back on the mutual love and loyalty between himself and Seamus, and between them and their comrades.

This was the room where they received the visitors with no names, only code words. That was how it was then. No more brigades or battalions or companies as in the old days. Only small units known as cells, none of them knowing about the others. They would be told when a new consignment of weapons would be arriving, when someone would come to collect them and what code word they would use. They never knew what they would be used for. They would hear it on the news, like everybody else. Later they would be told who would need a safe house and for how long.

Then there were the two others, the ones who came separately and never reached their destination. They were the ones Brendan invited out for a drink. There's a good spit-and-sawdust pub just over the other side of the estate, he had said. Plenty of blokes from back home there. An Irish folk band sometimes. We'll take a short cut across the waste ground. Don't want to waste good drinking time, do we?

Patrick and Ruth never went into the front room, not even to clean. The back room was theirs, where Patrick played his guitar and Ruth listened and smiled at him. It was Seamus's job to clean the front room and keep it tidy. Brendan had never had to spell it out. It was understood. Certain areas were off-limits to Ruth and Patrick. The front room, and the cellar, and the special bedroom for guests. She could go into that bedroom to dust and clean and make up the bed. But once a guest had arrived she had to keep out of the way. Three other bedrooms, one each for Seamus and Patrick and one for Brendan and Ruth. Though usually Brendan slept on the sofa in the front room.

He walked through to the back room. The traitor's room. Ruth's books on the shelves. English classics. Dickens, Trollope, Hardy, all that British imperialist stuff. But harmless enough, surely? Not exactly a traitor's reading. But then Patrick would not have read them. He was barely literate. There was an open drawer filled with notebooks, yellow pages, writing so faint now he could barely read it. He flicked through the pages of one of the notebooks. Poems, essays. Ruth must have written them, when she wasn't spaced out on booze and pills.

Was this what you came back for, Patrick, for the life you had here in this room, with your music and your mother's books, ignoring everything else that was going on? An imaginary life of the mind and the soul for you, while we were making a real life out of guns and explosives? Bloody hell! We were risking everything, fighting for our country and our future, and you were in here in a world of your own. And when you finally put your nose outside your own little world it was to betray your own father. You were the one we should have taken out for a drink, taking the short cut. You should have made that walk across the waste ground years ago. Then Brendan would still be alive. Unhappy about the course events had taken, the compromises, the continuing Partition. But at least alive.

He reached to the back of the drawer. Pieces of cardboard. What in God's name...? Home-made Christmas cards. *To Dad from Patrick. To Seamus from Patrick.* Childish handwriting. He had never given them or they wouldn't still be in the drawer. So why had the little creep made them in the first place? If Seamus had known they were there he would have rammed them down his treacherous throat before shooting him.

Anything else? Nothing. No records, no photographs, no magazines. Patrick had lived there all the years of a young man, alone, friendless, without intimacy of any sort. He didn't do what Seamus had done before he met Carlotta. He had no interest in prostitutes of either sex. He had been good-looking, breathtakingly so. But he might as well have been a monk. He worked in Soho. He came out of his bar in the early hours, surrounded by whatever opportunities for company he might wish for. He had wished for none. He had gone straight home.

So what were you, for fuck's sake? A eunuch? What happened to you to make the touch of flesh, even the thought of it, so abhorrent? When another's forbidden looks and caresses made you cringe, did you blame yourself for that ugly, misshapen need? Did you fear that if you let someone else into your life they would awaken those monsters of guilt and shame, by even the most casual raising of a hand to your skin?

He looked round again. It was not all as neat as he had first thought. The guitar was lying in a corner, broken. The body had been smashed, with a foot or a fist, the thin layers of wood splintered, the fretboard snapped back like a broken neck. Patrick must have done it. But why? And why had he left it there, when the rest of the house was so tidy?

He opened another of the notebooks. Jottings, short essays, poems. He started to read through one of the poems at the beginning of the book. There was no title.

The guns fall silent as the shadows lengthen.
Blood, cooled by the night air,
Congeals on flesh and stone.

He shook his head. No, Ruth could never have written that. Guns meant nothing to her, except as things which made a noise which frightened her and made her huddle in a corner with Linda and

Patrick. She could have copied it out of a book. But why? He looked at the Christmas cards again, then back at the poem. It was the same writing.

The next few lines were crossed through and he could not read what they had said. The rest were just about legible, though several words and phrases had been crossed out and replaced, some of them more than once.

A deafening scream falls
Soundless from each open, frozen mouth.
Through the night the screams gather,
Shrouded and hunched like birds of carrion –
Until dawn creeps in again,
Hiding behind a veil of mist,
Hoping the guns will not notice, will not begin again,
Because the faintest glimmer is all they need
To wake and greet
The sun's new fire with their own.

A date had been pencilled in beneath the last line. June 1972. Patrick had been fifteen at the time. Seamus walked back into the hall, a lump at the back of his throat holding back a rising tide of nausea. Had Patrick really written it? There could be no doubt it was his writing. Perhaps it was he who had copied it out from a book. He was so backward he was probably still learning to write, even at the age of fifteen. But why advertise that fact by putting in the date? He looked at the poem again. 'Carrion crows' had been crossed out and 'birds of prey' written in its place. That had been replaced in its turn with 'birds of carrion.' No, this was no writing exercise. He had been searching for the expression he wanted, and he had at last found it.

He had always thought Patrick was backward. Had he not left school early with no qualifications? He barely spoke. His only talent seemed to be music. Seamus had overheard him play from time to time. But it was not Seamus's sort of music, and he had no way of knowing if Patrick really had a talent. Seamus had always assumed his brother had never been aware of what was going on, protected by his mother from the harsh realities of life outside their front door.

But if he really had written that poem, then he had been aware and could find words to express himself. If he barely spoke to Brendan and Seamus, it was not because he was an idiot but because he knew that they had always despised him.

Christ, Patrick, I know how I behaved to you when we were young. But that was so long ago. You could have said something instead of letting me go on thinking you were simple. I know poetry was never my scene. But if I had known you were seeing things like that...I mean, we could have talked about it, couldn't we? And if we had, we might still be talking about it. And perhaps Brendan wouldn't have gone to prison. And you wouldn't be lying there in that fucking hole.

He realised that he had been talking out loud.

He returned to the back room and skimmed through all the notebooks. They contained some fifty poems, the earliest written when Patrick was thirteen, the last just after his nineteenth birthday. There was an empty, badly scuffed leather briefcase on a chair. Seamus collected the notebooks, put them inside and picked up the case.

Upstairs. His own old room, as empty of furnishings now as it had been then, the bedstead standing against a wall, the mattress on the floor. Patrick's, a narrow bed, still in use up to the night before, crumpled sheets and a threadbare blanket. What was that in the wall? He went next door, to his mother's room. The picture, of the Sacred Heart of Jesus, had been moved to one side. Patrick must have done it. Perhaps he was dusting in here and accidentally knocked it. The room was as clean as all the others. He had discovered the spy-hole his mother had made, blasphemously using the Sacred Heart to cover it up. He would have realised that throughout their time in that house she had watched him undress every night, watched him in bed.

Unless he had always known.

# FORTY-EIGHT

'So he smashed it. Left it there so he could look at it every day and remind himself how much he hated me.'

Her tone was flat, matter-of-fact. She stood up and started to walk away. He rose, caught up with her and held her by the arm. She stopped and turned.

'It was his way of smashing the chains that bound him to you,' said Seamus. 'Except the damage had already been done. You couldn't bear it, could you, the thought of him going away, meeting people like him, developing his talent in a way that had nothing to do with you.'

'He was there in the same house.' Her voice rose in anger. 'You could have gone out with him for walks. Talked to him. Found out if he really was backward or if he had something to say for himself.'

'You wouldn't have let me.'

'Come off it. Could I have stopped you if you had really made up your mind, when I couldn't stop you becoming a thug and a killer? You could have fought with me over him, told me you were his brother and you were going to take an interest in him. You would have defeated me if you had tried.'

'Why did he take it from you, Ma? Why did he put up with it? I suppose it was because it looked like love, sounded like love, even felt like it at times. When there's no other kind around you're not going to turn it down. Even when you realise it's destroying you. You made him into a eunuch. And he let you. Go on. Tell me how you came to part.'

'After I had told them about Brendan they brought him back into the room. They hadn't taken him away. He had heard everything. At last he found his voice. And it was a voice of hate. He was screaming at me, asking me if I knew what I had done. Those were his last words to me.

'After I had disposed of Linda I searched for him. I travelled round the country. I had no idea where to start looking. I suppose I thought that I would just run into him. What would I have said to him if I had? Would I have begged him to forgive me? Of course not. There could never be any question of forgiveness. I knew his hate would last as long as his memory. But by the time I did see him, from a distance, so many years later, I knew he had changed. The anger had gone. Maybe some of the pain had gone as well. Maybe he had in some way come to terms with what you and Brendan and I and the world had done to him. I even wondered if he had had a breakdown and forgotten.'

'He hadn't forgotten anything.'

'I know. But I took a little comfort in that thought, until I realised it was yet another delusion. It was so important that I didn't let him see me, didn't let the sight of me re-open his wounds. I had no hope that he no longer hated me. But love and hate can co-exist, like two halves of a soul. Anger and love cannot. Anger drives out love for as long as it lasts.'

'For God's sake, Ma! After everything you'd done and all that had happened between you, you were still dreaming that he might yet have some love for you. You had no right even to dream.'

'No, Seamus. I'm not talking about the sort of love anyone can expect, or even hope for. Not any love that two people can share. Of course I had no right. I'm talking about love as a gift, undeserved, not sought for, a love which only emerges from the womb of time, for someone from whom you have parted forever, someone who has harmed you as deeply as it is possible to harm anybody. I suppose the supreme test of love is to commit an act of love towards someone you hate.'

'What the hell are you talking about, Ma?'

'He hated me but he died for me. He never betrayed Brendan. I swear it. And he never betrayed me. He let you kill him in my place. It's easy to die for someone you love. I was ready to do that for

213

Brendan or for him. But to die for someone you hate…that must be the highest form of love.'

'You're crazy. Delusional. He betrayed my father. Not you.'

'Did he confess? In so many words?'

'No. He just said he knew why I was there. Said he'd been expecting me. We went straight to the spot. He knelt down and waited. Why would he do that if he wasn't guilty?'

'Because he was giving his life for someone else, that's why. You kept your gun all those years. Did you always think you would kill him one day?'

'No. I never planned it. I wanted to let the past stay in the past. I wanted to move on, make a new life. After I had given the bald man the slip I kept the gun handy in case he came after me again. It was never my plan to settle any scores myself.'

'So why did you settle the score with Patrick?'

'Brendan asked me to. On his deathbed. His dying wish.'

'Asked you to?'

'Made me swear. I couldn't refuse him. I couldn't refuse a dying man.'

'But why would he make you swear to kill an innocent man?'

'But he didn't believe he was innocent, for Christ's sake! Neither do I. Or you. In fact, you're the only witness to his guilt, apart from those men. You were there. So why do you keep on telling me it wasn't him?'

She turned away, climbed down into a valley, then up to the top of the dune on the other side. It was the last dune before the beach. He waited for a minute before joining her. They watched the scene together. The last glow of pink in the sky was on the point of disappearing. The massive sweep of mud-coloured sand was ridged and mottled with tidal pools. In the distance, foaming grey waters reared and crashed along the shoreline.

'There were donkey rides down on the beach, just below here,' she said, smiling. 'And a stall selling candy floss and toffee apples. The first time I realised there was an apple underneath the toffee, I thought I had discovered the secret of life. I thought this was the world and it belonged to us, to me, my friends, my family. Now it belongs to the wind and the sand. Is this what the world will be like when we've all gone, no trace of us, all memory of us blown away, just wind and sand and a sea that can scarcely be bothered to visit any more? What will God do when we're no longer here, without all the attention we give Him, without the prayers to join our cause, to vanquish our enemies, to forgive our sins? Shrug His shoulders and move on, I suppose. Which way is Belfast from here?'

He pointed. 'That way. As the seagulls fly.'

'And you long to fly with them, don't you, back over the sea, back to your past? Your heart is still there. If only we had never gone there. If only we had never got caught up in it all. You were a fool, Seamus. A simple-minded fool. You knew nothing and you understood nothing. You just followed those people into the nightmare of all that violence like a big kid going on holiday. Isn't this fun, you thought. Doesn't this just make me into a real man? I must be a real man now because my Dad took me to those whores and I fucked them and he paid. So what will I do now I'm a man? I'll go and kill some guys I know nothing about because those chaps tell me to, whether or not they're guilty. What next? Oh, I'll kill my Uncle John because, guess what, he's been playing one side against the other, as if plenty weren't doing the same just to get by. You killed him, even though he'd got your father a job and us a home. You killed him even though that meant we had no more protection and were going to be burned out. And why? Because it was fun, because it was being a man, something I would never understand. And of course it was something that weird simpleton, Patrick, would never understand in a month of Sundays. But I have news for you. And when I've told you this you'll see the truth at last. Do you want to hear it?'

'Go on, Ma. I'm listening.'

'I would never understand, but he did. What he really wanted, deep inside, was to be like you and Brendan. Not as killers, of course not. That could never have been his way. But to be part of what brought you together. To understand and share the cause. To believe in the future. To find a way forward. He would have understood you, even as he urged you to find other ways. He adored Brendan. I never realised how much, not until those men brought him back into that room and he was screaming his words of hate at me. I would have given anything for the tiniest particle of that love he had for his father. Brendan had nothing but contempt for him and Patrick adored him. I adored Patrick and he hated me. I suppose you find that funny.'

'No, Ma. It's not funny.'

'Isn't it? I'm sure God finds it funny. I was prepared to believe in God, a loving God I mean, until He put me in that room with those men and made me choose. But the only God I can believe in now is one with a warped sense of humour. No, Seamus. Patrick would never have betrayed Brendan. Never in eternity. You found his poems. I never saw any of those. Or anything else he wrote. Except a letter. He left it for me. I found it after he had gone.'

'Do you still have it?'

'No. I burned it. I couldn't bear to keep it. I couldn't bear the thought of it still existing. But I couldn't burn the words away from my heart.'

'What did it say?'

'It was very short. Just a few lines. He told me I had taken away his last chance to make a sacrifice for Brendan, to be accepted by him, loved by him. He didn't care what those men would have done to him. Because of me he had no place in the world. He was invisible, a spirit nobody could see or hear. He said nothing about where he was going. But I should have realised. It made sense, his going back to the house. It was where he had been closest to the two of you. Your shadows were still there, the memories of your voices. He needed to be surrounded by them.'

Seamus raised his hands and worked his knuckles into his cheeks until it hurt. How could he have been there in the same house with Patrick all those years and missed so much? How could he have been so blind? He struggled to imagine a different past, a different story of two brothers, one which a single word or look from one to the other might have created, instead of what had happened.

'For God's sake, Ma, why did he leave with you in the first place if he felt like that? He could have stayed with us, asked to be part of us, in his own way. We wouldn't have rejected him.'

'Wouldn't you? You know it was far too late. You had already rejected him, from the day he was born. You bullied him then ignored him. I wept for him. I knew his heart was breaking. So I gave him my love instead.'

'Too much of the wrong sort of love, for far too long.'

'Yes, you're right, Seamus. I am guilty. What I did to him was terrible. But I won't take all the blame. If you and Brendan had loved him as well in your way, as men, I could have given him what he needed from me to make him complete. I don't claim to understand it, but I know that a woman's love can never be enough for a man. A man needs to belong. That was all Patrick ever wanted. Just to belong. He thought he might have a chance, there in that room, when those men were threatening us. Maybe there was just a possibility that we would survive with the secret of Brendan's whereabouts still intact. And we could get word to Brendan that he was in danger. Perhaps one day Brendan would know what we had gone through to protect him. Then, if Patrick survived and came home, he could belong at last. It was all a fantasy, of course. But it was all he had left, and I took it away from him. My act of betrayal was a double one. I didn't understand, not until it was too late. I did what I did so he would be grateful and learn at last to love me. Instead I made sure he would hate me for the rest of his life. But he never gave me away. He went back to the house. He must have thought you would come for him one day. He never tried to hide. He waited all those years. When you came, he went to his death letting you believe he had betrayed Brendan. I was the one you should have killed. He died in my place. And that is God's truth, Seamus.'

He shook his head violently from side to side and moaned. She walked away.

# FORTY-NINE

———

When she returned after half an hour he was sitting on the sand, at the exact spot where she had left him. When he looked up she wondered for a moment if it was someone else. He seemed to have aged years in that half hour. His face was drawn with grief. There were grey smudges of tear-moistened sand across his cheeks. She handed him a tissue.

'Do you believe me now, Seamus? You were crying for him, weren't you, just now? For the brother you never knew. He could have done so much for you. You could have learned so much from him, discovered the best part of yourself through him. God placed an angel by your side to teach you. But you despised him and then you killed him. Yes, I killed him too. It wasn't meant to be like this. I brought you here to make you look into your own soul, not so you could force me to look into mine. But that's what you've done. We've been each other's Furies, haven't we, these past few hours? Do you hate me now? It should be easy. I seduced Patrick, my own son. I betrayed your father and my husband. A woman like that doesn't deserve to live. Go on, tell me you hate me.'

'I can't. Yes, I understand why I should hate you. But I can't. I can't feel anything anymore.'

'Come on. Let's walk back. Take my arm.'

He stopped at the foot of the dune.

'Go on,' she said, calmly. 'I think I know what's on your mind. Tell me.'

'All right. Explain this, if you can. Brendan never understood or cared how Patrick felt about him. But he would never have asked me to kill him. Not unless he was sure he was guilty. So what made him so sure? He said he had reliable intelligence from a senior source. So where could he have got that intelligence from?'

He was gazing intently at her. She stared back, shaking her head violently.

'You think it came from me?' She wrung her hands. 'After everything I've told you about my love for him, you think I was the one who fingered Patrick? I betrayed Brendan to try to save Patrick. So why in God's name would I put him in danger all over again?'

'I don't know, Ma. Maybe you got scared when you realised what you had done.'

'Scared? I had lost everything, everybody who ever meant anything to me. My life was over. What in God's name did I have to be scared about?'

'So what did you tell them?'

'When the police picked us up and took us to hospital they never asked any questions. I was puzzled about that. Then this man came to see me, just before we were discharged. Tall, in his fifties, briefcase, distinguished appearance, posh voice. He said he couldn't tell me his name or his exact position, only that he was a senior member of the security services. He'd obviously told the local police it was above their heads and he would deal with it. He told me Brendan had just been arrested. They were going through what was in the house. The arrest would be made public once they had enough evidence to charge him. He said he knew I was the one who had informed. He was sorry I had been maltreated. The man who had found me had exceeded his orders, he said. He was only supposed to locate me and bring me in for questioning. Unfortunately there was no prospect of finding him. He had absconded. I didn't believe him.'

'You were right not to. The bald man was still working for them when I went over to Belfast to visit John's grave.'

'I said I didn't care about myself, only about Patrick. He had to protect Patrick by telling Brendan I was the one who had shopped him. He promised. He also agreed not to tell Brendan about the torture, so Brendan would have no reason to find excuses for me. I had turned him in because of the life he had made me lead.

He had put me in a far worse prison than any I was putting him in. I had been loyal to him all those years, all for the sake of something I could never believe in. I had left because I couldn't stand it anymore. He had taken my son from me, reduced me to dependence on drink and pills, forced me to leave in the end, to lead the life of a refugee in my own country, poor and alone. Why would he be surprised to learn that I had finally broken, that I had decided to use what I knew to put him behind bars? He promised to tell Brendan all that. He owed me a favour, he said. I didn't tell him about the bodies on the waste ground, of course. I didn't want Brendan getting thirty years for murder. Twenty was bad enough. I thought he'd get fifteen at most. I only thought about those bodies later on. When Brendan was already dead and there was a danger that the knowledge might die with me.'

'Except that he never told Brendan, did he? That man from the security services broke his promise to you. He went to see Brendan, all right. I know that. But he told him it was Patrick and Brendan believed him. So why would this man set up Patrick?'

'Did he?'

'Of course. If it didn't come from you it had to come from him. He broke his promise to you and lied to Brendan. When Patrick left, you believed he was safe.'

'That's right. I still wanted to find him and watch out for him. But I never thought anybody would come after him. That's why I missed you when you came for him. When I realised you'd killed him, I assumed you'd worked it out for yourself. Worked it out and got it all wrong. I only knew an hour ago that the idea came from Brendan, when you told me. I couldn't understand it. I was thinking about it when I left you here just now. I'm beginning to understand now.'

'I still don't understand. You were in danger as well. The man from the security services told Brendan it was Patrick but the bald man knew it was you. If word on either of you had got back to the Army Council, they would have ordered both of you to be executed, just to be on the safe side, even though Brendan said there should be no reprisals on his behalf.'

'I was offered protection. A new identity. A fresh start. I refused. I made my own arrangements, as you know. Even if they had tried to find me, they would have got no further than Ruth Gibson's grave.'

'So why would he offer you protection and at the same time set up Patrick? His only concern was to find Brendan and have him sent down. Why would he want to do something which could lead to more killings? That would only reduce the chances of other informants coming forward.'

She sighed.

'It's all right, Seamus. I can explain why Patrick was set up, as you put it. Only it would be better if you worked it out for yourself. You're still much too disinclined to believe me.'

'All I want to know is why he told me to kill him. Why was he given false intelligence and why did he believe it?'

'Did Brendan tell you to kill him? In so many words? What exactly did he make you swear? What were the precise words?'

# FIFTY

---

For a moment Brendan's dimming eyes opened wide and gleamed.

'Do you know where he is, Da'? Is that it? Is that what you want to tell me?'

Brendan shook his head slowly. His hand dropped and his eyes closed. For a moment Seamus thought he had passed away. There was still a slight movement beneath the blanket. Brendan's eyes opened again.

'I didn't want to tell you anything. Just to hear you say something.'

'What is it, Da'? Anything you want.'

'Swear to me. Swear to me that if you get the chance you'll kill the one who grassed me up.'

'You mean kill Patrick?'

'Why not? You always hated him, didn't you?'

'Yes. So you want me to swear to kill him?'

'Swear in the way I said it. So you remember why you're doing it. You're not doing it because you hate him. You're doing it because of what he did. Swear to kill the one who betrayed me.'

Brendan's hand was clutching Seamus's again. He was clinging on to life for as long as it took to know his need for revenge would live after him. Only then could he go. He had only lived so long, weeks past the date predicted by the doctors, for this moment. Seamus had to release him. He had to give him the peace of mind he had craved for so long. How could he refuse him, at the moment of death?

'I swear, Da'. Brendan, I swear. Do you hear? I swear to kill the person who betrayed you. Do you hear? Nod if you hear me, you pathetic old man!'

Brendan nodded. Or he seemed to. But it could have been an involuntary movement. His eyes were closed and this time they didn't open again.

Now Brendan could no longer see him or hear him Seamus could afford to cry.

'You stupid old fucker!' he shouted, forgetting that the nurse was just outside the door. 'Why in the name of all we had and all we did didn't you make me tell you I loved you? I could have done it just now if it was the last thing you wanted to hear from me. If it was your last request. I could never have said it otherwise. You had your chance to hear it from me and you blew it! It's your own fault. Instead, you made me promise to carry on killing. All right, I'll do it. If I get the chance, I'll fucking do it.'

# FIFTY-ONE

---

'So you swore? Using exactly those words?'

'Yes.'

'Say them again, Seamus. Repeat your oath now.'

'No. I can't.'

'You know what an oath is, don't you? People have died rather than take oaths they don't believe in. You took it. You believed in it. So swear it again.'

'"I swear to kill the person who betrayed you." That's what I said.'

'And he heard you?'

'Yes. He was waiting for it. He had hung on so he could hear me say it. So he could die at last.'

'Why those words, Seamus? Why would only those words do?'

'He said I had to use those words so I would remember why I was doing it.'

'But of course you'd remember. He knew that. So why those words?'

Seamus screamed, sank to his knees and beat the sand with his fists. He looked up at last, his face contorted, his whole body shaking.

'He tricked me. The bastard tricked me. I meant one thing by the oath. He meant something different. After all we'd been through together, he lied to me. He tricked me into killing an innocent man, my own brother. I was always his real son, the one he loved and trusted. And I loved him. Christ, I loved him. No son could have loved a father more. It was my reason for living. There was nothing else. Nobody else. I was married, for a while, until she left me. I was in love. But that was just something that came and went. Nothing like the bond between me and him. That was from birth to death. I would gladly have gone to prison for his sake. I would have crawled into the mouth of Hell for his sake. And he lied to me at the moment of death. He knew it was you all along but he told me it was Patrick. He said he had reliable intelligence from a senior source. He said I had to trust him, the way we had always trusted each other. Fuck you, Da'! Fuck you! I hope you rot in Hell, where you belong.'

She moved towards him and stood over him.

'Tell me this, Seamus. If he had told you I was the one he wanted you to kill, would you have taken the oath?'

'Never. I wouldn't have believed him. And even if I had I would have refused. I would have told him that was a line I could never cross. The oath wasn't valid.'

'He knew you would react like that. But the oath was valid. You thought he meant you to kill Patrick. He did. And while you were saying the words, you must have thought, I'm still bound by this, even if I find out it's someone else. If you hadn't accepted that possibility, you wouldn't have sworn using those words. Admit that.'

'Someone else, maybe. Some cowardly grass. Someone I could have killed as easily as swotting a fly, without a second thought. But not you, Ma. Not you, for Christ's sake! But why did he do it? He must have realised I would go after Patrick if I could find him.'

'So what would happen then? Hasn't the penny dropped yet?'

Seamus put his face in his hands.

'Yes,' she said, softly. 'I see the penny has finally dropped. Shall I spell it out for you? The man from the security services, the one who came to see me in hospital, never broke his word to me. He went to see Brendan and told him everything I had asked him to tell him. He told him and Brendan believed him. Of course he did. Why wouldn't he? Brendan was the one who set Patrick up, when he made you swear. Patrick was still a legitimate target in his eyes. He would be…what would you soldiers of the good cause call it? Collateral damage, that's it. Wonderful expression. Inevitable in any war. And Brendan was still at war, remember. Innocent lives have to be sacrificed in the service of the greater good. That was what the two of you always believed, wasn't it?

'He would have assumed I was still alive but in hiding. He wouldn't have heard about my death any more than you had. Nobody was going to connect the suicide of an obscure woman in Liverpool with an IRA convict in the Scrubs. The man from the security services might have done if he had seen my picture in the paper. But he was hardly likely to pick up on a few column inches inside a Liverpool rag. Even if he had, he wouldn't have bothered to tell Brendan. The case was over as far as he was concerned.

'Brendan wanted revenge but he had two problems. He had no idea where to find me. And even if he could, he was a sick man, unlikely to be released in time to hunt me down and kill me himself. But what if he could get you to kill Patrick and I somehow found out? I would have to come out of hiding and tell you I was the one you wanted. He knew I would never stand by and let you go on thinking Patrick was guilty. You would be shocked to learn the truth. You would hesitate. You would say, no, this isn't what I bargained for. But in the end you were bound by the terms of your oath. And by your love for him and your loyalty to him. He knew what he meant to you. And he knew I meant nothing to you. Once you had heard my guilt from my own mouth you would have to go ahead. That's what he was thinking. You're wrong to be so angry with him, Seamus. He loved you and trusted you to the end. There was nobody else to whom he could have entrusted the task. Yes, it would be a terrible burden to carry, he knew that. But he was prepared to place it on you. That's a measure of what he thought of you. No father loved or revered a son more. You must believe that.'

He was sobbing. She crouched beside him and took his hand. He leant his head on her shoulder.

'It's not true, Ma,' he murmured. 'That you meant nothing to me. We had become strangers, you and I, that's all. Because of the times.'

'You know that now. I know it. But then? I was nothing to you then. And he knew that. He wasn't to know we would find each other again. Don't blame him for that. Seamus, my darling boy. Now we've been completely honest with each other. Now we can go on. We'll leave here tomorrow. As soon as we've got the car back. Let's go back to the hotel now.'

# FIFTY-TWO

She waited in the car while he paid the bill at the reception desk. As he was about to leave he turned back and asked the owner if anyone else had been staying there. The owner was in his sixties, unshaven, unkempt, wearing a permanent frown, as if he had long known the hopelessness of his situation but had no idea how to get himself out of it.

'We had two young couples recently but they checked out just before you arrived. It's a very quiet time of the year. Actually it's been quiet for years, ever since the camp closed and the golf club went bankrupt. I don't suppose we'll be able to stay in business much longer.'

'Nobody on their own? A bald man, for example?'

'No. Nobody like that. We did have one man on his own. Arrived just before you. He had a beer and a sandwich in the bar while you were having dinner. He went to bed early and left this morning at the crack of dawn. That was his car out the front, when you arrived. Not bald. White-haired. A very nice man. Irish. Accent like yours but not like yours, if you know what I mean. Wore one of those collars. I think he was a priest.'

'What was all that about?' she asked when he got into the car.

'I was wrong about the bald man. He's not after me. He probably did go to Africa when the trail went cold. I think I know who's been following us. My guardian angel. He's not bad at it, actually. Better than I would have thought, at his age. He's gone now.'

'I never had a guardian angel. There was a time when I thought Linda was mine. She guarded me from danger once. But guardian angels don't turn against you and betray you.'

'I'll be your guardian angel if you want, Ma. I'll stay with you, look after you. I'll never betray you again, I swear. I know you're not well. When you're better, you can decide if you want me around or not.'

She shook her head. 'No, Seamus. We can't be together. You have to give yourself up. I'm not going to get better. We both know that. I can't face dying on my own. And I can't kill myself. So there's only one way forward.'

'I can't kill you, if that's what you mean. All right, I always understood what the oath meant. I knew that if Brendan was wrong about Patrick I was still bound to kill his real betrayer. But I took the oath for one death. One final killing. I killed an innocent man. I accept that now. But I can't kill you. How would that make it right? Don't try to make me. There has to be an end to all this.'

'Of course. That's exactly what we're going to do. End it all. So we can find peace at last.'

'Peace? That was our tragedy, wasn't it? The Troubles didn't just divide us. Brendan and I fought for a cause we believed was right. We thought we saw and heard and felt our humanity all the more because right was on our side. But in the end we were blinded and deafened and our hearts were frozen.'

She started the engine.

'So, where are we going, Ma?'

'You know where. To the place where it has to end. To the Place of a Skull.'

# EPILOGUE

Now they are all gone. They were just two families among so many consumed by the fire which swept through the land. Peace came at last to the land but not to them, not until death had finally broken the circle of hate and betrayal which had closed them in. God has left me alive to tell their story. He has granted me enough strength to complete the task. When it is done I will commit my body and soul into His hands.

Seamus gave himself up and they found the bodies in that place, as he had told them. And Golgotha, the Place of a Skull, as she had called it, was sealed forever by concrete and tarmac. Over here they followed his directions to the even older remains in the fields of death where they had lain, fertilising the ground with their blood. They too found consecrated ground at last.

It was I who followed the two of them on their final odyssey. The local paper gave me the exact address. I hoped I would arrive in time to stop him killing or being killed. Imagine my relief when I saw him come out with Ruth, the mother he had told me was dead. I followed them some way on their journey before I lost them. I was not too concerned about what might happen. There seemed to be some distance between them but no threat. He had told me where he believed his mother was buried. I went to the grave, wondering what poor lost soul lay there in her place. By happy chance I saw them both. I followed them again. I saw them in the chalet and wondered what could have drawn them to that broken-down, deserted place. But I was sure by then they were in no danger. I left and returned to Belfast. For a long time I tormented myself with the thought that if I had not given up, if I had only pursued them to their final destination, I might have prevented what happened. But God did not will it. And in the end, when I heard Seamus's story, I knew why it had to end that way.

At Seamus's request the prison chaplain invited me to come over and take the funeral service for Ruth and Patrick. Seamus stood by the graves, handcuffed to a police officer, his gaunt features impassive. Nobody else who was present knew the part he had played in their deaths. The full truth only emerged later, when at last the police began to believe his story. Before that, the press had speculated that Ruth and Patrick had died in a suicide pact, a mother and son overwhelmed by the tragic events which had torn the family apart. What they could not explain was the chosen place of death.

No, the real suicide pact was between Ruth and Seamus, if that is indeed what we should call an act of mutual forgiveness and acceptance of death, when one party lives on only to tell their story. I have watched the scene in my mind's eye many times since he told me about it. They crawled to the place where Patrick's body lay. Seamus opened the trapdoor. They prayed. She led the prayers because he had forgotten the words. She told him she wanted to be down there with Patrick, among the rubble and the rats and the bones, in that desolate, sacred space. She was dying. He already knew that. She didn't want to die alone on the streets or in a hospital full of strangers. It was her fate to die at his hands. That way she would find peace, as would the restless soul of Brendan, waiting for the fulfilment of Seamus's oath. Then he would give himself up. In prison he would tell me everything that had happened. It was not an execution. She understood that he could not just put the gun to her head. So, at the final moment, her finger too was on the trigger, guided by his.

Without breaking the seal hiding what he said to me in Confession, I can now tell what I knew about Patrick, despised as a simpleton by his father and brother. Soon after they came here to live, Ruth brought Patrick along to see me after Confession. She told me he wanted to observe all the sacraments faithfully. But he had never been able to use the confessional box with the dividing curtain between priest and penitent. He was claustrophobic. The box made him nervous and tongue-tied. His parish priest in England had agreed to hear his confession in the sacristy. I assured her I would be happy to make the same arrangement. Ruth warned me that he might still be very reluctant to speak. I assured her I would do my best to help him overcome his nerves. So Ruth left and I heard Patrick's confession there and then. To my surprise he spoke in clear, measured tones, confessing to sins for which I was sure Seamus and perhaps Brendan were at least partly responsible. I sensed a deep, aching love beneath his words, a need to take blame upon himself. Seamus and Brendan may have despised him but Patrick had returned their scorn with a love more than worthy of the Christ whose image was on the cross in my hand. The thought that that love could have turned to hatred and a desire for revenge so horrified me that I refused in my heart to believe it. When I knew the truth at last I wept for his innocence in death but rejoiced that he had died as he had lived. That he went bravely to his death to save someone he had every reason to hate came as no surprise to me.

Seamus told the police where they would find the confessions and the maps he had left in his room in Liverpool. The police also found there the notebooks containing Patrick's poems. When Seamus asked for them, they agreed to let him have them, once they had satisfied themselves they had no bearing on his case. He gave them to me the first time I went to visit him in prison. I asked him why he had kept them. Because they were his gift to me, he told me, to me, his brother and his murderer. I killed and disposed of his body. Then I discovered his soul was still alive, back at the house, in those poems. At last I could begin to know and understand him, and know and understand what I had done. Those were his exact words.

As he and I read through the poems out loud during my visits, Seamus also grew to understand that they were not just Patrick's gift to him. They were for the world. It was not given to Patrick to be part of the times in which he lived, desperately though he may have longed for that. His task was a much harder one, to feel the grief and anger of others as if they were his own, to observe and record for those who would come after. Other burdens are placed on such men and women while they live, of misunderstanding, scorn, even hatred, of being unable to live like others. Though he was barely into his teens when he started to write, he had none of the obsession with self which drives so many at that age to write, and later to destroy what they have written when they come to maturity. He was never a teenager, any more than he had ever been a child. He never saw the world with the natural wonder of a child's eye. A vision of reality granted to very few of us entered his soul far too early for that. Like his poems he was ageless. While he lived he could not be loved or befriended for what he was. He was destined not to be known until years after his death. Now his poems have been published and acclaimed. I vowed to bring that about, as soon as I started to read them, barely able to contain my wonder and my tears. I have no doubt that the name of Patrick O'Hara will live on among the poets who chronicled those times, their words flowering from seeds of death like the blood-red poppies that bloom on fields where battles once raged.

Ruth made Seamus swear to tell me everything that passed between them during their last few days together, and to ask me to leave nothing out of my account. So I can say that I was the priest to whom she confided her earlier misgivings about her love for Patrick. I told her that love which possesses the soul of the lover will devour the beloved, body and soul. At the time she did not understand my words. But I know from what Seamus told me that she had at last come to see the wrong she had done. I never had the chance to give her Absolution. But I am sure that as she waited for death God looked into her heart and saw her sorrow and remorse.

I have tried to tell Seamus's story honestly, as he told it to me, slowly and painfully, during the last year of his life. I visited him many times before I felt I had understood enough to begin to write it down. But that was not the only reason why I went so often to see him. Not that, not even my love for him. I reminded him each time that I was not only his friend but his priest and confessor. He knew what I meant. At last, a week before his death, aware of the threats which surrounded him, he finally spoke the words I longed to hear from him. 'Bless me, Father, for I have sinned.' I blessed him and pronounced the words of Absolution.

His end came as he had foretold, when he and his mother had knelt by that hole in the ground. As a prisoner he was reviled above all others. They kept him in isolation. But they could not protect him when the riots came and he was dragged from his cell and beaten to death.

He came home here to Belfast, where his heart had always been since the day he first arrived. He is not buried in Milltown, among the heroes of the Republican cause where his father lies, but in an anonymous corner of the city cemetery on the other side of the Falls Road. I said the prayers over his coffin, nobody else there to mourn his passing. I visit his grave each week, the only one left to remember him as he was, a man who had indeed done great wrong, who had tried to crawl out of the hell he had built for himself to find an honourable place in a world of peace, only to find himself dragged back by demons he could never escape. Often I wonder about the man he might have been in better times.

Brother Carey, sick and bedbound in a nursing home, was horrified by what he had heard and read about the deaths of Patrick and Ruth and was desperate to hear the truth from me. I told him the whole story as Seamus unfolded it to me. When I had to tell him about his death and the way it had come about, he wept. I wept with him, remembering what we had both done, but I more than anybody, to bring him to the way of life which had destroyed him.

I have tried to be honest by admitting to myself and to whoever reads this that Seamus was the love of my life and had been from the day I first saw the wide-eyed fourteen-year-old boy at my presbytery. I also have to confess that because of him I could never remain aloof. When I heard what that Brother would have done to him if Brother Carey had not intervened, it was I who used my contacts to have him dealt with. But that got out of hand as these things so often do, God forgive me. I never intended or wished the Brother's death and it weighs heavily on me. No, I was never just an adviser or a provider of refuge. Once Seamus had come into my life I was in it up to my neck.

After a long and painful struggle with my conscience I gave up my own part in the armed struggle some years before the 1994 cease-fire. Too much had happened in the name of our cause which sickened me to the depths of my soul. I burnt all incriminating papers. Fox arranged for men to come in the dead of night to clear out the arms I still had hidden in my shed. They were taken to a secret weapons dump, where they were later put beyond use. I intended to give myself up, but Fox persuaded me to keep silent. He did not fear I might betray him or others. He told me that I was needed in a different role, one I could not easily undertake from a prison cell. Secret talks were underway. Peace might come in a few years. I was respected by both sides, and representatives of the British Government would listen to me. And, through my work as a parish priest, I could prepare the ground for the difficult time to come, when the communities who had so long been at war would need to learn to live together.

I played my part as best as I could. I rejoiced when the cease-fire came and fell close to despair when it failed. Still we talked. There were misunderstandings and setbacks to try the patience of a whole host of angels and saints. But in time peace did come, though not through my efforts but those of far braver and wiser men than I.

I retired from my parish duties as soon as I had returned from England, after following Ruth and Seamus on their last journey. When he came to see me to tell me he had killed Patrick some years before and was now being pursued in his turn, I was already feeling old and tired. His story and his plight aged me yet more years in that one night. My efforts to pursue them while remaining hidden drained the last dregs of my strength from me. I wonder now how I could have been so foolish as to embark on an adventure only fit for a much younger man.

I now live in a little cottage in the shadow of Black Hill. I tend my flower-garden and grow vegetables. My neighbours still greet me as 'Father,' though I no longer say Mass or administer the sacraments. Sometimes they come to visit me, seeking solace for the loss of loved ones. Others, from both sides of the divide, tell me what they did during the Troubles and ask for my help in salving their tormented consciences. I listen and try to speak words of comfort. They thank me and bring me presents, usually a bottle of whiskey, because they know how much I enjoy a little tipple.

Many would say my life is idyllic, but the truth is very different. I never paid the price for my crimes which the law of the land would have demanded. But I pay it every day in my own heart. I am being slowly crushed by the loneliness which comes upon me each evening when my last visitor has left, and by a weight of sadness for the loss of so much hope and youth and love and friendship.

So now the evenings find me here in my cottage, alone and lost in my memories. Yet as the whiskey begins to take effect I realise I am not really alone at all. The sadness that threatens to engulf me comes not only from within my own soul but from the ghosts of the departed and those who mourn them. As the evenings draw on I feel and hear them all around me. Their cries began to gather and resonate through the land when the guns finally fell silent. They well up from the sides of graves, real, sanctified places of rest for those lucky mourners who know where their loved ones lie, imagined patches of unknown earth for those who disappeared and were never found. They echo through the streets of the city, in the hills, through the towns and villages, fields and churches, in conversations recalled by firesides cold with absence, as trembling fingers and dimming eyes pore over fading photographs and worn-out leaves of letters.

At last I think I understand why the guns roared for so long. Because we were afraid of what would come to fill the silence they would leave behind.

*Father Peter Gerald*
*Belfast*
*January 2005*

Lightning Source UK Ltd.
Milton Keynes UK
UKOW04f1847250713

214353UK00001B/8/P